Alison Evans' first YA book, *Ida*, was published in 2017 (Echo Publishing). *Ida* won the People's Choice Award in the Victorian Premier's Awards 2018, was shortlisted in the 2017 Aurealis Awards, and longlisted for a 2018 Gold Inky Award. Alison is the co-editor of the zine *Concrete Queers*, which they started with Katherine Back in 2015. So far, the zine has featured over sixty queer artists. Alison has been an artist at Melbourne Writers Festival, Emerging Writers Festival, National Young Writers Festival, Reading Matters, and Feminist Writers Festival, and has done many library and bookshop events.

ALISON EVANS

HIGHWAY BODIES

echo

Echo Publishing
An imprint of Bonnier Books UK
80-81 Wimpole Street
London W1G 9RE
www.echopublishing.com.au
www.bonnierbooks.co.uk

First published 2019

Cover design by Jo Hunt
Page design and typesetting by Shaun Jury
Images via Shutterstock

Typeset in Janson Text LT

Printed in Australia at Griffin Press.
Only wood grown from sustainable regrowth forests is used in
the manufacture of paper found in this book.

A catalogue record for this book is available from the
National Library of Australia
  ISBN: 9781760685027 (paperback)
  ISBN: 9781760685034 (epub)
  ISBN: 9781760685041 (mobi)

echopublishingau

echo_publishing

echo_publishing

One

The logo on the news report is the same as the one on Dad's uniform. The telly shows a ton of body bags, like a fuck ton of em. All them people inside are dead an there's a couple people walkin round in them white suits. Dad's got the sound too low for me to hear from the kitchen; I turn on the kettle an drown out the rest.

Mum cracks her voice through the silence an he looks at her. She points her finger at him as she bends in real close, an her words leak out. They drip onto his lap an nestle next to the food stains. He jus sits there, sits there an watches the screen cause he don' give a shit.

Sometimes I used to try an talk to her when she got like this but she'd yell at me too an then say somethin she later'd say she didn' really mean. But I could see the look behin her eyes, the way she'd try an hide behin her fringe when I'd talk to her bout it. But we don' really talk bout that anymore.

An Dad don' talk to anyone anymore, not even my brothers. But they're never home so it don' really matter. When they do come home they stumble through the door, knockin over shit as they try an find their way in the dark.

The news report is still showin the factory Dad works at. There's a view from a helicopter but the footage ain' live cause it's dark outside but the telly screen is sunny.

The kettle switch flicks up when it boils an Mum turns her head, notices I'm here. I take in the skin an bones of her, the way her dress is so tight like a second skin. She doesn' say anythin an I break eye contact to make my tea. Out the corner of my eye, Dad changes the channel.

I say goodnight to Mum an she stares at me cause we don' usually say things like that anymore. Wait for her to say somethin back, but she don'. I take my tea back to my room without anythin more said. People don' really like my room; Mum comes in sometimes an tells me to clean it. But I like the dried gumleaves tied in bunches, the gumnuts linin the windowsill, bird feathers everywhere. The magpies hang out by my window cause I sneak em meat from the kitchen sometimes, an they got the prettiest voices.

Then I notice the books on my desk. We got a science test tomorrow an I really can' be fucked studyin. I know it all already; even though I skip school heaps I do pretty good so maybe that's why no one's kicked up a fuss. Dunno. I go to the river down the back a lot, it's nice cause no one's ever there. It's quiet an I can feel the water roll over the rocks, past the fish, never stoppin, jus keeps flowin down past the grass an the mud an the people.

Keeps rollin.

* * *

The next day after school Dad's still at work so I flop on the couch, disappear into the cracks of the cushions. The stuffin's comin out the middle one an makes everythin lopsided, itchin gainst my leg.

The telly's still set to the news so I flick to the next channel, but there's news there, too. The next one is black. Nothin else, jus black. I call out to ask Mum if the telly was workin before but she don' answer, might be out the back.

The next channel is showin cartoons, though, so by the time she's back in, stinkin of ciggies, I can' be bothered to ask. Maybe if she was anyone else's mum she'd ask how my science test was. It was fine. They're always fine cause I read the fucken book, not like everyone in my class. Sometimes I look at the others an can see my mum an dad sittin right by em, not learnin anythin an stuck in this goddamn town in the middle of fucken nowhere.

Might be pretty an there's fresh air out here, not like in the city, but what's the point when everyone's fucked? I'm gettin a scholarship to any uni in Melbourne that'll take me, in a couple years. It'll happen, then I'll never have to come back here.

I'd miss the river, the trees, the birds, that's bout it.

The cartoon on the telly starts gettin lines through it, flickers once, an then turns into another news report. I sigh, turn it off an start to go back to my room filled with the gumleaves an silence.

Mum comes round the corner an her face is crinkled.

'What?' I ask.

'Somethin's happened.'

I roll my eyes. 'What, though?' Cause like, really.

'They said all schools've bin cancelled.' Her face is drawn back. I can see the outline of her skull.

'Whaddya mean?'

She shrugs. 'I dunno. Somethin on the telly. Diseases.'

All them news reports. 'Where's Dad?'

'Work. He weren' sposed to go in, but his boss said if he didn' he's gon get fired.'

Cause we all need fucken money.

'An Joe?' That's me oldest brother. I didn' hear him come home last night.

She shakes her head.

'Right,' I say, 'I'm goin to the river.'

'Don' you wanna stay home?' She looks real sad. Maybe I should stay but I can' when she looks like that, so I shake my head an go back to my room to change outta my school uniform. I put on my only dress cause it's hot as shit outside.

When I go to leave through the back door she stops me. 'You wearin that outside?'

I nod. She don' like it when I do. Dunno if it's cause she wishes I still called meself her son or if she's worried someone'll see me an say somethin. Maybe both. But I walk past her an she doesn' try to stop me. At least there's that.

Funny how pieces of cloth can make you feel better. They're jus clothes. But they do.

The gumleaves crunch under my shoes as I make my way to the river. It's cool under the leaves, sunlight dappled an less harsh out here. No one comes down the river ever, so I'm always alone. If I go down the back of our property an take the dusty road then I barely ever see anyone.

I hear it before I see it, always. That mumblin as the water rumbles over the stones, smoothin them, quiet, always workin. I take off my shoes, then my socks that are already startin to get soaked by my sweat, an shove em into the toes of my shoes. There's a branch that fell across the river ages ago that I always sit on so I can dip my feet in the water. The bottom of it is covered in algae an it's so deep green an alive sometimes it's hard to believe it's real.

If I'm quiet an still I can hear my heart beat slow, slow, slow.

I watch my feet in the water, they're darker than the rocks down the bottom. I feel like the earth when I'm out here. If I close my eyes, I spin.

Lookin down at me legs I wonder if I should shave em. Other girls do. But I don' really see why, an maybe it's jus too much effort. I shave me beard but only cause it itches like crazy if I don', an if it gets too long then food gets stuck in there, an that's pretty fucken gross.

A kookaburra sits in a tree a couple over, an she starts singin.

***

The younger of my two brothers, David, isn' allowed to go to work today. His boss isn' like Dad's. He's bin blastin music since I got home, grindin electrics that throb in beats I don' understan. I put on my own headphones an try an do my maths homework.

Dad gets home early while I'm in the kitchen microwavin some food. His skin is sweaty an pale. I frown, pretend I don' see him come in the door. He don' see me, an like usual he slumps on the couch, but then he don' turn on the TV. Mum goes over to him an says somethin; he doesn' talk. She asks if he's sick.

He looks like he's bout to vomit as he opens his mouth, but nothin comes out. Looks up at her, won' blink. Doesn' blink, keeps starin.

She takes half a step back, an those eyes won' look away. His jaw works up an down but he don' make any noise.

I dunno what to do, if I should get David or stay with Mum. Maybe I should run.

Why ain' Dad blinkin?

The microwave starts to beep an he turns to the noise; I shut it off an then he looks at me.

Mum sees him lookin at me an then her eyes are on fire. 'Whaddya doin? Cut it the fuck out, all right?' As she speaks he looks at her, really looks at her.

David comes out from the hallway an sees us all, frozen. He looks from Dad to Mum an then he looks at me, eyebrows raised, but he don' say anythin. I widen my eyes cause if I make a noise Dad'll look at me again.

Dad's sweatin more, beads rollin down his face. He stands up slow, sluggish, an steps towards Mum. David goes forward, Mum an I go back – an then somethin changes again in Dad an he growls.

Can' explain it but it's like he's a fucken dog or some shit an he's gnashin his teeth as that growl leaks out from his ribs, an it's lower than any sound I've ever heard a human make. His arms don' move the way they should.

Mum backs away but he's faster an then he's tryina bite off her face. His teeth find her neck an her blood is so red. I dunno what to do, I watch an watch as the red keeps comin an it won' stop; it gets on his clothes an all over everythin, he's got my mother's flesh in his teeth.

David moves to him, thumps him on the back, drags him off by the shoulders. Mum's screamin, Dad's growlin. David an Dad roll onto the couch. Dad doesn' even try to get up, jus buries his teeth in David's ear, more blood.

Mum's not movin anymore – fainted? I still can' move. David's screams are different to Mum's from before; his ain' as wet, are jus pain. Well it's not his husban, is it.

David looks at me an his eyes are unfocused, an he tries to yell out but he can' make the words right. 'David,' I say. I dunno what else to say. He's my big brother, he's sposed to look after me. That's Mum's job, that's Dad's job – though he ain' done it in like ten years if he ever fucken did. An now he's really ruined everythin.

David's not breathin. He's not, *fuck*, he's not breathin. His chest has stopped movin. What do I do? My brother

7

is dead, but he's always bin there in the background, always, an I was angry at him before jus for his music.

Dad looks at me. Tears are fucken pourin outta my face as I try to breathe without drownin. He lets out a hungry noise, a low, on-an-on noise that makes my spine itch, an it's like spiders are under my skin. I pick up the closest thing, a spatula, an hold it out in fronta me. He lurches towards me, an I dunno what to do. I hit his face but he don' even flinch, keeps comin. I kick him in the shins, but it does nothin. His breath smells like blood an I didn' even know that had a smell til now. It's warm an rusty an makes me wanna spew.

He's still comin, faster, an my heart is beatin hard as shit. I see the knife block on the other side of the kitchen – I need to get to that. On the sink behin me is a saucepan so I pick it up with both hands an whack him across the face. His head goes off to the side an he stumbles a bit, then he rights himself an keeps comin like nothin happened. I hit him, harder this time, an I notice for some shitty reason the pan don' ring like it does in the movies. There's a dull *thuck* an that's it. Dad growls low again, an somehow I don' think it's my dad anymore, that's a fucken animal with human skin. Again I hit him, an this time somethin's different. He stumbles back, blinkin, an I dash for the knife block, get out the biggest one.

He comes at me again, an this time I raise the knife. I got no idea if this thing is gonna stick in him, but I take it in both hands. He don' even look at it, jus stares at me cause I'm made of meat. He takes a step, almost close enough, another, an then I stick the knife in his chest.

Barely any blood comes out. He doesn' react.

That's when I realise it's jus like in the fucken movies this time. I get another knife an plunge it in his eye socket. It's hard but I get it in there. Goo oozes out, clogged-up blood, an then he falls at my feet. A coupla his teeth drop out, skit across the kitchen floor, an then everythin's still.

He looks so small, still in his work gear. In the back of my mind I wonder if I'll need to get a job now we don' got Dad's money comin in.

Can I even get a job? Will they put me in jail? They're not gonna believe that I killed a goddamn zombie but … there's gotta be evidence he chewed off my mum's face, right?

I can' look at her. Her dress is ruined. Is she breathin?

I go up to her an she smells like her perfume. *Fuck*.

There's the bracelet she always wears, jus a gold chain that's probly not real gold but she still loved that thing. I kneel beside her an unlatch it from her wrist, put it on my own.

An then as I stand up I realise my knee is wet; I've kneeled in a pool of her blood. The warmth oozes down my skin, into my socks, an I vomit, I vomit all over her, an it stinks an I can', I can' … David's right next to me, lyin there, not breathin, an I can'.

Through the kitchen I get out the back door, covered in blood an vomit an whatever the fuck else I don' want anyone to see, where can I go? I hear a scream somewhere, far away, maybe in the town centre.

An so, lookin round for any of the neighbours, I run over to the treehouse cause I ain' bin in there in a billion years an it'll be safe. It'll keep me safe, off the ground. I can lie down an no one'll see me. They'll find the bodies but won' know where I went. I stink, can smell the death on me. It's an empty box, three walls. Me ole table an chairs is in here, from when I was lil an use to crawl up here fore I found the river.

I lie down on the cool wood, peel off my clothes so I'm just in my undies an a singlet, an stare up at the treehouse roof, at the leaves. I killed my father.

Two

Poppy's singing to herself; her words escape down the highway as her curly black hair tangles in the wind. She turns to me, grins, and points to the packet beside me. 'Pass the chips, would ya.' I sling them over.

The trip's been long and the van stinks like feet. The aircon died twenty minutes after we left Melbourne, so the rest of the way we've had the windows rolled down. Even with the wind it's still boiling and I'm melting onto the seat.

'I think that was the turn-off,' Zufan says from the passenger seat, turning to Jack. He doesn't stop driving but tells Zufan to look at the map again. She waves her phone around. 'I *am* looking at the map.'

'So where are we, then?' Jack slows the van and glances at the phone. He's always been bad at taking directions.

She points to the screen. 'There, just after the road.'

'Why do you think that was the road? There wasn't a sign.'

She points again. 'The angle, Jack. Come on. If it's the right one we're almost there, and I need to pee real bad.'

Poppy takes off her seatbelt and leans over to have a look. 'She's right, Jacky boy.'

He sighs, huge and long, but nods. 'All right. It'd be nice if these roads weren't so fucking bumpy. Jesus –' Right on cue, we go over a huge pothole. 'I'll find somewhere up here to turn round. Please put your seatbelt back on, Pop.'

As we continue on, we get a view of the valley we're in; it's so full of trees I can barely believe it. They stretch out, far, and there's a river in the distance. Above, the sky is bluer than I've ever seen it.

Poppy catches me looking. 'See, Dee, told you it was great out here.'

'Maybe,' I say, grinning at her.

This was all her idea. She came here once with her parents when she was little, when they all still got on. But now we've just finished high school, and we're our own little queer family. This holiday is a way for us to recover after the exams, and try to maybe write some more songs so we can record something.

Me and Poppy aren't related, but we always introduce ourselves as sisters. With my pale freckly skin and her dark Ethiopian skin, we laugh at the people who seem confused, like it's any of their business. We grew up in each other's homes, and then when her parents decided her being a lesbian was the end of the world, she spent almost every night at my place. Not that my mum was better, but at least she wasn't home as much.

When we realised I couldn't sing but Poppy could, I

tried and failed to learn guitar. She kept telling me I'd be good at something. It ended up being the drums. She learned guitar and then we practised all the time, writing terrible songs.

She met Jack through choir at school, and I met Zufan through a boring IT class. We all came together because Poppy had lights in her eyes and Zufan's brother owned a bass guitar.

Jack turns around eventually, after the view disappears behind the trees, and we go back over the potholes, find the sign and turn into the road.

'Pop, I swear to god,' Jack says, 'if everything's as dusty as this road, I'm going to die.'

'It's not,' she replies. 'Promise.'

The road's more of a driveway that goes for about three kilometres and ends at the house. It's surrounded by gum trees, and leaves are everywhere. The house is mudbrick with a tin roof; it looks like one of the houses that are photographed for those Australia calendars.

Jack pulls up into a carport that's made of corrugated iron and four wooden poles. It leans to the side, and if the wind was strong enough I reckon it'd fall over in two seconds. In the space where a second car could fit, there's a bunch of chopped-up wood.

'Isn't it great?' Poppy takes off her seatbelt and jumps out of the van. She's already got the front door keys in her hand. She's good at seeing the potential in everything.

'Give us a hand with the shopping,' Zufan says, opening the back when I get out.

We brought enough food for two weeks because we don't want to drive all the way back into town.

After the supermarket we loaded up the van and then realised we were half-dying of thirst. We went into the closest pub, mostly empty except for like a group of old sunburnt guys; they looked like they'd never left there in twenty years, they looked like ghosts.

We sat at a dusty table out the back, started hearing weird noises inside. I poked my head in and saw a guy stumbling around. Nothing the other men were saying was making him listen; it was like he couldn't hear them. *Calm down, mate*, one of them was saying. *How much have you had?* His skin was grey under all the red splotches. He must have been really drunk, I guess. We finished our drinks then walked back to the van to avoid the guy, cause after a few minutes the shouts inside were getting louder.

And now, with armloads of groceries, we make our way into the house. It's cool inside because of the mudbrick keeping all the hot out.

'Poppy,' Zufan says, 'this is perfect.'

The room we walk into is huge. It's got straw matting instead of carpet, and it smells like earth. To the right is the kitchen, so we chuck our shopping bags on the table.

'I'll go get the rest,' Jack says, heading out, and Zufan follows.

Poppy takes it all in. 'It's so nice being back here. I

can't wait to get started – it'll be so awesome. We can really start working on some stuff.'

'Do you want to have a look around first?' I ask. 'I can go help the others with the rest of our things.'

She nods. 'Maybe just for a little bit.' But she starts putting away the cold things in the fridge as I go outside.

Jack has started unloading the instruments from the trailer. I take my drums in one bit at a time, and it kinda feels like we're setting up for a gig. We've played a few at local festivals and schools, but we were usually asked to do covers. Me and Poppy sometimes busk in the city and in Werribee or Footscray, and once Zufan has her eighteenth birthday we'll be able to play more venues. We've managed to convince a couple of places to let us play – mostly it's them deciding to pretend they didn't hear us say Zufan is seventeen.

I set up in the corner of the main room, and soon everything is in its place. Zufan goes to take a nap and Jack disappears to have a shower. I pound the bass drum a couple of times, start hitting out a beat for I don't know how long, and eventually Poppy emerges from a side door that I hadn't realised was there.

'Sounds good,' she says, smiling. She's got a couple of red and green kangaroo paws in her hand. 'I'm just gonna find a vase for these, then I'll come and join you.'

Jack comes out of the bathroom, long black hair still wet. 'We playing?' He runs a hand through his hair, combing it out of his eyes.

Although I'm mostly not really into dudes, Jack is

pretty attractive in the way that his face is nice to look at. If we went out I'd probably be sick of him in about three weeks, and I'm sure he feels the same about me. I'm bisexual, just with a heavy preference for people who aren't boys.

Poppy picks up a guitar and strums it a little, mumbling a song to herself as Jack tries to find a power point in this huge room. When he finally finds one, he strums out a tiny explosion of music before Poppy joins in on her acoustic, singing nonsense words. I tap out a slow beat, and together we fumble our way through a song we're not sure of.

I've always loved hearing Poppy sing, ever since that first time in my room when she was trying to get me to recognise a song. The sound is clear, ringing out under the electric noise. Jack picks out something that sounds vaguely familiar, and then suddenly we're playing one of our own songs, one that Poppy and Jack wrote together. Poppy sings first, Jack joins in, their voices twirl against each other, Jack's brushes against Poppy's, and hers reacts, climbing higher and higher before breaking breaks off, silent, the guitars also stopping. Only my drums remain, *beat, beat, beat, beat*, then Jack's voice is low, rumbling out the words. Poppy's guitar starts, then her voice, Jack's guitar, before everything stops with a final strum of her acoustic.

We play for a little longer, then Poppy and Jack go into their writing mode; they write the bones of our songs. Now they're going back to the thing we were making up before, talking about chords. I've got no clue what those are, so I tell them I'm going for a walk.

The air outside is a bit cooler now, but it's still warmer than in the house. Under my feet the dried gumleaves crackle, and I hear cicadas everywhere. If the leaf litter isn't a fire hazard then the leaf-choked gutters are. But the height of fire season isn't for a couple of weeks, so we should be right. And it's not like there's a million people out here, anyway, so hopefully no one's going to start a fire any time soon.

When I get back to the house, I hear quiet music. As I come through the back door, Poppy is sitting on a chair in the corner, singing away. I sit beside her and she smiles at me around the lyrics.

Three

Rhea's groaning and I can see the whites of her eyes. She comes towards me, arms raised, and I dodge, run around her back. She turns, lunges out at me, and then a dribble of spit falls from her mouth and she starts giggling.

Her irises return to their regular places and she turns to me. 'Gross.' She wipes her chin with the back of her hand.

'You'd make a shit zombie.' I kick a stone down the footpath. The walk home from school wouldn't be the hell trip that it is if it wasn't forty freaking degrees and the council hadn't cut down all the trees to make the neighbourhood *neater*. My back's all sweaty from my bag, and I stink. Soon as I get home I'm gonna take off my shoes, hopefully I won't gas myself in the process. Good thing about family is they tell you if you stink. Bad thing about family is that Rhea's told me at least a hundred times since we left school.

'Wow,' she says. 'Rude, Jojo.' Intercepting the stone, she kicks it far.

'Wanna do my homework for me?' I ask.

'Not really. Unless you want to do mine?' She raises her eyebrows at me. There's still faint scars where Mr

Marshall made her take out her eyebrow piercing. 'Glover's given us heaps of trig work. Fuck. That.'

'So drop maths next year.' I kinda like maths. It's not particularly interesting but like, at least it's not English class. I like reading, I guess, but it'd be cooler if we stopped reading books by dead white guys and instead analysed the Twitter feeds of celebrities or something. Something relevant.

'Super sibs don't need to do homework,' Rhea says. 'Probably.'

'Super sibs,' I repeat.

'You love it.'

And I do. When I told her I wasn't her brother any-more she asked if I was her sister and I said no, and she said okay. Just her sibling, her twin. That was a couple of years ago, before I knew the words. Non-binary. I like it. Sounds maths-y, a little bit. I like maths because there's a right answer. Everything else, not so much.

Rhea gets ahead to kick the stone some more. Her school dress is shabby and I can see where she's patched it a million times. Next year the school's bringing out new uniforms and we won't be able to afford them, though Mum would never say that.

We reach the start of our street and I can't see Mum's car sticking out from behind the fence like it should be. 'Did Mum have the afternoon shift?' I ask.

Rhea shrugs and checks the mailbox. A couple of letters, look like bills.

Through the front door, we dump our bags on the

ground with loud thumps. This amount of homework is going to give us back problems, I swear. Rhea heads straight for the fridge and gets out the rice left over from yesterday's dinner, shoves it in the microwave and stands there bouncing on her feet as she wails about how hungry she is. 'We need more breaks at school,' she says. 'I'm literally starving.'

'Literally.' I reach for the TV remote on the coffee table and try to find the PlayStation controllers.

The microwave beeps and she picks up the bowl, yelps cause it's too hot. She plonks down on the couch beside me.

'Controllers?' I ask as I watch her shovel rice into her face. My stomach growls.

'Bluh,' she says through the food as she points. One's wedged between the cushions, the other's fallen on the floor. We select our options, and even though she's pausing to eat she kills me twice as much as I kill her.

'You know this is super unfair,' I tell her. On my right hand, the two outermost fingers were cut off when I was like, five. Before Dad disappeared, a lot of *accidents* happened. That one was the most drastic.

'You say that literally every time we play, Jojo,' she says. 'And you don't even need those fingers with these controllers.'

'Anyway, I'm just sad cause I'm literally shit at games,' I tell her, just as I manage to hit her with my rocket launcher. Her avatar goes spiralling off the map.

'Maybe I'm just really good,' she says, waiting to

respawn. 'Maybe I'd have some sympathy if this,' she gestures to the scar across her face that just misses her left eye, another *accident*, 'had hit something important.'

We continue shooting each other and Rhea keeps winning, but it's fun. Eventually she hands me the bowl of rice, says she's full, so I start eating the rest. Saves me from making my own. We quit multiplayer and she goes into solo mode, shooting the enemy grunts with ease on the highest difficulty as I cheer her on, with my mouth full of rice.

My pocket vibrates. Ahmad's texted me:

Half the internet won't load wtf. Is yours good?

Bringing up my browser, I search the first thing that comes to mind: rice. It takes a while, but the search results page loads. I type back:

mines fine. looks like youre just shit.

You suck

luv u xoxo

Whatever (jk ilu)

Sometimes I wonder if we have a thing. Maybe.

Rhea takes on a huge group of enemies and she's too smooth, doesn't miss any shots. Her tongue sticks out the side of her mouth as she concentrates, and by the time I'm finishing my rice she gets the last guy by butting him in the back of his head with a pistol.

'Wanna go?' she asks, pausing the game and handing me the controller.

I shake my head. 'You keep going.'

'Keep on keeping on,' she says. It's something Mum started to say whenever she had to do something she didn't want to do, but now we just say it whenever we hear the word 'keep'.

I stretch out my toes, cramped from my shoes, and lean back into the couch. My eyelids sting when I close them but I keep them closed, feel the hot sticky faux-leather of the couch swallow me up. It'd be great if we had aircon but it's too expensive; on really hot days we stand in front of the fan and spray ourselves with water.

'Gonna make a cake.' If I sit here while a pool of my own sweat gathers around me for much longer, I might do something awful, like start my homework. 'I'll leave you to your childish games.'

'Fuck off.' She grins. 'I am the official taste tester, don't you forget.'

So I get out the eggs, the flour, everything, and start up. Halfway through, Rhea comes over and decides the cake should be green and squeezes the bottle too hard and gets the dye all over her hands. I'm laughing, so she smears her fingers all over my face.

'Art!' I yell as I grab the blue dye and get her forehead.

She lunges for me again. I dodge, but she's too quick. Then I get her again, and we can't breathe from laughing while we cover each other in dye. I get her arms and she goes for my legs sticking out of my shorts.

There's the keys in the door and Mum comes in, her hair everywhere. She had the morning shift at the hospital, should've been home hours ago. Her eyes dart everywhere before she sees us in the kitchen. She cries out and rushes over, takes our hands. 'You're all right?'

'Mum!' Rhea says. 'What's wrong?'

She keeps staring at us and her eyes are tired. 'Of course, you never check the news.' She puts down her bag and places a hand on her hip.

'Excuse you!' Rhea says.

'We check Twitter,' I say, although we haven't since we got home.

'Why would there be news on Twitter?' Mum asks.

Rhea and I make noises of protest while Mum laughs and apologises. 'Shouldn't you be blogging like normal sixteen-year-olds? It should be all over the internet. They were talking about setting up a quarantine at the hospital, so I left.' She shakes her head. 'They tried to make me stay. No way I'm spending my annual leave working.'

My mother is made of steel. Mostly it's a good thing, but sometimes she makes me worry. 'Won't you get in trouble?'

She shrugs, just like Rhea; they're both in a perpetual state of shrugging, telling the rest of the world they don't care. 'They can't make me stay longer than a fifteen-hour shift.' She runs a hand through her long black hair that has too many greys for her age.

There's a knot in my windpipe because she won't look either of us in the eye.

'I'm putting on the news, okay?' she says as she finds the remote and sits down. The paused game menu changes to a woman with a serious face telling us no one knows what's happening. News crews are being denied access to the hospital where Mum works, a couple of suburbs away; some food factories out in Woop Woop and other places I don't know. Reports of internet blackouts, and I didn't even know that was a thing that could happen.

'Some kind of disease outbreak,' Mum says. 'Everyone's freaked out. It'll be fine, it always is.'

Down the bottom of the screen, words scroll past.

Estimated hundreds injured in factory explosion // Police presence strong in Bundoora, Mill Park and Diamond Creek // Social media blackout // State MP declined to comment, seen in talks with army officials

And it just keeps going.

'Something to do with the food,' Mum says. 'They were bringing people in with …' She frowns, stares intently at the news reporter even though all they're talking about is how we don't know anything. 'They said it was food poisoning or contamination or something … Everyone looked … I don't know if they were telling the truth.'

I remember Ahmad's text and open Twitter on my phone. *Tweets cannot be retrieved at this time*. Facebook, everything is the same.

I text Ahmad:

my internets broken
       Fuckin told ya. Seen the news?
weird. military coup or military coup?

I'm texting as I watch tanks appear on screen. The footage is blurry, maybe taken with a shaky camera phone. It's only a few seconds long, but those were definitely tanks. Do we even have tanks in Australia?

'Why won't Twitter work, though?' Rhea says. 'How can they block that?'

'Science magic,' I tell her, grinning. But it makes no sense – other crises around the world have always had social media working.

Ahmad replies:

No that only happens in movies.

There's an update on the television, then it switches to our state's MP. She gives a nothing speech about how the area is dangerous, and she denies there's a military presence, says there's *no need to panic*. All I can think as I watch her shiny forehead, her hair that looks like it was neatly styled with copious amounts of gel but is now tousled, loose, is that if there's nothing to worry about then why is she giving this statement on live television? Mum flicks through the other main channels and they're all showing it.

Mum's phone buzzes and she looks at its screen, frowning. 'It's your school.'

Rhea sits down beside her; I lean over the back of the couch and check out her screen.

'My kingdom for privacy,' Mum says, placing a hand on her forehead.

The text says school is cancelled tomorrow, and any student who needs can stay there under supervision. A curfew's been put in place. The TV doesn't say a curfew's been announced, but it does say people are encouraged to stay indoors; anyone wandering around the streets without *sufficient cause* will be questioned by police. Especially around our area, in the city and some country town I've never heard of, but they show it on a map.

As Mum reads the text, her work calls. As soon as the caller ID pops up, she locks the screen.

'Mum –' Rhea starts, looks at me.

'– you sure it was okay for you to leave?' I complete.

She smiles at us, tight like when we were little and asked for things we couldn't have at the supermarket. *Maybe next time*, she'd say.

'It's fine,' she says. 'They wouldn't have let me go if it wasn't.'

'You didn't like –' I start.

'– sneak out?' Rhea finishes.

I *was* going to say something a bit more tactful.

'You know, when you finish each other's sentences it doesn't help your "we're not a demon" theory.'

'I think that's your theory, Mum,' Rhea says. 'We *know* we're a single entity of dark forces – the sooner you accept it the easier your life's gonna be. But why can't we go to school?'

'Not that we really want to,' I say. 'But y'know. What with the military presence at your work, well. Questions just seem to pop into the mind.'

'Naturally, naturally,' Mum says. 'But no, me leaving work was fine.'

'So you did sneak out,' Rhea says.

'I just ... left without really telling anyone. Not exactly same thing. I should have been out of there hours ago, anyway.'

'Will you get in trouble?' I ask.

She shakes her head. 'They can't make me go back now.' She smiles, almost genuine this time. 'Come on. I'm on holidays. Endless parties, all those things the youths are into.'

'Gross,' Rhea says. 'I'm going to bed.'

'Jojo and I are gonna party all night long, aren't we?' Mum says, patting my arm.

'If by party you mean bake a cake and watch *Prime Suspect*, then yes. Yes, we are.'

And after Rhea goes to bed, that's what we do. Halfway through the episode, Mum gets a call. It's from work again, and I watch her as she watches the screen. 'I am so not answering that,' she says, locking the screen and chucking her phone on the coffee table. After another couple of minutes it's ringing again, buzzing against the wood. It happens again and again, until she grabs it. 'What?' she says, spitting into the phone. She listens for a second. 'No. Find someone else.' She doesn't wait for a reply and hangs up. 'Fuckin rude.' She turns off her phone and puts it in her pocket. 'Want a drink?'

'Isn't that the irresponsible serving of alcohol?' I ask, smiling sweetly.

'Yes, I firmly believe you have never had a drink up until this point. You're sixteen, Jojo, not five. I know for a fact you got drunk at Suzie's party on the weekend.'

I narrow my eyes. 'You know too much.'

'And I meant tea. Would you like tea?'

A police car drives past the house, slowly, its white paint reflected under the streetlights. The two cops look at our house, see us looking back, and continue on their way. Our street's a dead end, so they have to turn around and drive past again; this time Mum walks up to the window and watches them not watch us. She closes the curtains, and when she turns around she doesn't look at me.

'Gimme a coffee with some Baileys,' I say. I know my grin is forced.

'Baileys?' She wrinkles her nose. 'Don't be disgusting.' She turns on the kettle, and the home phone rings. 'Fuck off,' she mutters, but answers it. Then she's nodding, her grip getting tighter around the phone. 'Uh-huh,' she says, over and over. About a minute ticks by until she stops, mouth tight and eyes tighter. 'I'm not coming in,' she snaps, voice cracked metal. 'Megan, I'm on annual leave. I know you're busy with this shitstorm but I've had this planned for months. I need a break. Don't ask me again.' Megan says something; Mum balls a fist. 'I know, Megan. I know. Sorry. Look, I have to go, bye.'

Mum is shaking her head. The kettle boils, but she doesn't go to make the tea.

She looks at me. 'I might go to bed. We can finish watching tomorrow night.'

I nod and she kisses my forehead, walks into the lounge and turns off the TV. I wait until she's in her room before I make two cups of tea, one for Rhea because I don't think she's asleep. Sure enough, when I go into our room she's in her bed on her phone, staring intently at the screen. I hand her the tea and she looks up. 'Thanks. Look at this.' She's got Twitter open on her phone, and there aren't as many tweets as usual for this time of night. Most are complaining about the weird curfew thing, but some are from our school friends.

Ahmad: My bus couldn't get home usual way, did an hour detour!???

Kate: No school tomorrow! Shame about the impending apocalypse (apparently).

Margaret: there was a fire down the road, heaps of army guys showed up. screams? gonna go look

'Has Margaret said anything else?' I ask Rhea. She shakes her head. 'Has anyone said anything else?'

'Not really. This took, like, half an hour to load. Someone seems to be jamming it. I don't know ... There's not really anything else that'll load. All the other tweets are the same, and whenever I try and refresh it, it just says tweets can't be retrieved at this time.'

'Mum's work called again, like a hundred times. She finally answered and they want her to go back in.' I hope she doesn't, but then I dunno. She wants a holiday but always puts other people before herself. 'I hope she doesn't cave in.'

'She won't, will she?' Rhea frowns. 'That's such bullshit. There's probably nothing going on anyway – everyone's just freaking out.' She looks me right in the eye as she says it, but I know she doesn't mean what she's saying.

Four

The sun comes up an I dunno if I slept. I lie still as I can. No birds singin an there's still that yellin, people everywhere shoutin, an I dunno what to do. Shoulda paid more attention to the news maybe so I'd know what the fuck was hapnin.

Dogs are howlin an once it's cut off in the middle, an I don' even wanna think about it. Vomit rises in my throat but I can' let it out, maybe the smell will give me away to whatever's out there makin everyone scream. I wonder if neighbours tried to tell us. Did Dad know he was sick? Did his boss know what was hapnin? Why didn' anyone let us know?

Startin to feel hungry again. It went away in the night, jus like the heavy feelin that means I gotta pee, but both are back now. If I lie here more, maybe they'll go away again. The cicadas start but it's not nearly enough to drown out the yellin.

After hours, minutes, I dunno, I piss meself. Can' move, don' wanna let no one know I'm here, so I jus do it. Try not to think about it, an the air's hot enough I don' notice the warmth gainst my leg too much.

There are less screams as the sun moves across the sky.

To the left of me, there's the little table an chairs I used to play with when I was small. Their yellow paint's all cracked an faded. Too big to use em now.

Shoulda paid attention to the news. What's hapnin. Dunno.

The sun continues its path an shines right in my face; my skin tingles but I don' move. Can'. Weak as shit, so fucken thirsty.

Time passes, dunno how much, but it's gettin dark an the mozzies is comin out. I hear buzzin fore I feel one land like a tiny cloud on my skin. I turn my head to look at the insect an I can see its body swellin, gettin redder an redder. The pinprick of its spike hurts but if I move someone might hear me an I dunno how I'll tell em what I did to my family.

It's summer so the nights ain' as cold as they could be, but when the sun sets it's still enough to make me shiver. Don' wanna be anymore. Inside is warm an my bed's there, but he's still there. Covered in his own blood an I'm covered in it too. I wanna rub it off, red dry smudges gone brown. I dunno if I'm sorry that he wasn' proper alive.

The cicadas ain' as loud now, an there are more mozzies. I feel em land, pinpricks all over my flesh. Covered in bites but I don' move at all. Dunno what to do. I'm fucken hungry, me guts hurt. I need to piss again. It's cold. I can' move because there's a scream, sounds like it's nearby. Wonder who's dyin. The scream cuts out an then only the insects are makin noise.

There's a rustlin noise an my body turns cold, down to me toes. It's close. It's right under me. Can' look, can' move. Maybe it's the wind. Maybe it's a cat. Probly. It's fine.

I dunno what to do but it's fine. The rustlin will stop. It's fine.

The wind picks up, creepin through the planks of the treehouse, an it's dustier than I thought. I'm gonna sneeze, I can feel the ticklin, so I rub the tip of my tongue gainst the roof of my mouth; the sneeze dies between my teeth. Breeze brought the smell, too. I can' even gag, jus lie there an try not to think.

I keep goin to sneeze but stop cause the noise at the bottom of the tree's got louder an I dunno why. I could turn an peek through the floor but ... dunno if I wanna know. An really, I fucken know what's down there. I seen the movies, an if it works like it does in them, well.

I can see the mozzies flyin round the treehouse, an I shouldn' be able to. It should be dark. Need to see where the light's comin from, an if I don' move now then maybe I ain' gonna again. Pain shoots down into my toes, an my whole body is pins-an-needles, an I can' cry out. I draw in a sharp breath an then there's different noise below, a human noise. An I don' look, can' look.

The streetlight down the road's turned on. Coupla moths flyin around it, huge brown ones. Under the moths, a kid's walkin, all by herself. An that's when I notice all the screams have stopped. Everythin's quiet as, no more cicadas, only the sometimes mozzie.

The kid's walkin funny, shamblin, cause she only got one foot now. She's from a couple doors down. Her parents was pretty nice. Did they turn first? Maybe she turned em. If she was comin at me, teeth bared, I dunno if I could stop her.

Easier to stop a fuck who's bin a shit your whole life to ya, but not a little girl. Could never do that.

My stomach growls, empty an yawnin, so I lie down, try an trick it with gravity. It ain' gon work, but I'll be fucked if I can get the courage to go into the house when I can' see shit. I close my eyes an they burn. Jus glad I don' snore.

***

I wake up curled in a ball. It's warm again, an I'm sweatin; it's mixin in with the blood. I stink, I stink so fucken bad. He's everywhere, he's all on me.

It's different. The birds are singin all round, an I could drown in their song. Magpies is the prettiest; a bit fucken terrifyin in swoopin season but they sound pretty.

The rustlin's still at the bottom of the tree, less now. I lie still, eyes open. My cheek presses the wood under me. It's warm from my sleep an covered in dried blood mixed with me sweat. I take a deep breath, then look down through a crack. An I wanna scream, run as far as I can til I can' no more an my legs feel like they're gon fall off.

David's there, Mum right next to him. Their eyes are blank, misted brown, an the tips a their fingers is bloodied from clawin gainst the tree.

I musta proper killed Dad cause he ain' there.

Down there, that's my mum. That thing was my mum an now she's jus … What even is she? She sees me starin at her through the crack an lets out a low moan that doesn' sound like anythin anyone ever. Jesus Christ.

First thing I think is: I could jus go down there an they could bite me. Then I could crawl back up here, maybe, so I wouldn' get eaten. Turn in peace. Gettin eaten alive is like the worst way to die. In the movies that was what scared me the most. Don' wanna die like that.

But it'd be pretty fucken easy.

An then I know I don' wanna be stuck in the fucken treehouse for a second longer. I can go upstairs an barricade the staircase. Get the food that's in the cupboards, make a camp in the bathroom. Might be a bit shit but least there'll be water, an the door locks.

I squint down at the ladder through the crack, tryin not to see David's face as it stares up at me. I'm not gonna be able to get past em fast enough. Who knows how fast they can go? They still got all their limbs. Maybe they could run super fast. It's different in every movie, anyway.

I crawl over to the tiny chair an take it in my hands. I could break it maybe, use it to stab. Or use it whole, hit em with the legs. It'd keep em away from me, anyway. Could leave enough room for me to get in the house, then I could jus lock em out.

Fore I can move any further, I hear a car. It's goin slow. I duck, though I know they won' be able to see me from the road. Keepin low, I peer through the treehouse window an see the car drivin. It's full a white guys, an one is hangin out the window with a cricket bat, ready to whack some zombie heads.

Hopefully zombie heads, anyway. As they drive by they're too far away for me to see their faces, but they sound like the kinda bogans that ya don' wanna cross cause they'll fucken kill ya jus for lookin at em weird – not even weird, jus in a way they don' like.

The car disappears behin the houses an trees, but I hear em brake. I think maybe they seen me. I can' feel my body anymore. They're gon kill me, I jus fucken know it.

But then the car starts again an I can hear em laughin, tyres kickin up clouds a dust as they go.

Mum an David've turned to the noise, but I guess they can still smell the blood on me cause they ain' moved. So they like noise. An maybe they jus like blood the most, cause otherwise Mum an David woulda left me by now.

Sometimes I hated their fucken guts. I dunno. When Dad went all weird as shit I realised I didn' hate them. Think I might hate him. I guess that's not so bad, considerin he's dead an I'm a murderer now. Does it count as murder? I don' fucken know.

I gotta get outta this fucken treehouse. I chuck the table down into the yard, away from the ladder, an Mum an David turn to it, probly tryina figure out what's hapnin. I get down the ladder an I got the chair in me hands. They ain' gonna mess with me today, fuck that.

Mum comes at me first, gnashin her teeth. They're bloody an I wonder if she's bin eatin somethin. Musta started to eat David before he turned, then jus lost interest.

Her hair is tangled an I wanna comb it, make it better. She reaches for me an I whack her arm away with the chair. David comes at me now. He's taller than I am, but I'm bulkier, stronger. An so I hit him over the head with a chair an I remember when we used to do this with pillows; he'd pretend to be a bear an I'd have to defend myself. As I hit him again, I let out a sob, can' help it, an now I almost hate myself but I hit his head again an he goes down, down, down, an he don' get up cause those chair legs splintered, a chunk got lodged in him.

Mum comes at me again. This time I mash the end of a chair leg at her face an a coupla her teeth get knocked out. She can' shout anymore. I hit her with the leg again, harder, an she stumbles, falls on the ground. I feel the crack of her skull.

I take two steps then gotta spew. Prickly grass under me hands, I heave, though I dunno if there's anythin to throw up. The tug at my guts don' let up an I feel it through my chest, twistin inside. Spit dribbles out, an my eyes strain like they're gonna pop. I cough, throw up more nothin. I stand an my knees are shaky, but the throwin up's stopped. I swallow a couple times an then start toward the house.

Inside, it reeks like off meat. Flies are everywhere, big black ones you can hear.

I need to look at him to get through the kitchen to the rest of the house. His blood's thick on the floor tiles, an his face still looks empty. Empty, but manic as shit. I can' handle it an then I need to chuck again. More eye strain, more spit, no vomit.

If I wanna stay in this house, I'm gonna have to get him outta here.

I take one a his legs an drag him – or try to, anyway, he barely fucken moves. Weighs a fucken ton. I take a huge breath then pull as much as I can with both arms. He slips on his blood an somehow I get him out the door. When he's outside I can' drag him across the grass so I jus leave him there.

Gonna have to sort somethin out with the bodies. They'll start attractin the wildlife an I don' wanna get no diseases, specially what they got, cause Christ. For now, I slide the door shut an draw the blinds so I can' see him.

I scoff half a packet of Shapes from the pantry, fore realisin I should probly save some if I don' wanna starve. I grab a jug an fill it with water, then skol three cups.

The house's so empty that I dunno what to do first. There's no one to avoid.

I start by lockin the front door. When I walk to the lounge window, crouchin low, I don' see anyone. Hopefully that means no one sees me either. I close a window that was open, then shut all the curtains.

There's no one here, I realise, again. No one. I can do what I want.

I go to my mum's room an look through her wardrobe. She has so many dresses, better than mine. One's smooth, pale blue, an it slides across my skin. When I look in the mirror, I see I'm covered in old blood. My body turns hot; my dad took everythin away without even tryin. It's not all his fault, I try to remind meself, but he fucked us all up.

Still, the dress swirls round me like water runnin through my hands. In the bathroom, I let the dress slip through to the floor an it feels good to let it do that, it feels pretty.

The tap works when I turn it, an I wait with one hand in the stream; the water starts to warm up. This might be my last hot shower for a long time. The water runs over my body an turns pale pink as it runs down the drain. I close my eyes, put my face under the warm water an rub off the blood.

Maybe I jus didn' think the news report was real, maybe that's why I didn' pay attention when I shoulda.

Will the electricity work much longer?

I wonder if this is hapnin in other countries.

I guess the police won' be comin for me after all, then.

The shower relaxes my back, stiff from lyin on the hard floor all last night. An by the time I'm clean an the hot water has started to run out, I can almost pretend to forget what's happened.

I pat dry with one a the good towels I'm not sposed to use, an fluff me hair up. I comb it through, gettin out all the knots. I never really cared til this moment an it takes a while, but then my hair is smooth an shinin. With the dress back on, I'm cleaner, more me, than ever.

I turn off the lights an go back into the lounge. The telly will be too loud, so I dunno what to do. There's no study to be doin, an I don' really know how this works. I've always bin studyin, so what happens when it goes away?

Outside is quiet. I can' hear anythin movin about, which is nice for a change. There's no screams, no dogs barkin. No cars.

Birds've stopped singin, too.

An I miss that, an everythin ain' as good as it was a coupla seconds ago. The birds've stopped, an that ain' a good sign. I go into the next room an get the fire poker, hold it close to me. I figure goin upstairs is best. Can defend the stairs if I need to.

But nothin happens, an soon the birds are singin again.

I don' have a lock on my bedroom door, so I move my bedside table in fronta it, an lie on my bed with the poker beside me. Can' be too careful.

It's weird havin no one else in the house. No one's yellin, there's no telly. I stare at the shapes the streetlight makes on my curtains an I can' sleep, not like this. Wonder how long I can go for.

A long while, if I need to.

I close my eyes an don' let go of the poker til mornin.

Five

The marshmallow Zufan is toasting catches on fire before she blows on it. As she takes it off the stick, the pink goo oozes out under the charcoal, melting down her fingers before she scoffs it. I take a marshmallow and eat it raw. 'That's not how you do camping,' Zufan says, waving her stick at me. Her face is orange from the firelight as she grins.

'I think renting a house is *also* not how you do camping,' says Poppy. I look at her and she's out of her camp chair, lying on her back.

We've camped before, with school in Year Nine. The mission was to build a raft and then sail it down the Murray, and we did pretty well. Poppy fell in more than any of us, and she dragged me in a couple times too. Me and Poppy shared a tent, and that was when we came out to each other, in a quiet private world.

Zufan toasts another marshmallow and Jack joins her. He lets his go brown before eating it; Zufan's catches fire again.

'Look at all the stars,' Poppy says. I turn my head up to see the sky is half silver. These clouds of stars were in the sky the whole time, and now I can finally see them. So much I didn't know about.

Everyone's quiet as we look at the stars. I wonder how much else we can't see up there. Maybe I could get used to this, the stillness, the bright nights, the soft animal noises in the background, never ceasing but somehow relaxing.

Poppy is right, she's always been right. We can do it. It had all seemed like something other people would do. Other people could make music; other people got played on the radio. Other people got fans and could make art for a living. I'd have to be in an office that I hated, and everything would be mediocre.

But now, looking up at all of the night, anything is possible, anything at all.

***

Over the past week, I've only wanted to punch Jack about three hundred times, so things are going better than I expected.

'I think it's working,' Poppy says. We're sitting in the backyard on a fallen tree, and she's strumming her guitar, mumbling to herself. Jack tried to help her last night, because they mostly write all our songs together, but no. This one is Poppy's.

She's been working on it forever, on and off, and there's always something not quite right about it. But now it sounds better than that very first time, when we were kids and playing our own crisp song back to our ears. Better than that.

Jack shouts something inside, and Zufan's calm voice

sounds out in reply. I peer through the windows but can't see anything, and Poppy doesn't even look up. I lie back on the trunk, my spine digging at the wood. A sugar ant runs across my fingers, and I watch its tiny quick feet and don't feel anything. Another ant joins it, scurrying over my skin.

'Sounding good,' I say to Poppy.

'Finally.' She doesn't look at me, bites her lip and keeps playing.

'It's always sounded good, you know that.' I hold up a hand and block out the tiny pricks of sun coming in through the trees. 'It has.'

'I suppose.' She taps out a beat on the body of the guitar. 'But, y'know, not the way I mean it to.'

I guess I don't really know, *really*, because I just bash out a rhythm and hope for the best. Some drummers really get what's happening in a song, but I'm more of a guesser. Plus, Poppy'll tell me if it sounds shit. Jack will too, but I don't always listen. The thing with Jack is that he wants us to be a certain thing and we don't always fit. He does have a point, though, about us trying to market ourselves to a certain audience – but does that really matter? Poppy's a genius so she'll go places no matter what she does. Jack's just practical. They're both good at what they do.

'Hey, can you grab some sticks, Dee?' Poppy prods my leg. 'I need you to do a thing.'

There are so many everywhere among the dead gumleaves. I pick the straightest two I can find.

'Okay,' Poppy says. 'Can you tap on the trunk?' She pats it, and I start.

She strums a bit slower than me, so I adjust and follow. Something's different, the lyrics have shifted and the music is like waves rolling out under the words, sometimes taking over but always retreating back under. Poppy sings like restless colours, lost things, storms. It's like diving into a cold pool after this heat, immersed, and everything's silent but not, completely in the moment.

When she stops I wanna cry, but instead I grin at her because she's grinning huge, eyes crinkled up. 'It's totally ready,' she says. 'Come on.' She grabs her guitar around the neck and jumps off the tree trunk, not bothering to put on her shoes as she runs inside.

I follow, still with my sticks in hand.

'Zufan,' Poppy says when we get inside and she's alone in the room, sitting on the floor, reading something on her laptop. 'Come on, we gotta play.'

She shakes her head. 'Power's out.'

'Power's out?' Poppy repeats.

I walk to a light switch and flick it. Nothing. 'Since when?'

Zufan shrugs. 'Twenty minutes ago?'

'Goddamn it,' Jack says as he walks into the room. 'What're we sposed to do?'

'We'll just call someone, hang on.' Poppy walks off into her room, comes back, and waits for her phone to turn on. After it boots up, she sighs. 'No reception, duh.'

'I am dying without wi-fi, I hope you realise,' Zufan says. 'I now understand the extent of my addiction and I need help. This place is like some kind of awful rehab.'

'Sorry our program isn't working for you, Zufan,' Jack says.

'What about the power, though?' I ask. 'We can't play without it.'

Jack scrunches up his face, thinks. 'Oh! The landline. Those are a thing that exist.'

We eventually find the house phone in the kitchen next to the fridge. It's dusty, and as I hold it to my ear I don't hear a dial tone. 'It's not connected.'

'Goddamn it,' Jack says. 'Fuckin bush country shit.'

'You sound pretty country right now, mate,' Zufan says, grinning.

'Oi, nah, fuck off,' Jack replies. 'Seriously, though, we need power. Our food's gonna go off, for one thing.'

'I need to get my song down quick before I forget it,' Poppy says.

'We can drive into town. Come on, Jack, you and me. Pop, maybe you can show Zufan the new bits to the song? Just so she's got it too.' I sigh. 'And write it down because you never do and I always tell you to and it sounded so fucking good, Poppy. So please do.'

She grins. 'You're too kind.'

'All right,' I say, 'gimme your phone.' She hands it over and I nod. 'Come on, Jacky boy, let's get this show on the road.'

'Don't get lost,' Zufan says.

Jack sticks up his middle finger.

'We'll be back soon,' I say as we leave.

Jack gets in the driver's seat cause I don't have my licence. And besides, Jack's dad will kill him if anything happens to the van. Thought the only thing that's going to happen to the van is that it'll get covered in dust.

It's a half-hour drive into town, and I wish we had some music. But the system broke a while ago, and Jack's dad could never be bothered to get it repaired.

'I've got reception,' I say when one bar finally appears.

Jack seems pissed off. He doesn't reply. Then he stares up the road and brakes, leans forward. 'Something's weird.'

'What?' I look up.

A car is parked across the road, door open.

'What?' I say again. 'Just a car.'

'Yeah, but the door's open, and … that's blood.'

I look at the stain on the dirt, dark, too red. 'What.'

'Come on. We should go take a look.'

'People out here are fuckin weird.'

'They might need help, Dee.' Jack pulls over and turns off the engine. 'I'm gonna go have a look.'

'No, wait. Let's call the thing and then go together.'

He makes to move out of the van.

'Please.' I realise how quiet it is and I think he does too, because he doesn't move. He looks out of the window and keeps moving his head at the slightest noise.

In Poppy's phone address book, I tap the house owner's number and wait.

The number you have dialled is not connected. Please check the number and try again.

I swallow. 'It's not working, Jack.' I try again but get the same result. When I type *electrician* into the search bar of the internet browser, it won't search. I refresh, and nothing. 'Something weird's going on. Internet's down, the number isn't connecting.'

He glances out the window again. 'I think we should go take a look at that car.'

That's the last fucking thing I want to do, but I nod. Without needing to consult each other, we climb out and don't shut the doors – quicker to get away. We move slow, walking down the edge of the road. Twigs crack under our shoes. There's no other noise.

'This is weird, Dee,' Jack says, slowing.

'No shit, son. Come on.' I grab his elbow. 'This was your idea.'

It takes us forever to get to the car, and sweat is running down my back in the heat.

When we reach it, I peer inside. I don't scream but I inhale a whole bunch, more than I thought I could all at once, as Jack cries out.

There's a person in the passenger seat, bloodied mouth, knife wound in their chest, and in their skull, right through the forehead. I can tell it's a knife wound because the knife is sticking out.

I clutch Jack's arm as he takes a step back. 'Don't fuckin leave me,' I say through gritted teeth. I can still feel a scream in my throat. Jack's panicking so I have to not panic. That's how we work: when one of us isn't able to function, the other one does. That's why he comes to me when a boy breaks up with him, and why he helps me get through exam nerves.

'What the fuck,' he says. 'What the fuck.'

'It looks like it's been a couple days, maybe more.'

'We've only been gone like two weeks!'

'Keep quiet, Jack!' I whisper fiercely. 'Jesus.'

'What the fuck.'

I can't look at the face anymore, so I look at the seat. Blood's splattered over it, onto the dirt below. Whoever killed the passenger must have been hurt, too. I frown and look around the car and towards the town proper. I can't see anyone moving, no signs of human life. It's a small town, but there should be at least one person out, right?

'We have to get the others,' I say. 'Something's wrong – I mean, more than this.'

'Okay,' Jack says, but he doesn't move.

'Jack,' I tug his sleeve, 'come on. It's okay. We just have to go now.'

His eyes are wide, but he nods.

The whole ride back to the house we don't speak.

Six

Everything is suddenly super fricken boring when there's no internet. I want to read fanfic, do some blogging, talk about gender with randos, do literally anything instead of try to beat my sister on PlayStation at games she's amazing at. We don't have a lot of games and only, like, three are multiplayer. Mum tried the radio yesterday, but it wouldn't work. Not even the car radio. After six hours of this, I'm going to explode.

I put down my controller. 'I'm gonna go read a book or some shit.'

Rhea scoffs. 'Nerd.' She doesn't mean it.

I chuck a cushion at her. 'Gonna go see if Twitter works again, too.'

She shakes her head. 'I couldn't get anything while you were asleep, so dunno if it'd be working now.'

'What time was that?'

She shrugs, blows the head off an enemy. 'Maybe like three or four?'

'Didn't you sleep?'

'Dunno how you did, especially after that police car you told me about.'

'Did Mum get up at all?'

'Haven't seen her.'

'It's like …' I check the time on Rhea's phone. 'Eleven. She never sleeps this late.'

I knock on Mum's door and there's no answer, so I peek inside. Curtains are drawn. 'Mum?' There's no response; I take a step closer. 'Rhea!' I go back into the lounge and I'm so cold, my bones are heavy in my chest. 'She's not home.'

Rhea just kinda stares at me, then the thoughts click into place and her eyes widen. 'Did she go to work?'

I shrug. 'Don't think she would've.'

'Where did she go?' Rhea runs a hand through her hair. She cut it a couple of weeks ago, shorter than mine. From the back, she's mistaken for me all the time at school, and a sometimes by Mum. From the front we're pretty much identical even though we're fraternal twins, except Rhea's got the face scar, I've got the fingers. Or, y'know, the lack of.

Now it's my turn to shrug, and then the house phone rings. I jump at the noise and Rhea laughs briefly before we remember who'd be calling.

'Fuck off,' I mutter. The phone rings out, the only noise in here. 'I guess if they're still calling then she's not at work? Like, they're calling to intimidate her, I guess,' and I snort because no one can intimidate my mother, 'so like, yeah, she's not at work.'

'Was she kidnapped?' Rhea says, then laughs as she runs a hand through her hair. 'We need to chill out.'

I take Rhea's phone off of the coffee table. 'I'll call her.'

The phone won't connect the first time, goes straight to message bank. I try again, the same thing. 'Maybe her phone's off,' I say – she forgets to charge it all the time. 'Maybe she's doing secret spy work and can't answer right now.'

'I would actually believe that,' Rhea says. 'But she'd tell us if she was a spy.'

'Maybe she was sworn to secrecy by some shady characters.'

'She wouldn't be reporting to shady characters, Jojo. Our mother has integrity.'

'We could go have a look. Just like, go for a walk.'

Rhea grins. 'Yes. Super siblings power up.'

So we put on clothes that aren't pyjamas, and I grab my last five dollars and the house keys. 'So, our super valid and important reason for venturing outdoors in these troubling times is to scavenge for food, correct?'

'Yes, indeed,' Rhea says with a sharp nod. She holds the front door open for me and we step outside. The air's hotter, stickier. Over in the distance there's a thin plume of smoke, and I smell its sharpness on the breeze.

'What's over that way?' I ask Rhea.

She narrows her eyes, thinks. 'No idea. Maybe one of those places the news was talking about. Maybe there was a riot or something.'

There's no one on our street. Which is kinda normal, because it's usually quiet at this time of day. But when we make it to a bigger road, and there are way less cars than normal, maybe a third of usual traffic – it's not right. A couple of birds are singing in the park, but we don't see very many life forms. *Life forms*, I snort to myself. *Like a sci-fi movie*.

'Should've worn balaclavas,' Rhea whispers as we pass someone walking their dog, aggressively not making any eye contact with us.

We round the corner and on the main road are four cars in the car park; usually it's at least half full. There's a couple of cops with their backs to us. One's smoking; the other points, slaps the smoker on the chest, and they watch as an army truck drives past. It's that khaki colour, and I don't know how many people could fit in that. Maybe the cloths on the back are hiding more passengers, maybe they're hiding guns. Or both.

'Rhea,' I say. 'Did you –?'

'Yeah.'

'Maybe we shouldn't be here.'

'We're out of milk,' she tells me. 'Come on, it'll be fine.'

'I dunno.' But she starts walking and I can't not follow her.

So we go up to the supermarket; the police still haven't noticed us. The guy behind the counter looks at us, grunts to himself, and goes back to his paper. There are literally no other people in the shop. I swat a fly out of my eyes. There's usually aircon in here, but it must be broken because the air is slow and boiling. It's musty and smells like old shoes. The guy barely looks at us as he takes the money for the milk and hands back the change.

Outside there's more smoke than before.

'Mum totally set a building on fire,' Rhea says.

I snort and she giggles, nudging me with her shoulder as we walk down the car park, away from the cops who still haven't noticed us.

'Don't let them hear –' I stop, grab Rhea's hand to stop her walking onto the road. A car speeds past and the wind makes us take a step back; a police car follows close with its light flashing but no sirens.

'Shit,' she says. 'Mum's accomplice.'

I giggle. 'Shh, don't.' Something at the back of my mind wonders if the cops can hear us somehow. But they don't, and we get home sweaty from the sun. Everything still smells like smoke, but the plume is getting smaller so we're probs not gonna die.

There's a couple of bags of chips in the cupboard so we eat those and all the biscuits as we watch DVDs because the internet's too clogged up and slow to be anything but the most annoying thing ever.

After two movies, Mum comes home through the back door. I cry out and Rhea stands up, shushing me.

'Where did you go?' I ask Mum, my words hissing out.

'I thought it wouldn't take that long,' she says. 'Didn't want to worry you.'

'Well, you did,' I snap, my nails digging into my palms. There are knots in my stomach, in my throat. 'You should've told us.'

'Jojo, worrying is *my* job. I went to the hospital, it's fine.'

'Why?' Rhea asks, biting her lip. 'Didn't they see you? We saw an army truck when we went to get milk.'

'Why didn't you leave a note?' I ask.

'I don't think so,' Mum says to Rhea. 'There's a perimeter around the hospital, army trucks. I couldn't get in, and then a couple were parked near me for a while. That's why I was so late.'

'Mum!' Rhea and I shriek.

'You two,' she says, trying not to laugh at our serious faces.

Rhea and I look at each other.

'Apocalypse?' Rhea asks.

Mum shakes her head, sighs. 'Does anyone want a cup of tea?' She moves past us to the kitchen where she puts on the kettle. 'I'm sorry. I should have told you I was going.'

'You shouldn't have gone at all!' I yell.

'What did you see?' Rhea asks.

'The perimeter.'

'What else?'

There's a pause. She looks up at the ceiling. 'I think they're burning people.'

I don't know what to say, so I say nothing. Rhea goes up and hugs Mum, then makes her tea. We all watch a movie, and nothing else is said. I text Ahmad a couple of times but I don't get a response.

***

The next day, the news 'recommends' we stay inside, and I'm not sure what that means exactly. The only things on TV are the news programs saying nothing and reruns of old shows, one that I half remember from watching Mum watch as I was growing up; I recognise the theme songs and know a lot of the words.

I start reading a book in my room because I can't watch any more TV. Rhea's been in the bathroom for about an hour, even though I heard her turn off the shower ages ago.

Mum wants to go out again, I can tell. Through my open door, I see her wandering around, making sure the doors are locked, looking through the windows. Fidgeting, deciding we need things at the supermarket but that she can't go outside.

'Nice cake,' Mum says, holding up a piece as she stands in my doorway. The cake looks like alien snot, which is totally Rhea's fault.

I smile at her. 'Thanks.' I'd forgotten I made it.

'Internet working?'

I shrug. 'Only one tweet loaded – Mags said she has no food in the house and everything's shit.'

'Well, she's not wrong,' Mum says.

'We have some food. You're literally eating right now.'

'Literally.'

'Hey,' I grin, 'that was the proper use of the word.'

'I know.'

There's a knock at the door, firm and too loud. I shiver, drop my phone, and Mum turns to stone. I don't hear anything from the bathroom.

The knock comes again.

'All right, all right,' Mum says to whoever it is. 'I'm coming.' She gestures to me and says quietly, 'Stay in here.' She disappears from my doorway, and I hear her open the front door.

'We're going to need you to come to the hospital, Ms –'

'I'm sorry, but who are you?' Mum asks. The fire is there in her voice. I'm constantly grateful my mother is on my side.

I peek around the doorway. Two people are there, taller than Mum, looking down on her. She's got one hand on her hip, the other holding open the door.

'We need you to come back to the hospital.'

'What if I refuse?' When she speaks, I feel my pulse in my throat.

'I'm sure you could be persuaded.'

And then Rhea comes out of the bathroom, typing on her phone as she dries her hair with her other hand. She stops and the two people look at her, look back at Mum.

'Well, have a good rest of the day with your daughter.' They leave.

Mum closes the door, looks at us, and she's shaking. 'I'm just a nurse. Why do they need me so badly?'

Maybe she's been exposed to some kind of virus; maybe she knows too much.

'It'll be fine, Mum,' Rhea says.

The phone rings and we stare, watch it ring out. It starts again.

***

In the end, Mum unplugs the phone and swears under her breath for about fifteen minutes before having a shower. The bathroom's the only room in the house with a lock, the one place we can't see her face; she must be tired of us looking at her, tired of looking at us.

My veins want to explode because we're trapped, and I never thought I'd wanna go outside willingly, but here we are. I can hear loud cars – trucks? army vehicles? – driving past on the main road nearby. We could probably see them from the roof but we're *not allowed*. Fuck off.

Rhea's pacing between the stove and the couch, which isn't very far, and this just makes me madder because it's so fucking pointless – but I don't say anything because if she's not pacing she's going to go off.

I turn on the TV again; the news is on. Again. I turned it off because nothing was happening, but now there's something. It's a reporter I haven't seen before; they must be rotating heaps because there's never anything else fucking on anymore. The reporter has a pimple on their cheek, and I know I shouldn't focus on it but I can't help it. They're saying there are *troublesome youths* – they legit use those words – around the region where I live, particularly Bundoora where the hospital is. They briefly cut to a small crowd, where protesters are holding signs and whatever, and they're chanting about not being told anything and being cooped up. In the background, a bunch of police are watching, alert. Then there's some tiny bullshit story about Gen Z and how we're ruining something-something … I mute it.

Rhea's still pacing, didn't even turn around when I turned on the TV.

'I think we should sneak onto the roof later,' I tell her. 'Get a view of the town or whatever.'

'If they catch us we'll get in trouble.' Then she grins. 'Super sibs, doin cool rebel shit.'

'We should totes do a stakeout. Take snacks.' Already, the house feels bigger and I can breathe.

'Heck, yes.' Her eyes light up as she sits next to me. 'The streetlight outside is still broken, so we probably won't be seen if we wear dark clothes.'

Mum comes out of the bathroom, looks at us. We turn and look at her, and she stares right back, straight face. 'I heard nothing. Carry on.' Then she just walks into her room.

I wonder how many calls have been missed from our house phone, and I wonder if those men will be back. They're not calling her mobile because no calls have been getting through either way.

I can tell Rhea's upset because the internet's not working at all anymore, so she doesn't know what her online friends are doing. They don't know if she's okay, and that's stressing her out more than anything. Would a lockdown in a tiny Australian town make international news? It might not even make the news in other states – maybe only Victoria cares. *If* they do. She picks at her nails, bites them.

It's like a blackout but worse; everything turns on but nothing works the way it's supposed to except the fucking TV, and if I watch another news report I'm going to cry. I'm so used to being soaked in information, and now it's gone I feel like I'm wandering around in the dark. A really fucking annoying kind of dark.

On the TV, someone's just thrown a glass bottle. I don't know what's going on because the sound's still off. Then another bottle's thrown at a storefront. It's only a couple of people, and I turn the sound up. The reporter's talking about the violent mob – any talk of *protesters* is gone, replaced with *rioters*. The two throwing the bottles are middle-aged white people. One looks a little like the reporter, and they're laughing at each other while they stumble about.

I turn off the TV, and watch Rhea pace around and around and around. *Just stop*, I want to tell her but I don't say anything. Just glare. We make eye contact.

'If I'm annoying you so much,' she says, still fucking pacing, 'then get lost.'

I'm sick of my own company anyway so it makes sense she'd be sick of mine, really. I go to our room and pick up a crime book, read the first page about ten times before giving up. I'm not gonna be retaining any fucking information. I think I hear a knock on the front door and I tense up, but it's Mum tapping on the open door to my room. 'Tea?'

I nod. 'You all right?'

She breathes out all the air in her lungs. 'Yeah. Book good?'

'Dunno.'

Then she leaves, I'm left staring at this fucking book that I want to burn. Goddamn it. I pick up another, but it's the same. I end up lying on my back, staring at the ceiling for hours, seeing if I can feel my heartbeat without using my hands. I can't.

* * *

When the sky is orange, there's a *boom* in the distance. My eyes shift to the window, but I can't see anything unusual out there.

Rhea comes in, eyes wide. 'Roof?'

I nod, and we scramble out the back door. Mum's watching the news but I don't pause to see what's happening. There's almost a breeze. I feel the prick of a mosquito on my neck and swat it away, itch at the bite that's forming.

One wall of the carport is concrete bricks with patterned holes in them, perfect for climbing. Rhea goes up first. When we first started climbing onto the roof, it was harder for me cause I had less fingers to grip with. It's easy now; I know the pattern to the top, exactly where to place my feet.

Something flashes, then there's another *boom*, louder though maybe that's just because I'm outside. Although the news said the riots are in the Bundoora town centre, these flashes aren't there; they're in the middle of some houses in the opposite direction. Another flash, a little further from us. No sirens, no other sound except for my and Rhea's breathing as we watch the sky darken, a fire starting. Sometimes a scream is loud enough to carry, but that's all.

Seven

From the pantry, I take all the biscuits, rice, pasta an that upstairs to the bathroom. I take all the creams an shit off the shelves behin the mirror an put what food I can in there. Not that it really matters where I chuck it now, but it's kinda like a pantry, somethin like how it used to be.

I tried turnin on the telly but there was no signal an so I got no idea what's hapnin anywhere. Cars drive by sometimes but they never pull over. Guess the houses round here look so poor they figure there'd be nothin to steal, an there are so many of them dead people that it's more effort than it'd be worth.

I've raided some houses for food, had to kill a few zombies but now I got heapsa cans an that. Stole a couple can-openers case the one I got broke. Kinda weird that I call it stealin – is it stealin if everyone round here is dead? No one to ask.

I pick up the cricket bat I found in the next-door neighbour's backyard an I take a look up an down the road. Only dead ones around, so I walk to a couple houses down. I ain' raided this one yet an I think they might have some food; they had kids so I'm guessin they needed a lot. I get a green bag hangin on a door handle an fill it with cans from the pantry. They got heapsa fresh veggies but they gone rotten, same with the fruit. Some tomatoes are all right, wrinkly but I take em. Bag's heavy by the time I leave the house.

If I move fast enough the zombies are too slow to bother with. Never let em follow me home, I jump fences an that. I think they like noise, an they like blood. Like when Dad got fast. They're unpredictable.

These cans with the rest'll probly last a few weeks if I don' pig out. They rattle so I stuff in an old shirt to try an keep them from clankin as I walk. I turn into a backyard, an then I see her.

She's got almost-shaved-short hair, an she looks Indian. She's thin, really thin, scary thin. An she's surrounded by zombies, a knife in her hands. But there are so many, an the fences behind her are too tall.

She stares at me an I stare at her. My whole body's been dipped in ice. My blood's in my ears, there's no other sound.

She springs back into action, tryina get the ones near her away, get at least one down. I drop the bag of cans. The closest zombie to me turns round an I whack it in the face with me bat. It goes down, I get another one. She grunts as she sticks the knife into one's neck.

We get rid of them pretty quick, an then we're jus starin at each other.

If she wants to kill me, she can do it easy as shit. The cricket bat is loose in my hands.

She still hasn' said anythin an I dunno what to say.

I realise I'm wearin the dress an maybe I look weird to her cause I ain' shaved my beard in so long. Grows fast as shit. But I shouldn' assume she's a she. She might've – they might've assumed I'm a boy.

'You're alive,' they say. Their voice is lower than I expected, cracked but steady.

'Yeah.'

'You,' they breathe, each breath echoin the *you*. 'You're alive.'

'Well shit, yeah?'

They jus keep lookin into my eyes. Their hair is all dusty an they look like they havn' showered since all this happened. Am I the first person they've seen since then? Somehow I don' think so. They look hard.

'You need some clothes?' I ask. Theirs are all ragged – all right in summer, I guess, long as you got somewhere to stay at night, but when winter comes round they're gonna freeze.

They nod. I pick up the bag of cans an lead them to the house. We go upstairs, an I get all my beddin out of the bath an give them a change of clothes. A bit big, but they don' say nothin.

'Here,' I say.

They nod again. 'Thank you.'

I wait in the hallway an listen to the water runnin. They can sleep in the bedroom down the hall, I guess. Do they wanna stay? I don' wanna be alone.

The water turns off, an after a while they open the door. 'Thank you,' they say again.

'You hungry?'

They nod, an so we grab a packet of chips off the bathroom cabinet an sit on the floor gainst the wall, silently eatin. Their arm gainst mine is nice; they're warm an I've missed other people. We don' move after the chips is finished, don' say anythin, an then I scrunch up the wrapper, the only sound I can hear cause they breathe so quiet.

'I'm a girl,' I say to them. 'Just so ya know.' I cough once, tryina keep my breathin steady. I never said it out loud before.

'I know,' they say. 'And me too. For the record.' Then she asks, 'Have you been on your own this whole time?'

I nod. 'Bin real quiet round here. Sometimes people drive past, but I think they wouldn' be ... I don' let em know I'm here.'

She nods slowly, her eyelids heavy.

'You alone the whole time?' I ask.

An she looks at me, an I know she hasn' bin. She's had to do things like I did, but I think worse. So much worse. So I don' ask. If she wants to tell me, she will.

Then she does somethin no one's ever really done before: she rests her head on my shoulder. She breathes low, deep, an then she's asleep jus like that.

I stare at the wall an see us reflected in the grimy tiles. The sun is beginnin to set an it's gettin hard to see anythin at all. I wonder if she's gonna kill me when I fall asleep, but right now it's jus nice havin someone in the same room who ain' a half-eaten body or a zombie.

My bum is gettin sore so I nudge her awake, an she blinks a coupla times before proply wakin up.

'Do ya wanna bed?' I say, an she looks at me.

'Please don't leave,' she says.

'I won'.'

I show her down the hall to the double bed in my room. She gets in the right side an I get in the left, an then we pull the sheet up over us.

She's lyin so she's lookin at me, so I lie so I'm lookin at her.

'It's been so …' she says, an closes her eyes.

I find her hand under the blanket an take it; she doesn' flinch. Her hands are warm gainst my cold ones.

'Thank you,' she says for the third time.

I realise how close we are. It's not cold out, but she's so warm, an so I put my hand on her waist an she smiles at me, cups my elbow.

An in the mornin she's still there, her arms wrapped round me, an she don' leave. I don' bring it up, she don' either, an so we keep like this.

Eight

When we get back to the house, the two of them are laughing inside. Poppy's wiping a tear from her eye and Zufan is explaining something, gesturing huge. But when she notices my face and Jack's quiet, pale panic, her hands drop. 'Poppy,' she says, and points at us.

Poppy looks at me, and her laughter is wiped off her face. She knows this look, the *everything is awful* look, except now it's not about school or a crush but something much, *much* more, and I think she can see I don't know how to bear it.

Jack opens his mouth but then just shakes his head. 'Nope.' He shakes it some more.

'When we went into town,' I say, and pause. How do you say something like this?

'They were dead,' Jack says. 'They'd been killed. No one was in town and there was this person and they were dead.'

They stare at us.

'Who?' Poppy asks. 'Did you call someone?'

'The phones wouldn't connect to anything,' I say. 'We couldn't get through.'

'But the internet?' Zufan asks.

I shake my head. 'Wouldn't load at all.'

The two of them keep staring at us. I look at Jack; he looks at me.

'Should we go get help?' Poppy asks.

'Where from?' Jack says.

We're silent again.

'We should go see what's going on,' Poppy says.

'I don't want to,' says Jack. 'It was freaky. Ghost town.'

'We can't just stay in this house forever,' Poppy says. 'Maybe no one knows what's happened in the town, but we should find another place with people. And what about home? We have to make sure everyone's okay.'

I don't know who she's talking about. Zufan's brother, maybe? Not her parents, not my mum. Definitely not Jack's dad, who's the most biphobic person I've ever met.

'But the internet wasn't working,' Jack says. I know he doesn't want to go back; his dad has left marks on him. 'I think it's way bigger than this town.'

'We need to find out what's going on,' I say. 'What if everyone's been evacuated for some reason?'

Zufan starts nodding, and Poppy follows. I need to know why that person in the car is dead, because I can't get their blood-covered face out of my mind.

Jack's just staring off at something above my shoulder.

'Jack,' I say, 'we gotta leave here, okay?'

He looks at me, nods. 'They were dead, though. Like, *dead*-dead. I don't want to die.'

'I know,' I say.

'We're not going to die,' Poppy says. 'We just gotta go have a look, find out why they're dead.'

'What if someone's murdered everyone?' Jack asks. 'You think we'd have a chance against someone like that?' He's so pale.

'We'll just go, find out what we can, and then we'll leave, okay?' I say. 'We can come back here if we want.'

He nods again, and stands. 'I'll drive.'

Poppy looks at me and frowns, and I shrug at her. He's in a weird mood, he might freeze when we're driving, but it's his van. 'I'll take shotgun,' I say, and soon we're in the van and I'm beside him. I'll snap him out of anything if we need to. I can grab the wheel.

The drive back into town takes ages. When the car that's in the middle of the road comes into view, Jack slows down to walking pace.

'Drive past, Jack,' I say.

His knuckles are white, gripping the wheel, but he nods, jaw set, firm. He doesn't blink.

I'd never seen a dead person before. Every funeral I've been to has been closed casket. But because Jack has freaked out I need to not, and somehow I can do that. When I look at his panic, I feel like I'm standing on an island in the middle of a sea that can't be still.

He inches past the car, and as I look back I see the passenger side window is splattered with blood. From the inside.

We continue on, and I point at the car park round

the back of the pub, on the edge of town. 'Let's go there. We can leave the van here.'

Jack complies without a word, and when we get out of the van we shut the doors quietly. We kick up red dust as we walk.

The pub's back door is open, and the place is covered in blood. Gluggy pools seep out from under bodies and into the floorboards. There are swarms of fat black flies, their constant buzz underlying everything.

I clap my hand over my nose and mouth, and Jack goes out to vomit. We leave the way we've come, then look at each other.

'We should search for survivors,' Poppy says, but none of us makes a move to. How could there be survivors?

'We should keep driving,' Zufan says. 'This is fucked up. Whoever did this is … This is so fucked up.'

Jack gets back in the driver's seat and we head to the highway. We're surrounded by trees, and the engine is so loud. If whoever did this is out here, we're making ourselves really obvious. Someone could easily be between the trunks, watching.

'I have to pee,' Zufan says.

'We can't stop.' Jack doesn't even turn his head.

'No, like, I really have to. I'll be two seconds. Please.'

'Jack, pull over at the lookout,' says Poppy. 'It's not far, I just saw a sign. And maybe we'll be able to see something from there.' Her voice is calm, soothing. She knows how to handle this situation, I realise. It makes sense; she's looked after all of us at one time or another.

He nods.

When we get to the lookout, no one's around, no cars, nothing. We climb it and Zufan rushes to the drop toilet on the edge of the clearing. As I look out, I see trees, more trees, trees everywhere. I can't see any signs of human life – except for plumes of smoke in the distance.

We wait up there, not saying anything, and then Zufan joins us. 'Oh, I just remembered,' she says. 'Last night I was woken by an explosion.'

'What?' Poppy says, eyes wide. 'Why didn't you tell us?'

Zufan shrugs. 'Forgot until now, it kinda blended into my dream. But yeah. It was faint, didn't really wake me exactly, and I was already half awake. But I definitely heard an explosion.'

I look at all the smoke plumes. 'Did it sound close?'

She shakes her head. 'I'm not really sure. I only heard one, though.'

As we gaze at the sea of trees, I wonder how many people are out there.

Nine

In the morning everything is quiet. Sometimes I hear a car on the main road, but none on our street. The phone is still unplugged. Mum's set up a nest on the couch, where she just sits and watches the news. She's drunk too much coffee but I don't want to tell her to stop. At least she doesn't smoke anymore.

The fires went out eventually, but it took a long time. We didn't hear any sirens, so I don't know if it was firefighters or just regular people who did the job. Now the news broadcast is fuzzy and it says there were *minor explosions* in town, caused by *rioters*, and I feel like my skull's been hollowed out. Because I don't know why they're telling us this.

'Tea?' Mum asks in an ad break.

On screen, colourful patterns are trying to sell me toys made for three-year-olds. I feel like I'm not real anymore. I nod. 'Or coffee,' I tell her, my words dry in the air. 'Hitting the hard stuff.'

She smiles, tight, and I try and smile back.

In the kitchen she watches the kettle boil, tapping her fingernails against the counter. *Tap. Tap-tap. Tap-tap-tap.*

Tap-tap-tap-tap-tap-tap-tap. The kettle switch flicks up and she makes one coffee. Hands it to me.

'Where's yours?' I ask.

'I'm going out.'

I stare at her. 'You're not serious?'

'Something's going on, and I need to know. What kind of bullshit is this?' She points at the TV and shakes her head. 'I'll only be gone a little while.' She's planning something.

'Maybe the explosions *were* in the town centre,' I say, but last night Rhea and I told her exactly what we saw from the roof. 'I mean, it was dark.' I swallow. 'Could have been anywhere.'

She says, 'Johannes –'

Rhea emerges from our room and looks at both of us. 'Mum, are you really gonna go outside?'

Mum nods.

Rhea looks at me; her eyes are tired.

'I won't be long, just gonna check out the hospital,' Mum says, and then Rhea and I hug her. I bury my face in her shoulder, memorise her perfume, her warmth, and then she lets us go. She doesn't take anything except a Swiss Army knife that she's had forever. She hugs us again, tells us she loves us, before she slips out the back door.

I sip my coffee, sit in Mum's spot on the couch and watch the news for two seconds before remembering it's bullshit. I turn on the DVD player, and Rhea and I watch shitty sitcoms for the rest of the day. We don't talk, just laugh and cringe, and only leave the couch to get food, drinks and go to the toilet. When I get up for the fifth or so time, I see we barely have anything in the pantry; if we keep going like this, by the end of today we'll have nothing left. But I don't mention this to Rhea because I'm sure she's realised too, and we just keep drinking caffeine. I remember I've got a chocolate bar in my desk drawer, so we split that.

It gets dark. Mum hasn't come home. I lie awake in our room and wait for her, but she doesn't come. At every tiny sound I think it must be her, but it's not. When the sun rises, I figure I may as well get up. I glance over and see Rhea has been awake too, judging by how tired she looks.

I check the whole house, but Mum isn't anywhere. I know she's not, but still …

'Jojo, please stop,' Rhea says when I go back into Mum's room for the fifth time.

'Where is she?' I can feel tears forming, and I'm too tired to make them stop. Rhea just hugs me.

We spend the rest of the day napping in shifts, showering, trying to read – anything to distract us from the fact Mum isn't here. I even plug the landline back in, but no one calls.

'We should go look for her,' Rhea says.

'Where would we even start?' I ask, though I already know I'm game. The thought of leaving our house is terrifying but I miss Mum, I want her to be safe.

'The hospital, duh.'

I swallow and look at the clock on the wall. She's been gone almost twenty-four hours. 'All right.'

***

The sky is dark when we slip out the back. Rhea grabs the keys off the hook next to the door and holds them in her fist as a weapon.

The hospital isn't far, though it takes maybe an hour for us to walk there. The whole time I'm starting at any noise, whenever a car goes past, whenever we see a bird, and I'm sweating from nerves by the time we're halfway there. We get to the hill before the hospital, and the crest of it is just high enough that we can see the buildings. We crouch down. There's lots of fences surrounding the hospital, and army trucks, and people in white hazmat suits.

'What *is* this?' Rhea asks. 'Disease breakout?' She edges closer. 'This is intense.'

I didn't realise it was this bad. What if Mum's stuck in there? What if she's infected?

'We've gotta find Mum,' Rhea says. 'Come on.'

We keep low, scooting behind fences and over drains, and get a bit closer to the hospital. It's very quiet. We stare at each other, and Rhea looks just as scared as I feel.

'Where is everyone?' I ask.

She just moves closer to the fence.

'Rhea,' I hiss, but I follow her.

We reach a wire fence, one that's been put up around

another one. No one says anything or comes to stop us, they're all with the trucks. She slips through the fence; I yelp.

'Rhea!' I say louder this time, and she turns.

'Come on, Jojo,' she says through the fence. 'We've got to find Mum.'

'We could get in trouble.'

'She could die.' Rhea's eyes are bright. 'Come on.'

So I follow her.

There are a few shipping containers around, lots of medical supplies, a few gurneys, and ... a lot of body bags.

'Rhea,' I grab her arm and point at the pile.

'Fuck,' she whispers.

'We should be wearing masks or something – we don't know what's happening. Mum said there was a quarantine. We could get sick.'

'You're right.'

We cover our mouths with our shirts and dig through the medical supplies lying around. I can't find anything useful and go over to what looks like a little office, a temporary one like I've seen at building sites. The door is locked.

'Here.' Rhea smashes the window with a rock. She reaches around the frame and unlocks the door from the inside.

In the first drawer, we find a packet of masks. We put them on and look at each other.

'Doctor,' Rhea says, nodding at me seriously.

'Mm, yes, Doctor,' I reply, nodding at her in acknowledgement.

Someone says something outside, and we freeze, duck away from the window. The door's still open, but there's no time to shut it.

'They're going to have to close this place,' someone says. 'They've already shut down the others in this area. We've got no staff left.'

Does that mean Mum? Did she go back to work, to help?

'We've got no control anymore. The disease is out of our hands.' Whoever it is must be on the phone, because there's no second voice.

Rhea sticks her head out. 'It's someone in an army uniform. This is real bad, Jojo.'

I swallow. Where is Mum? 'They said there's no staff left.'

'We can't let it spread,' the army person says. Silence for a few moments. 'Yes. We'll commence evacuation.'

I realise I'm crying again because Rhea looks upset when she sees my face.

The army person goes around the corner.

'We've gotta find her,' Rhea says, and we dash to the closest door to the hospital.

The corridor is deserted but filled with body bags, rubbish, random medical supplies. There are bodies that aren't in bags, too. I flinch every time I see a nurse's uniform, but they're never Mum. Besides, she wasn't in her uniform, but the sight of it …

'Rhea, she's not here.'

Rhea's ahead of me, and she keeps ducking into rooms as we come up to them. There's the distant sound of a crowd, but I don't know where it's coming from.

'Oi!' someone shouts from up the corridor, and I scream. Where did they come from?

'Quick!' Rhea pulls me back and we dash down the corridor past the bodies. We break through the door and into the bright sunny day. I shield my eyes, and there's a whole bunch of people next to us, behind a chain-link fence. The crowd we heard before.

Rhea and I both scream some more then flee around the corner where the army person talking on their phone went. No one's there. The crowd follows us along the fence, picking up the pace now they've noticed us. A lot of them have open wounds and clammy skin. They don't look like people anymore; they don't look alive.

'Rhea, Mum can't …' What can I say?

The crowd is closer, some people leaning on the fence that separates us from them.

'We'll find her,' she says.

'What if we do and she's –?'

Rhea flinches. 'Come on.' She takes my hand and we walk around the perimeter. The crowd follows us, sometimes getting a burst of speed. 'Gotta get rid of them somehow,' she says. Some are trying to fit their hands through the chain-link fence. I can feel my heartbeat, too hard, too fast.

'They like noise,' I say.

'And they like us.'

'Maybe if we hide from them for a bit. They might forget we're here.'

'Hmm.' Rhea jogs over to the nearest garden bed and picks up a rock, weighs it in her hands. 'I'm gonna smash a window. Come on. We'll find some cover, I'll chuck this, and they'll –' She chokes, her face crumpling.

'Rhea?' I turn to where she's looking. There are just the people. 'What is it?'

She points, her hand shaking, to just behind the crowd. A couple more people are coming to join it, and one of them, in the green jumper that's so ugly but loved, is Mum. She's not her. Her skin is dull, hair everywhere. As she gets closer, I lose her in the crowd for a second. When I spot her again, she's close enough that I can see her eyes are glossed over.

There's blood in my ears, my head is so heavy and light at the same time. I can't feel my legs. This isn't real. That's not real.

'Mum,' Rhea says, and she takes a couple steps forward as she drops the rock.

'Rhea!' I grab her arm. 'Don't get close.'

'But she's …'

'I know.'

Rhea tenses under my hand; I know she wants to keep walking towards Mum. 'It's so dangerous, Rhea.'

She turns to look at me, the hard fire in her just like Mum.

'I can't lose you too. Please.'

She softens. 'We should bury her.'

'She's still, she's …' I don't know how to say it. 'Still walking. We'd have to …'

Rhea nods. 'Yeah. She always wanted to be buried under a tree, though. Remember? She said to chuck her in a cardboard box and make her plant food.'

I nod. I don't know what to say. Whenever Mum talked about that kind of thing, I never thought it would actually happen. After her mother died, and they had a big fancy funeral with a glossy wooden coffin, buried in a graveyard, Mum knew she didn't want that. But she didn't want this.

Rhea and I hold hands and watch Mum because we don't know what else to do.

The ground under us rumbles; the sharp tang of smoke starts to brew.

'Let's go,' Rhea says, face streaming with tears.

I swallow hard, take one last look at Mum who is not Mum, and then I follow.

Ten

We use water in buckets now; grab it from the river.
We're almost halfway through our food supply after
bout a week, an it's scary how quick it goes. When it was
jus me I guess I didn' notice how much I ate. We done
rations but really we got maybe two or three weeks' food
here. After that we're gonna need to make bigger trips
further out soon cause I've searched almost all through
my street. Still haven' got the nerve to go through other
places in town – too many dead ones walkin round out
there, an fuck knows how many alive ones.

Sometimes when I go to the end of the street I hear
voices. Deep voices far away. Harsh. Dunno what they're
talkin bout; whenever I hear the faintest bit of anyone's
voice that ain' hers, I jus get the hell outta there.

It's nice havin someone to talk to. She's Pakistani,
she said, an from the inner suburbs. She almost died a
million times tryina get outta Melbourne, but she made
it. Dunno how, lots of luck.

An now, standin at the edge of my street behin a few
trees an that, I look out at the next road. The little girl
is wanderin round an I wonder how good her smellin
is. Can' tell if they can smell me all the time or if it's

blood. There's a couple others I can see; one's only got one foot an the other's lost half its guts. It's easier to not gag now, but it's still fucked.

I go round the back of the first house an see the carcass of someone's dog they left tied up that's bin half eaten. Poor bugger. I try not to look at it an go test the back door. It's open; guess no one really had time to lock their doors when they got out. The people who lived here didn' get out, but. They're still in their lounge, torn to bits. Like me, they didn know nothin, I'm guessin.

I raise my cricket bat – maybe the zombie's still trapped inside. I ain' made much noise yet, so it mightn'ta heard me. Hope not. I haven' got one since I found her.

I step into the lounge an one of the dead people looks at me. Steppin backwards, I don' scream. It uses its arms to try an drag itself off the chair it died in, cause its legs don' work. I bring me bat down over its head, an the *crack* that comes out is the worst sound I ever heard. I have to do it five more times til the thing stops movin, my bat gettin covered in more blood. Should clean it but can' waste water.

My heart's beatin like anythin an I breathe heavy, breathe in the death smell, breathe it all in. I would chuck but everywhere smells like this now, every house. Maybe not so much ours, though ours is pretty musty; we only use the bathroom an the bedroom. Sometimes we open the windows a tiny bit. They're weak points – people can see em open, an noise can get out. We've got heavy curtains over em, coverin every crack. We could light candles in the night, but we never do.

Last night we slept in the bathroom; I was on the floor an she was in the bath. After everything that's happened, I needed a smaller space. But then I couldn' sleep without her, so she came onto the floor with me. An it was cold an I felt like a kid but she didn' complain, didn' say anythin. She jus knew. She knows a lot a things without askin, she knows I'm a girl, she knows when it's gonna rain. She watches a lot, listens to everythin an stores it away. She took my hand in the dark an I smiled to meself, an I knew that she knew.

I fucken hate writin, but that changes when she's here. She makes me wanna write poetry.

I dunno if this will work between us. Maybe it's only like this cause we don' got no one else. Maybe we woulda killed each other or gone our separate ways, I think, but then she's so different to anyone I met before. I dunno where she's from; I think she's come a long way from home cause she don' talk like people from here. She knows a lot. I bet her school was fucken great, an she didn' have to study as much cause her teachers knew what the fuck they was on about.

I hope she's okay. She went down Coop Street to see if there's anythin useful. Dunno what's gonna happen when we run outta food – pretty fucken sure we're gonna die. I stare at the beaten, bloody skull an brains spread out in fronta me, splattered all across the couch an walls an me.

The one I killed worked at the supermarket. She'd bag our groceries an never smile, always looked so tired. I wonder why her legs didn' work anymore.

An that's too much, I can' fucken handle it, an I back up to a corner, drop my bat an bawl my eyes out. I knew her, I *knew* her, I didn' know her at all, an I jus smashed her face in. The movies say the people are gone an only the zombie is there, but what if that's not true? What if they're trapped in a weird frenzy, what if they're aware of everythin they're doin?

Can' think that, can'. Gonna die if I start thinkin that. They're not people, you can see it in their eyes.

I look in the cupboards an grab a coupla cans an some packets of dried pasta. The fridge's full of rottin veggies. On the counter is a mouldy bowl of fruit, an little flies are buzzin around it. An there are blowflies, all flockin to the dead one that was proper dead, but now they're settlin on the lady from the supermarket too. She's got a ponytail in.

I go back out the door an almost step in the dog. I notice little maggots wrigglin in its eyes, an cough. Can' let meself vomit. Vomit smells too strong.

But it's still noise, shit. I put down the food, grip tighter on my bat, an flatten meself gainst the house, look left an right. After a coupla minutes, no zombies appear, no people either, but I don' let my bat down as I pick up the food. Keepin close to the side of the house, I poke me head into the street to see if anythin's comin my way.

'Fuck!' An old nail, juttin out from the buildin, just tore a hole in my arm. 'Fuck.' I drop everythin an look at the cut. It's deep, blood's fucken everywhere. My hand's covered in it, sticky an red, an they're gonna fucken smell it. I take off my t-shirt an wrap it round my arm, no time to do it proply.

I pick up my shit with my free hand an make my way home. My arm is stingin. Was the nail rusty? How does tetanus work? I can hear my blood rushin through my body too fast.

A zombie lurches at me from behin a car, air hissin from its lungs. I yell out, drop everythin, my bat slippery with the blood pourin out me arm. I try to hit the zombie in the head, but it's got a busted ankle an I keep hittin its shoulders or missin.

'Fuck, fuck, fuck.' I'm tryin not to make too much noise. But the blood an the shout from before have drawn a group of them down the road. They're lookin bitier as I bleed more, and I wish me heart would slow down. Dunno how long I can keep this up. I finally knock the first one down, but then two others come at me with their hands an teeth an moans.

Then she's runnin up the road to me. She jabs at the heads of the closest zombies with her knife; they fall forward an she grabs me, starts runnin til we can hide. 'Come on,' she says, takin off her shirt an wiping at the blood on my arm. 'They can smell it.'

'I know.'

She wraps the shirt round me tight, an we walk into

the trees for a bit. Not too far, jus enough so we can' be seen by the zombies on the road.

She's lookin at me funny. 'Are you bitten?' From the movies an the way my family turned, we're guessin that bein bit is how it happens.

I stare at her an can' form words. She's gonna kill me. She is ready to kill me right now.

Her grip tightens on the knife. 'Are you bitten?'

I shake my head, finally. 'Nail on the side of a house.'

An then she drops her weapon, lets out a sob an falls into me, grippin the back of my head as she tries to breathe. 'I thought you were …' she says into my neck before we kiss.

I pull her closer an feel my cut break open again. 'You were gonna kill me,' I say, voice shaky as my damn legs.

She grips me tighter. 'Yeah.'

'Good.'

'You have to promise you'll do the same.' There are new tears in her eyes. 'You have to promise.'

'I do. I promise.'

She nods once, twice, an then laughs as she's cryin, tears fallin down her cheeks, her neck. 'We gotta be quiet,' she says, more to herself.

After a couple minutes, we start to walk back to the house. We come to the river first, an I lean down to wash the blood off my arm, soak her shirt.

***

'I'll clean it for you,' she says when we're home, upstairs. She dabs at the cut with a face washer, an it's not as bad as I thought. 'You probably shouldn't go out for a couple days,' she tells me. 'Let it heal. It might start bleeding again if we're not careful.'

I nod. 'Find anythin when you was searchin?'

'I went further than I should have. Didn't find any food, but I found that place you said your dad worked. It's crawling with zombies – I don't know how he got out.'

'Musta bin one a the first bit. He was home early that day.'

She nods. 'Well, we shouldn't go near it unless we really have to.'

'Kay.'

She cuts up some bandaids, sticks em on my arm. An then we see the window's still open, this whole time. We've bin too loud.

Eleven

As we start back to the van from the lookout, the cicadas get louder. The sun's getting higher with every gumleaf I crunch under my shoes, and I smell terrible. Jack's aircon is busted, still, so the drive won't be much better.

'There must've been a mass murder,' Zufan says, weirdly sounding like that would be a good thing. 'That has to be it.'

'There weren't any other cars on the road, though,' I say. 'Like, when we went through town the first time, there were heaps of cars. It's near the highway, so people would be passing through.'

'There was no police tape or anything,' Poppy says. 'The bodies should have been found by now.'

'And the internet isn't working,' I say. 'Or the phones. We had that blackout. There's nothing.'

No one says anything, and suddenly I'm hyper aware of how tired I am. Guess finding blood-covered bodies in the middle of a deserted town takes it out of a girl.

A smell on the wind makes my face curl. I hold up a hand and everyone stops. 'Can you smell that?' I ask.

Poppy sniffs as she peers round at the trees. 'Like off meat.'

'It's getting stronger,' Zufan says, whirling around.

Jack takes a couple of steps forward, raising his hand to shade his eyes against the blinding sun. He stares down the path back to the van. 'I think someone's coming,' he says, half a whisper.

A person is walking down the leafy path towards us.

'Shit,' Zufan says, shrinking back. 'They're the mass murderer and we're gonna fuckin die. This sucks.'

'What do we do?' Poppy looks at me, then so do the others.

'It's cool, be calm,' I say, though I want to run. 'We can just ask them what's happened.'

Poppy nods. 'Maybe everyone's been … evacuated.'

As I look to the person, I see they're limping. Their pace remains constant and they make no sign they've seen or heard us, other than walking straight towards us.

The smell gets stronger.

It's the murderer, Zufan is right. We're going to die. Jesus fucking shit Christ, we're going to *die*. There are four of us and one of them, but they murdered *a whole fucking town*.

'Hello?' Poppy calls to them, her voice clear over the cicadas. I want to make her stop, but they've obviously already seen us – although what if they're not alone? Poppy clears her throat. 'Can you tell us what's happened?'

They don't respond.

Zufan takes a few steps forward. 'Are they … they …

holy shit.' She turns around, her eyes wide. 'They've got blood on them. We have to go.'

'Wait,' I say, clutching her arm. 'What if they're injured? Just cause they've got blood on them doesn't mean they're the killer.'

'It's around their mouth,' Poppy says, as Jack makes a noise of disgust, stepping towards the person to get a closer look. 'Are you okay?' she calls out.

I freeze.

'We have to get back to the van,' Zufan says. Jack nods in agreement.

But I join Poppy in peering closer, curiosity getting the better of me. The person is still shuffling towards us, a bit quicker now we're talking to them.

'This is so not fuckin safe,' Jack says.

'Holy hell,' I say, as I get a proper look at the person's bloody mouth. I keep my voice low. 'Okay, we'll backtrack to the lookout, and maybe we can get around them through the bush and to the van.'

'But they might need help,' Poppy says.

My panic is rising like bile, but I swallow and push it down. This isn't real because stuff like this doesn't happen in real life. And that's how I keep calm. As long as we get back to the van, we'll be all right. Jack starts to go back to the van, and the rest of us follow.

'They stink,' Zufan says softly. 'Why do they smell so bad?'

'Maybe they're carrying something gross,' Poppy says.

'*Where*, Pop?' Zufan replies. 'They don't have a bag.'

'I just don't think we should abandon someone who might need help.'

'Something's gone wrong here, it's not safe.'

'Keep walking,' I remind them, especially Poppy. 'They're getting closer.'

'They don't look like they've noticed us properly,' Poppy says. They're getting too close to her. 'They keep opening and closing their mouth. Maybe they *do* need help.'

'Come on, Poppy,' I say. 'They're too close.'

A breeze picks up and the full stench of the person hits me in the face; I gag, Jack retches. Poppy gives him a look of sympathy before walking a bit faster, but still not fast enough. Jack's soon past her as she trails behind us.

'Come on,' I tell her again. 'They might actually be the one who killed everyone.'

'They've got blood all round their mouth,' Zufan reminds us. She snorts. 'Maybe they're drunk?' She waggles her fingers at the person, and she laughs, but no one else does. 'Come on, mate,' she calls, 'let's get you a taxi.'

'Look at them,' I say. 'They look mindless.'

They're close, ten metres away.

'We could help –' Poppy starts, while I say, 'We're –'

Jack cuts in. 'One of their legs is broken.'

The person lets out a low, wheezy snarl, snapping their jaws. Their teeth are bloody too. They raise their arms towards us, and their hands are covered in dried blood.

'Jesus Christ,' Zufan says. 'I'm fuckin running.'

'Wait, Zufan –' I grab her arm again. 'We shouldn't split up.'

'Let's all just duck through the trees,' she replies.

'I am *really* fuckin scared,' Jack says. 'I like Zufan's plan. It's a good plan.'

And my body is telling me I should; I can feel the blood pumping in every vein, through my heart, down my arms. I look at Poppy and she looks at me, and she nods. 'Okay.'

Zufan bolts off, Jack close behind her. Poppy's next, and I bring up the rear. We run into the trees; sticks cut into my legs and a branch gets me across the forehead. My eyes water, but there's no time to stop. Poppy yelps as she gets a branch to the face too, and we run faster. We get back onto the path, and the person is having trouble turning ... though now that we're moving they're walking faster, lurching around but getting close.

Jack gets the keys out of his pocket, drops them, and Zufan is screaming at him.

The person is moving even quicker now, and the foot of their broken leg crunches under their joints. A low breathy growl whines out of their lungs.

Finally Jack gets the van's doors open, and we pile in. But the engine won't fucking start. We're all yelling – we're gonna die because of his dad's shitty van. He yells at us to shut up, and after another failure he pauses.

'Give it a sec,' he says, voice higher than I've ever heard it. 'Lock all the doors, wind up the windows if any are –'

There's a loud slap on the side window, right in front of me. I scream and shuffle back against Zufan. She puts an arm round my torso and drags me closer. The person outside has their face pressed to the glass. Blood smears onto the window and everyone screams, me included, and I can't feel my throat anymore. I can't feel my head, my feet; I'm dreaming again, that's all. I hear Zufan right close in my ear, her breath is warm, and I hold on to that thought: *Zufan is alive, I'm alive.* My heart is pounding against her arm.

Finally, Jack gets the van running.

'Go!' I scream.

He seems to startle out of shock and slams his foot on the accelerator. The van lurches forward, the person's face crushed to the window.

And then it's gone. We're back on the highway in a cloud of dust. There's no one else around.

'What the fuck,' I say. 'What the *fuck*.'

'I just about fucking pissed myself,' Zufan says. I'm still leaning into her, we realise, and she lets me go. I put on my seatbelt. 'They looked like a zom–'

'Don't be ridiculous, Dee,' Jack says. 'There's no such thing.'

'So what, there are just rabid people wandering the woods?' Zufan asks.

'They looked like a zombie, Jack,' Poppy says. 'Dee's right.'

'That's so fucked,' he says. 'That can't be it. Maybe some disease … Can, like, rabies be in humans?'

'They'd probably just gone bush, living off the wildlife,' Zufan says, 'and we wandered into their path. They probably saw everyone in their town die.'

'And they wanted to eat us,' I retort. 'I'm telling you, that was a fucking zombie.'

'Who says they wanted to eat us?' Jack asks.

'Um, they implied it pretty heavily with their tooth gnashing. Did you see the way they pressed up against the glass? Their leg was broken. They clearly didn't feel pain.'

Jack is silent.

'Their teeth were coming loose against the window,' I say.

'We have to find someone,' Poppy says. 'What if no one knows yet? We have to tell people.'

'Where?' Zufan replies. 'And who's going to believe us?'

'We can drive around and see who's out there,' Jack says.

'That doesn't solve the problem of this all sounding ridiculous!' Zufan snaps.

'We'll figure something out. We can't hide in the bush for the rest of our lives. We just have to find the next town.' I wonder what my family are doing. Are they safe? Do they know? Are they worried about me? I don't know how I feel about them maybe being dead. I don't think my mum deserves to die. What if she needs help?

'The fuck we gonna go?' Zufan says. 'We don't have maps.'

'We can find one,' Poppy replies. 'Someone'll have a Melways.'

'Going to the next town is the shittest idea I've ever heard,' Zufan says. 'All the towns around this one will be some of the worst ones hit.'

'It can't hurt to have a look, Zufan, you don't have to be so shitty,' I say. 'We made it through this town and it was completely deserted.'

Zufan rolls her eyes but she doesn't respond.

We keep driving, then when the next turn-off appears we start to go down that road. On the other side, the exit ramp, we see all the cars.

They're backed up, all blocked by a truck on its side. Its cargo has spilled onto the ground, and I don't know what it is but it's made dark patches. There are birds circling it, and Jack slows down.

'They were trying to escape,' Zufan says. 'Why did they all die here?'

A couple of cars on the on-ramp have veered off the road, upside down or abandoned, empty or filled with bodies. I wonder how many cars made it out before someone panicked and crashed into the car in front. How did that truck roll?

Poppy sighs. 'There are so many.' Her voice is heavy.

It looks like a lot of them crashed into each other after the truck rolled. But some of them are just sitting there. A few have open doors; a few bodies are lying around. Lots of cars have windows spattered with blood from the inside. I can't understand what I'm seeing. How did all this happen? But how do you find information that isn't on the internet or the TV?

'One of these cars must have a map in it,' Poppy says, and I really wish she hadn't because she's right. There are too many for there not to be a map. People probably have food with them, too, and blankets and water.

Jack looks around at us. 'Do I drive closer?'

'Maybe we can back it in,' Poppy says. 'Then we can make a quicker getaway if we need to.'

'Someone should stay in the van,' Jack says.

'You do it,' I tell him. 'Keep the engine running.'

Poppy and I pair up; Zufan stays in the van so no one's on their own. Jack found some tools in the back, Poppy's got a wrench and I've got a thing that might be a jack. But we don't really know how to use weapons, so we just gotta keep a good lookout, I guess.

The first car we pass has three people in it, pressing their faces against the windows, obviously wanting to get at us. They grow more frantic as Poppy stops to look at them close up. Their eyes are milky; their skin looks dead, all dull and loose. They're covered in blood – I think it's from one another. The middle one has chunks of flesh ripped out, and there are lots of teeth marks.

'What are you doing?' I ask Poppy. I'm standing a few metres back, glancing around in case one tries to sneak up on us.

She's silent for a few moments; the cicadas hum. 'Wondering who they were.'

Again I wonder what's happened to my family. Maybe they tried to escape like these people. A thought drops through my chest: *They must be dead.* I can't think about it. I can't. Squash those thoughts.

Poppy swallows. 'It's just, like ... what if they're self-aware?'

'What if they kill you?' I say, and that thought chokes up my whole body. The world without Poppy doesn't exist, I'm sure.

'They're behind the glass, it's okay.'

'I meant other ones.'

And she doesn't reply for a whole long while. There's a teen in there, our age, snapping their jaw at Poppy's face, then her hand as she reaches up to the glass. 'I wonder who's still alive.' She keeps staring at the people in the car. 'I don't feel bad if they're not.'

'Your parents?'

'I'm more sad about people at school. Like Mr Eades.'

He's the teacher in charge of the music department. He always let us into the rooms at lunch, even though officially we were only allowed in them once a week. The music teachers were the best, and they're the people I'll miss most from school.

'Zufan's brother, I'll miss him,' I say. 'Her family.'

'Your mum?'

'Maybe.'

I watch the car window for the tiniest hint that it

might break. It doesn't, and the growls from inside get louder the longer she stands there.

She straightens, looks at me. 'Come on.' The next car is upside down, driven off the road. There are two passengers: one still in their seatbelt, dangling from the roof, and the other crumpled into a heap. Both are dead, and we check them properly. At least we know this means the zombified people are probably created while they're still alive.

'Should we go back?' I ask.

'Back where?'

'Home.'

She looks at me. 'I don't know.'

I drag one passenger out of the car by the feet and realise this is the first time I've touched a dead body, and I wonder if it will be the last or if there'll be more soon. We leave the one dangling from the driver's seat, and all I can feel is how cold those legs were.

'Here's a map,' Poppy says, reaching over. 'It's from like 1994 … Still, better than nothing.'

We go to the next car, doors open, empty of people in any states of life. (Or non-life. Un-life? This is ridiculous.) The car has a torch in the glove box. I flick the switch and it turns on; I grin and show Poppy. 'Nice one,' she says. 'I found a bag of Minties.' She throws one at me and I catch it. She's already chewing.

'Excellent.'

As we walk to the next car, further away than the others, it could feel like a normal summer day – only it doesn't. The smell has started to creep up on us, and as we get closer to the exit ramp and all the cars piled behind the truck, I see masses of flies everywhere. We're gonna have to get used to the smell.

The next car is filled with bodies ripped to shreds. The red inside is darker than I thought it would be. I swallow, again pushing down the vomit that wants to rise.

So why were we the ones who got out? We're not special. This must have happened not long after we arrived at the house; these bodies look pretty old. How far does this go?

Is everyone dead?

'I didn't write down my song,' Poppy says. I turn to her. She's looking at the exposed organs of the people in the car, strewn all over the leather seats. 'I don't even remember it.' There are tears in her eyes. After a quick glance around for zombies, I take the three steps between us and hug her, tighter than even the time her grandma died. I feel her sobs but she barely makes any noise, only breathing in wetly. She clings to me with both hands, and it's like we're the same person.

I don't cry because I know that if I do I will never stop.

I wonder who turned first in my family, or if they got away. Who killed who? Did they kill each other or would they just let themselves be turned? Maybe they were killed by bandits. Would there be bandits? Do we count as bandits, stealing from these dead people?

Poppy lets me go, and I don't want her to; I want her to cling to me forever so I can keep clinging to her. But forever is too long, and I don't say anything.

The next car has nothing, but the one after that is stocked with food. It's smashed into the one in front; the driver looks like they were pinned by the steering wheel. As we approach, they look at us and their eyes aren't human. They growl, low and long.

'They'll get us,' I say.

They're struggling but can't get out from under the wheel.

'We can't,' Poppy says.

I look at the food behind the driver, everywhere. There's so much. My stomach pangs.

'You're right,' I say.

A few cars down is a boot filled with food. It's already been popped open, or maybe it popped when the car crashed. Either way, we grab the food; two big cardboard boxes of cans.

The car beside it has guts strewn on it. At first I think they're on the inside but then the smell gets me, the shiny smooth purple-red of it. 'Gross,' I say, and this time the vomit comes up, splashing onto my shoes. I manage to not get any on the food, at least.

Poppy shakes her head, lips drawn tight as she groans, tries not to vomit herself. After a few minutes, when I've chucked two more times, she repeats, 'Gross. That was the most disgusting thing I have ever smelt.'

'But now we get to enjoy all this delicious zombie

food,' I say, gripping the box close. 'Make sure we find a can-opener, otherwise we're gonna die.'

She nods, and sure enough there's a can-opener in one of the boxes.

We take the boxes back to the van, and we crack open one of the bottles of water. The sun is hot and bright; it must be the middle of the day, and the others get out of the van because it's heating up.

Then we hear the distant sound of a car approaching, and I don't know what to do.

'Should we hide?' Zufan asks.

'Maybe we can get information,' I say. 'We still have no idea what's going on.'

We don't know what to do.

'They could help us,' Poppy says.

'I dunno,' Jack says, but he doesn't move. Zufan makes to say something, then she just closes her mouth.

The sun shines on the windscreen as the car gets closer, and then closer, and slower, and then it stops maybe a hundred metres away. A really tall person steps out of the car. Then another person, maybe the same height as me. The tall person stays at the car, and the other walks towards us. Poppy grips my arm, and we don't say anything. Jack ties up his shoulder-length hair; he does that when he's nervous.

'Do you need help?' is the first thing the person says when they're close enough.

'What happened?' Jack asks.

They stop walking. 'You don't know?'

'We were camping.'

'Oh.' They look back at the tall person, wave them over. Nobody says anything as we watch them get a toddler out of the car and walk to us. Cicadas, the sound of everyone breathing, that's all. Then, 'Hasib, they don't know what's happening.'

Hasib's brow furrows in concern. 'Do you kids need help?' Hasib sighs. 'Do you know anything – at all, about what happened?' The toddler tugs at Hasib's hand but doesn't say anything.

I don't know what to say. It's something bad, and I don't want to know how bad.

'It's, uh, how do we say it?' Hasib asked.

'A zombie apocalypse?' says the other person.

'She's always been better at words than me.' Hasib tries to smile but can't do it properly. 'We're not sure really, what happened. There wasn't a lot of information, but everyone's –'

'Dead,' she supplies. 'There was a lot of death. A *lot*. I don't know how many people have survived – we hid for a long time. But then there were fires, you know how hot it's getting, and then we've just been driving, trying to find a safe place.'

'Where did you come from?' Zufan asks.

'Hoppers Crossing.'

We live around there, spread out through the west of Melbourne. Zufan's uncle lives in Hoppers Crossing. 'Our high school is in Werribee,' I say. Mostly because I want her to say, *Oh no, Werribee was perfectly fine. Very safe.*

She and Hasib look at each other. 'Do you want to come with us? We don't have any food or anything, but it would be safer to stick together.'

Zufan speaks first. 'I want to look for them,' she says. 'My family.'

And despite what I thought before, I don't want my mum to be dead.

'It's really not safe,' Hasib says.

But we can't say no to Zufan.

'I think we have to,' I say, and Poppy nods. Jack's face remains still, but he nods too.

'All right. If you're sure?' Hasib's eyes are wide, like they're pleading with us. They think we're going to die.

Zufan swallows, wrings her hands. 'Yeah.'

'Thank you,' I tell them. When you've got nothing, it must be hard to offer to look after five other people.

Hasib and the woman nod, then Hasib picks up the toddler. They walk back to their car. And then they're gone.

We find some more things in cars: blankets, a big box with a goon sac of water inside, more tins. We all get back into the van, and Jack drives off down the empty highway, towards something we don't want to find.

Twelve

'Fuck off, Jojo. I just want to sleep.' Rhea glares at me. We've been walking for hours and it's dark.

I know why she wants to sleep, it'd be nice just to not have to deal with everything for a little while, but my mind won't let me stop. Mum's gone, we're on the run from some kind of disease that's like ... killing everyone. We went home and grabbed some stuff, but we didn't really have any food left.

Will we go back home, ever? Mum's dead. She's dead. We didn't get to bury her.

'We can't,' I say, 'we've gotta keep moving. Something's happening.'

'Fine.'

We haven't spoken about Mum. I don't think we will yet.

There's a rumble in the ground, and more orange flares up in the distance.

We walk across the park; the moon is new so there's no light. I stumble in a hole in the dirt and fall into Rhea, but I haven't twisted my ankle and we make it across. I feel exposed like everyone's watching, when probably no one is.

'I think to get further out we're gonna have to cross the Ring Road,' Rhea says, scrunching up her face.

That's a big road. If the army or whatever need to transport things, they're probably using that. It's near the hospital, which we would have passed if we didn't decide to go east to avoid it.

'We must've been walking parallel to the road this whole time,' she says. 'We should grab a map, find out where we are.'

We've been walking the whole night and we're barely out of the suburb. Fuck. Off.

'A map's a good idea,' I tell her. 'Maybe if we can figure out where we're going, it won't take us so fucking long.' Seriously, I've never walked this far in my life and we've made negative three million progress. It's quiet and not a lot of buildings have lights on inside. Have people evacuated, like that army person said on the phone? Do they know what's happening?

'Maybe someone's left their car unlocked,' she says as we make it to the edge of the park and onto a small street. We walk up to a couple of parked cars – there aren't many – but they're all locked. When we round a corner, we see a big barricade that bars off the street. The houses behind the barricade all look abandoned; there are smashed windows and open doors, lots of biohazard signs. But no bodies, no greyed-out people moving behind it.

Rhea peers through the barricade. 'There's another

fence. I think this one might be like a precaution or something.'

I wish we still had those masks.

We keep walking down the street, and none of the lights are on here either. There's a noise up ahead, and Rhea drags me into someone's front yard. The bush smells strongly like citrus, though I don't know why exactly; I breathe through my mouth it's so pungent.

We wait, peering through the bushes and the fence, and then we see someone shuffling down the road. They're joined by another person, and then a few more. I don't know where they're going, and they seem pretty aimless. They're not walking with any purpose, just … drifting. We stay completely still as we watch the small crowd walk down the street. They take ages, and some have the open wounds that the people at the hospital had. It's too dark to see if they're all dull and dead looking, but I'm sure they must be.

We wait until we can't see them anymore, then emerge from the front yard. We wander some more and come across no one. The streets seem to be deserted now. We pass a burnt-out car. The next street over, the houses have been looted, there's shit everywhere.

And a few bodies.

Rhea yelps when she sees the first one, turns her head away.

'We gotta keep going,' I tell her, touching her shoulder. I wonder if Mum is a body now, or if she's still wandering around. 'Let's find a map.'

We go through cars, smashing dozens of windows. There are only two cars left when we find an old Melways. It's from 1997, covered in food stains with some pages ripped out, but it'll do. Rhea looks at the maps while I glance around; everything is so dark and every shadow could hide something. I can't believe how quiet it is. Is it like this everywhere? Why did these people leave, when in our area we were told to stay put?

There's a low growl somewhere behind me. I whirl around, and one of the diseased people is standing there. They've got blood all down their front, around their mouth, on their hands.

'Yikes!' I grab Rhea. 'We gotta go!'

'Oh jeez,' she says, and we pissbolt. Rhea leads the way, thrusts the maps into my arms. 'We're on McLean – find out where that is.' While we run and I look at the map, she makes sure I don't bump into anything.

'I literally can't read while running,' I say, trying to catch my breath. 'We should go north though, away from the hospital.'

'The fuck way is north?'

We're a couple of streets from the diseased person, so I grab Rhea's arm and we stop for a bit. We look at the map under the streetlight. 'And if we keep on the way we're going, we'll cross Greensborough Highway.'

She looks at the map while I keep an eye out for anyone. 'So if we wanna get away from ...' She pauses, because really, what are we running from? We have no idea. 'We can go up to either Whittlesea or Kinglake, or take a detour and go somewhere else.'

'Kinglake has all that green around, though – look.' I point at the map.

'That's where all those fires were, back in 2009,' she says.

'Still, more hiding places.'

She considers it. 'I want to steal a car.'

'We can't even drive.'

'How hard can it be? We're not gonna crash into anybody because no one's outside. We'll be fine, just gotta make sure we get an auto and not manual. All we have to worry about is the accelerator and the brake, right?'

I sigh. 'Maybe?' I've got no fucking clue. 'If you reckon you can drive, go for it.'

'We need to steal one first.'

'Stealing the maps was hard enough.'

She twists her mouth at me. 'Well, your negativity isn't helping,' she says, trying not to grin. 'Come on, let's keep walking. Maybe we should sleep during the day.'

'If we're going to Kinglake,' I start, 'then if we go kinda like … halfway between these two bigger roads,' I point on the map again, 'there must be more traffic.'

'More houses, but,' Rhea says. 'More people, maybe.'

'We'll be right.'

'Unless we run into the police or whatever.' She pushes me to the side.

I nudge her with my elbow. 'Or firefighters,' I say, thinking of the burnt-out cars.

'Hot firefighters.' She pushes her foot into the back of my knee. I start to fall and grab her, but she ducks out of the way. I hit the dirt.

'You're the worst,' I tell her from the ground. 'No hot army dudes or ladies *or* anyone else for you, you bisexual pervert.'

She giggles, gives me a hand up, and I push her to the side. 'As if you can talk,' she says, 'you're also a bisexual pervert, for fuck's sake.' She's running to the end of the street. 'Come on, let's …'

We can see the highway from here and there's heaps of cars on it, all parked. They've been pushed out of the way to let army trucks past. A truck's going through now, headlights on. They're driving away from us, they can't see us. Beyond the truck, the sun is rising.

'We should get some rest,' I say. 'I'm about to fall asleep.'

'I don't want to cross the highway in the daytime.'

'It's almost day now.'

She frowns. 'Let's go check it out anyway. We can make a plan – maybe find a car to steal. There's a lot there.'

They look like they've either crashed or been abandoned, or both, but we don't mention it. By the time we get to the highway, the sky is turning pink, but above our heads is still a dark blue. There's a couple of bushes we hide behind, but then we can't see shit.

'Let's get behind one of those cars,' Rhea says. 'It'll be fine – they won't be looking for people, anyway.'

'If we get caught I'm going to kill you,' I say, but I follow her, crouched across the grass, the bitumen.

The car stinks. I raise my head to peer through a window to see why it stinks, and clap my hand over my mouth. I slap Rhea's side with my other hand, again and again because I've forgotten how to do words.

'What?' she hisses, then sees my face. She leans up, looks in the car, and leans back down. 'Okay.'

'They've been dead a long time. Fuckin *maggots?* How long has this been going on?'

'Shut up.' Rhea keeps swallowing, holds her chin up. 'I'm gonna vomit. I'll vomit on you,' a deep breath, 'if you're not careful.'

'Are all these cars filled with people?'

'Not looking, don't care.' The highway is quiet except for a couple of crickets. 'Let's just cross.'

We crawl over to the front of the car, stick our heads out and look both ways. The road's empty, so we run across. Rhea stops in front of a car. 'This one's empty. And it's got the keys in the ignition.'

'It's got blood in it!'

'Only a little, you can sit on a towel,' she tells me.

The blood's on the passenger seat.

'What, *you're* driving?' I ask.

'Of course. I'm older, I'm the responsible one.'

'Oh my god. You're literally the worst.'

'Literally. Come on, let's steal our first car.'

'We're stealing a car. From the second-biggest road. That has some dead person's blood in it.'

'It's a bonding experience.' She taps me on the head. 'Come on, we need to get outta here. This car has possibility written all over it.'

'It might not even start.'

'Jojo!' There's a barely hidden urgency that I didn't see before. Her hands are fists, her knuckles light. 'Come on, before someone finds us.'

She's just as terrified as I am. Which, in a way, kinda calms me down.

We get in the car. She looks in the rear-view mirror, adjusts it to her height, and sees no one coming. 'Okay.' She lets out a deep breath and runs her hands along the wheel. She turns the key and the engine rumbles; the radio broadcasts static.

'Let the key go,' I say, and she does. The car stays on. 'Mum always lets the key go after that first rev bit,' I tell her when she turns to me, confused.

'All righty.' She looks at the gear control or ... whatever it's called. The stick that you move to make the car do stuff. 'So it's in P. That must mean park.'

'R is reverse ... no idea what N is. But D! Must mean drive.'

'What about the other ones?' Rhea asks. 'Can you blow up a car being in the wrong thing?'

'You said we just need to know how to go and stop. This is how we go. Trust me, I'm actually a scientist.'

'I hate you,' she says, but she puts it into D. 'Get me

some D.' Then she turns the wheel and we start going forward, lurch when she puts her foot too hard on the accelerator. 'It's ... sticky,' she says, when we're driving down the highway.

'Oh!' I see ... the thing. 'Behind the gearstick thing. Brake thing. Handbrake!'

'What?' She turns to me, puts her foot on the brake. 'Handbrake. Right.' She depresses the little button on the end and pushes the lever down. The car gets a little faster. 'That's better.'

'Headlights?'

The windscreen wipers come on. We're both giggling, and I find a CD in the glove box. It's a burnt one, unlabelled. We keep the volume super low but it's nice listening to music, even if we don't recognise the song.

'We should turn at some point,' I tell her. 'Get off the main road.'

'Tell me where, and then I guess Kinglake here we come.'

There's a huge noise. It seems really close but when I turn around the plume of smoke is a few kays away. The hospital, maybe? I can't tell where we are anymore.

'Kinglake it is,' I say.

A car zooms past us. Rhea's driving slowly, and soon more cars zoom past. I look at some of the passengers and they're yelling at each other, kids are screaming. Some cars are totally packed with people and things, more than is safe.

Another explosion rocks the road. Another.

'But, y'know, if you could go a bit faster,' I say, desperate to avoid looking in the rear-view mirrors; I don't want to figure out where those explosions are. 'That would also be good.'

Another *boom*, and more cars.

'Please,' I add.

'It's my first time driving,' she snaps. 'I don't want to kill us.'

'*They're* going to kill us. Come on, Rhea. You can do it. Look how good you are, and it's been two seconds.'

'Literally.'

'Almost.'

She grins then gets her eyes back on the road real quick. 'All right, let's do this.' She puts her foot down a little, and the speedo goes up.

'Turn left at the next road,' I say after about five minutes. We're passing fewer cars. Four more explosions have gone off. I put the music up a little louder; people are going to hear the engine before they hear the music, anyway.

We keep driving through the quiet suburbs, and the other cars have peeled away from us. We see a cat every now and then, a couple of foxes. A few drifting people. No army. No police. 'Maybe this was one of the areas they tried to evacuate,' I say.

'The newsreaders kept saying *tried*. What does that mean?' She frowns. According to the clock in the car, it's about seven in the morning.

I don't know how to answer her question, so I talk

about directions. 'There are two ways to Kinglake – the big road or the back way. It goes through all the towns, if that's okay?'

'The big road'll do that too, probably. With bigger towns, I guess, so we're probably safe.'

We don't say anything else until we get to the first town centre. The traffic lights are off. There are more drifters here; they like the sound of the car, it seems, because they turn to us when we pass. Lots of cars are crashed or parked on the roads, and we have to drive slowly between them, and some of the drifters are slapping our windows.

As we go on, we reach a car crash in the middle of the road. There are bodies in the car, on the ground. Abandoned.

'Zombie apocalypse,' I say, and it feels ridiculous.

'Don't be silly. If it was the apocalypse, we'd be better dressed.'

'Hmm.' I think about it. 'That's true. Our hair would also be stylishly messy, instead of greasy and tangled.'

'And we'd be less sweaty.'

We pass through heaps more towns. Sometimes we have to take a detour to get past the main streets, with too many cars and bodies. Theoretically we could just drive over the corpses, but like ... I don't want to do that and I don't suggest it to Rhea.

'Welcome to Kinglake,' I say, reading the sign as we drive into town after hours on empty roads. At first not running into any living people was good, but now

I just want to see one person, any person. It feels like we're the only two left alive. At least we can't hear any explosions from here.

'We should steal some food,' Rhea says. 'I'm starving.'

There's one of those stores that's like a tiny half supermarket, only stocking the essentials. We get a whole bunch of canvas bags from next to the counter and fill them with food, toothpaste and other stuff we'll need. The freezers and fridges are off, and a smell's oozing out, but we snag some Schweppes cans. There's almost nothing left on the shelves, only the shitty cheap lollies and canned stuff like peas and glacé cherries. I was hoping for beans, or tuna, *something*. I bend to check under the shelves. 'Hey! Jackpot.' I pull out a five-pack of two-minute noodles. 'Maybe we can boil some water,' I tell Rhea.

'Matches and shit,' she says. 'We'll need those. And batteries.'

We pack our bags to their fullest and get back in the car.

'This what being an adult feels like?' Rhea says.

'Guess we dunno what that'll mean anymore, do we.'

We drive until we find the entrance to the forest park and leave the car next to a couple of other parked cars. 'See?' Rhea says. 'Hide the thing in the forest with the other things.'

'Pretty sure that's exactly how the saying goes.'

We've got sleeping-bags but no tent, but it's summer

and warm enough that we probably don't need one for a while. To keep out mozzies, maybe.

We find a place to camp in the forest, after maybe half an hour's walking, that's a little off the path. The morning sun is bright as anything, but we fall asleep tucked under a bush in our sleeping-bags, as close as we can get to each other even though it's super warm.

***

When I wake up, Rhea's half asleep. I shake her properly awake and she mutters swears at me.

'Maybe we can find like a barbecue area to sleep in,' I say. 'Set up a mini camp.'

She nods, then reaches for a canvas bag with food in it as she blinks away sleep.

'I'm just gonna go pee,' I say.

'Don't go too far.'

'I won't.' I don't really want to leave her at all, but I'm not gonna let my sister see me pee. I walk maybe a hundred metres; the bush isn't very dense so it takes me a while to find a place. I undo my fly and then scream. There's a random just walking around in between the trees. They've seen me and start walking my way.

'Sorry,' I say. Now there's another person, the fear is back. Being alone, being with someone – there's no comfortable point. 'Do you know what's happening?'

They don't reply, just keep walking closer. Their face is really dirty, maybe they've been out here a while. Maybe they're a wild person, brought up by wombats.

Calm down, Jojo.

'Are you all right?' I ask, but then I realise they're greyed out like the others.

They're closer and they really smell, holy fuck. And then I see they only have one hand; there's a bloody stump where the other's been ripped off. And they've got, like, a fuckin knife stabbed into their stomach. And the dirt on their face isn't brown but a really dark red, dried-blood red.

'Zombie!' I yelp. 'Rhea! They're really fuckin zombies!'

'Fuck off,' she calls out. 'We need to be quiet.'

'Seriously!' I'm walking backwards so the zombie doesn't touch me. Slow walkers, thank fucking Christ. 'Look.' It gets quicker as I speak, and I run back to Rhea. The movement seems to make it pick up the pace even more.

She stands up, gets a knife that we brought from our kitchen. She holds it out in front of her. 'Watch out, buddy. If you're not a zombie you better lemme know, cause I'm about to stab you.'

The zombie keeps coming forward.

'Oh my god,' I say. 'It's got maggots in one eye. That's so fuckin rank.'

'Shut up,' she says, nudging me in the ribs. 'I gotta kill it, don't make it look cool. Or me vomit.'

'It's a zombie, Rhea. It's already cooler than I will ever be. And why do *you* get to kill it?'

'Because I'm older, fuck you.'

She swipes out with the knife, and the zombie growls in a way that turns my bones to ice. I see Rhea shudder and realise I'm doing it too. She lunges out again, into the neck this time. The zombie snaps its teeth.

'Get a branch,' Rhea says. 'Push it away.'

I find a big stick next to us and prod the zombie in the shoulder. Doesn't stop it, but now it's coming for me. 'Rhea!' I yell. 'Hurry up!'

'All right, all right.' She goes behind, plunges the knife into its spine. *Crack*. The head topples over, but it's still attached. The zombie swings around and lunges at her; she dodges.

'What the fuck,' I say. 'They kill them so easy in movies.'

'We need something heavier or … longer.' She dodges again to avoid its arms.

I kick its back, and it falls over. I stomp on its skull, which is fuckin hard. I don't know why I thought it would be soft. Maybe I'm not pressing hard enough because like … it's still looking pretty human.

'Pin it down,' she says.

I kneel on its back; it's scrambling. I manage to keep it down despite my spindly arms, while Rhea severs the spinal cord. Well, she severs something and there's zombie blood everywhere; I guess the spinal cord must be stuffed cause it stops moving. I get off it.

Rhea takes a few steps, keeps her chin up and starts swallowing again. 'I am *not* vomiting,' she says to herself. 'Not over a fucking zombie.'

'I think that's a fair enough reason,' I say, then vomit all over my knees. 'Gross,' I say after I stop retching. 'Covered in blood and vomit.' Then I realise I don't need to pee anymore. 'Oh my god, I fucking pissed myself.'

She looks at me and grins, then her eyes move to something behind me and her face hardens.

I turn, and there's a group of people looking at us.

Thirteen

I slam the window shut, which was probly a shit idea. All I can think about is the fact we're gonna die if anyone's heard us.

She looks at me. 'That was loud.'

'That was real fucken loud.'

'We should shut up,' she says, an I can see she blames me. She's jus gonna sit there in silence, an there's nothin to do cept sit opposite her.

So we wait, an there's nothin. We wait, an the sun sets. It always happens faster than you think. Sun's there, give it five minutes, it's gone.

Dunno how much time goes past til we hear a voice. A deep voice, an they say somethin about breakin the door down. She looks at me an I can' fucken breathe.

'We have to go,' she says.

'They might not come upstairs.'

'We should get out.' But she don' move.

'We can hide.' These walls've bin so safe til now.

She looks at me, waits, an then her face sets. 'We can't. We're taking the knives. We can lock the door or something, stay in here, don't make a noise. All right?'

'Right.'

She hands me my bat an clicks the lock. 'Hopefully they'll just give up. But you've got to be ready to fight them, all right?'

I never met anyone like her. She's so hard. I nod.

She gets out the knife she keeps in her belt, an then we wait. I hear them rummage through the kitchen drawers; knives an that clack to the floor. The fridge opens an one of em coughs, closes it again. One laughs an says somethin I can' hear proply.

'They're loud,' she whispers. There's a crash like someone fell into somethin an knocked it over. That means they ain' afraid of bein caught.

They're gonna get us fucken killed. I look at her an she's thinkin what I'm thinkin. Maybe they're gonna be the ones to kill us stead a zombies, who knows. But I know she ain' gonna let that happen, cause right now she's crouchin like a cat, coiled tight, an her knife is glintin. She lightly touches the back of me hand, an waits behind the locked door. The lock is tiny, cheap metal, an it's not gonna hold.

Jeez, the way they're talkin, they're gonna draw every fucken zombie in the street. We've bin seein more as the days go on, like today. Shoulda bin more careful.

I can' even hear her breathin. She's jus waitin, eyes wide, not movin, an it's not true but I wonder if she's turned to stone. Then I'd be alone again an I dunno if I could handle it. I wouldn', I know I wouldn'. It was all right fore she came cause it didn' feel real. When I was alone it coulda bin a dream, but she's the most real person I ever met in my life, an I know she ain' a dream. She's realer than blood.

One of the people downstairs yells out, calls to the others to have a look. They musta found the lounge, still covered in blood. I cleaned the kitchen cause we go through it to get upstairs, but didn' bother bout the lounge. It's hard to get tea outta the couch, so I reckon blood'd be harder. I jus closed the doors an mostly ignored the smell, an all them flies; sides, if someone broke in from the front, maybe the sight of all that blood'd make em think twice.

They're all talkin downstairs. Then they're on the staircase, an one line sticks out bove all the rest, I can hear it like they're whisperin right in my ear: 'Someone's cleaned out the bodies. Musta bin this house where we heard the voices.'

The bathroom is at the enda the hall, so I'm hopin that they check us last. Bedrooms first, though I hope they don' fucken touch our bed. We ain' slept there in a couple a nights but it's still our bed.

'That blood downstairs,' one of em says. 'There was a fucken lotta that, musta bin heapsa them.'

I didn' do any a that, was all me dad. An there's so much blood cause they was alive when he killed em, still had blood pumpin through proply. When I killed em for real it was gluggy blood. When I killed that lady from the supermarket, there was even less, though maybe cause she wasn' movin, jus sittin on the chair her legs was stuck to.

'Shut up,' another person says. 'They can probly hear us.'

'Fuck off,' the first one mutters, an the other musta heard but nothin happens. Maybe they're mates. Maybe they gotta be mates, otherwise they'd all kill each other.

They go into the first room in the hallway, shout at each other for a while, then go back into the hallway. She's still breathin but I can' hear, I'm breathin so hard through my nose I'm sure the people out there can hear it. Breathin, the walls is breathin, the floors – where's the breathin comin from? They can' tell; they're searchin for the breathin, searchin, searchin. They go into the next room, our bedroom, an I ball my fists. She looks at me but I don' move.

'This bed looks slept in,' one of them says. 'An look, chip packet. This is the house. Dead ones don' eat.'

'Coulda bin here since the start,' another says.

'Maybe there's only one of em.'

'All that blood, but. That's a lotta killin for one guy.'

Now she's ready to go at em, break down the door an rip out their throats. The way she looks at the door with her knife gripped in one hand, her legs ready to spring up – she's done this before, I think. I hear em walkin towards our door; one's laughin at another one's joke or somethin. They reach another door an open it but don' find anythin.

'One left,' the one that's nervous says.

'Fuck's sake, mate,' another says. 'Stop fucken talkin,

right?' There's a thump – they musta hit the other one. 'Come on,' they say.

The doorknob's bein turned. I'm close enough to hear the person's breathin on the other side. I stand up, an if it wasn' for the door between us we'd be face to face. I swallow an look at her; she nods at me, grips the knife tighter, an gets ready to spring.

'Locked,' they say. Bet their breath smells like beer, like Dad's. I imagine the smell an it's right there, overpowerin, like it's the only thing I've ever smelt.

I can' breathe, I've stopped time.

The person takes a few paces back, so does she. She's in the shadows. The door breaks open cause the lock is shitty an can' hold that much, an then I see their face an they see mine. Ain' noticed her, yet.

We stare at each other, then they seem to remember what they're doin an raise their fists.

'Just a kid,' the shorter one says, but they're ready to back up their mate, I can see.

An then one runs up behind, up the stairs. 'We gotta get the fuck outta here,' they say, outta breath. 'Heapsa zombies is comin, a fuck ton of em!'

We all stare at them, an they yell somethin none of us understan. They run down the hallway, grab the nervous small one's arm an start to drag them away. The bigger one looks at me, eyes a warm brown, an I wonder if they were gonna kill me if that other one hadn' come upstairs. 'Lucky day, kid,' they say, an I wanna spit in their face. They run off with the others. I hear em fall over a bit down the bottom, then there's an engine revvin an they drive off. I picture the dust cloud, red an dry, dirtyin the leaves everywhere.

'A fuck ton,' she repeats, comin outta the shadows. 'We'd better go an have a look. Bring your bat.'

The window doesn' give a view of any zombies, so we go down to the kitchen. An we can' see anythin, but there's a smell.

'Fuck,' she says. We crouch low, go out the front an sneak a look over the fence. An there's heapsa them. 'Those dickheads musta drawn em,' she says.

I wonder if it was them or my fault, for leavin that fucken window open, for runnin round with me arm bleedin fucken everywhere.

'We haveta get the fuck outta here,' I say, an look around. How much can I carry? We need backpacks – where are the backpacks? I can' even fucken remember.

'We could hide upstairs,' she says.

'If the zombies don' get us, them guys is gonna come back.' An I don' wanna leave, it was good havin a safe place without yellin or other people, a place where we could fall asleep without worryin about anythin, but now that's broken an gone. 'We can' stay.'

She has a think, then I see she knows I'm right.

'Can use me an me brother's schoolbags.' They're bigger, can carry more stuff than normal backpacks.

'Where are they?' she asks.

We find em, stuff em full of food, blankets an things like can-openers an matches.

'Okay, we need a plan,' she says once we put the backpacks on. We peer out, an the zombies is on the road in front of the house. 'Do you know how to drive?'

I shake my head.

'Me neither. All right, so do you have bikes?'

'Nah, but the neighbours cross the road do. They got two kids, both of em got bikes.'

'Know where they keep em?'

'Nuh.'

'Right. We'll take your cricket bat, smash some windows, find the bikes, grab them and then we'll just ride, all right? Outrun the group.'

'What if them people find us?'

'Then we deal with them.' She tightens a strap on her backpack 'We can. It's okay.'

Is it? But I don' say anythin.

'We'll just run to the neighbours' house, okay? And we'll have to be quick. I'll go first, you back me up. I'll find the bikes and you smash the window or whatever. Then we'll ride somewhere – back toward the street you went down, I guess.'

'That's the way to the town, jus so ya know,' I say. 'Might be more there.'

'We can't go the other way.'

'Jus sayin.'

'All right. So, you ready?'

We go out on the road. The first zombie notices us, so I whack his face an he stumbles back – an that surprises me, I mean me arms ain' that muscly or anythin. As she continues on across the road, I hit anythin that looks at her. There's only like five around us, but down the road there's a huge mass of em, lurchin closer. The stink is fucken awful, an I breathe through my mouth an I can taste the death. Vomit's in my throat again, but not now, can' do that now.

We make it to the neighbours' backyard, an there's another dead dog. This one's smaller, an its little legs look so sad.

The bikes is jus sittin in the yard. One's a lil rusty but they seem fine. They're a bit big for her, but she says it don' matter, an then we get on em an ride off.

Before times, I woulda bin puffed as soon as I got outta the backyard an onto the street, but right now cause of all the walkin an runnin we bin doin, my body can handle it. With the backpack it's a bit hard for me to balance, but nothin that'll make me crash. An she's speedin off so I pedal faster to catch up.

'You know this area better than me,' she says, once the zombies are far behin us. 'Do you want to lead the way?'

'Where we goin?'

'Away from here. I don't know. Anywhere.'

'We shouldn' go to town,' I say, an brake. She stops with me. 'We gotta keep away from them blokes.'

'Right. You know another way?'

'If we cut through one a these houses, yeah.'

So we get off the bikes, an the hardest part is gettin them over the back fence. We pass over the backpacks an then I climb right up, an she springs over, light as anythin. We wheel our bikes round the house an then check the road, which is empty cept one zombie that ain' noticed us yet. We need to ride in the opposite direction anyway. Pretty soon my butt is hurtin from the seat; standin up on the pedals is better, but hurts my legs. She's hurtin too, an soon we're barely pedlin, jus tryin to go slow as we can without losin our balance.

'We should probly stop soon,' I say when I feel like I'm really dyin.

She nods, an I can see the sweat on her forehead. We go into the nearest house, only three rooms: a bathroom, a kitchen-lounge an a bedroom. It'll do for now, so we lock all the doors – but not the front cause we broke it to get inside.

'You think it'll be all right?' I say.

She nods, points to a coupla houses cross the road. 'They've got broken doors, too.'

When we're in the bedroom, we move the chest of drawers gainst the door, jus in case. It's dark now, an the streetlights ain' comin on anymore. Not sure when that happened exactly. Time is hard, now.

We leave the curtains open an look at the stars, cause no one's gonna see inside. The moon's only a sliver so everythin is super dark, can barely see anythin.

'Shouldn' a left that window open,' I say, quiet, when we're lyin in bed, almost asleep. It's the first time we spoke since gettin to the house.

'It wasn't your fault,' she says. 'Did you see the uniforms all the zombies were wearing? They were from the factory you said your dad worked at, where I said there was heaps of zombies. I mustn't have been as quiet as I thought. I led them straight to us.'

'I still let them guys know where we was, though.'

She looks at me, closes her eyes an breathes slow. Her breath's on my eyelashes, slight, barely there. 'What do you want me to say? You'd forgive me for bringing the horde to our door.'

'People are more dangerous. Jus tell me it was my fault. Don' bullshit me.'

'Fine. Maybe it was.'

My stomach rumbles.

'You want some food?' she says.

I shake my head. 'In the mornin, maybe. Don' wanna make too much noise.'

She nods. 'All right. Breakfast of champions.'

We don' speak again, but I dunno if she's asleep. How mad is she at me? I'd be mad. I'd be fucken mad. But she's not takin it out on me, not like Dad would.

***

I can't sleep. The curtain, I should close the curtain. In the mornin the sun's gonna rise an people'll be able to see in. I get outta bed as quiet as I can an draw it across.

A shape's movin in the backyard. I duck, peer over the windowsill the tiniest bit. It's a uniformed zombie but not the one we saw when we rode in.

I dunno if I should wake her up or not. We could have one last night of peaceful sleep fore we die. Well, she could. Then we'd wake to bein eaten. Not the best way to go, but there are worse.

I shake her awake an she opens her eyes wide, ready to fight. 'What is it?'

'A zombie in the yard. With a uniform on.'

'Shit.' She throws off the covers an pulls on her shorts. 'More might come. Let's go.'

'It's dark – we won' be able to see.'

'We can take our chances. What if more are coming? We should have ridden further, fuck.' She picks up her backpack. 'Ready?'

I nod, an pick up my bag an the cricket bat. It's not as hard as I thought it would be, ridin with it in my hand; a back strap wouldn' be too bad, but.

It's dark as shit but we find the bikes easy. The zombie comes at us an I snap his neck with a jab of my bat. I must be stronger than I thought, I realise, as the spine crunches. Wasn' that bad at school cricket either.

'Which way?' she asks, an I lead us left. We're pedlin slow an nothin springs out on us, everythin's empty. My tyre hits a rock an I wobble, but we keep goin an nothin happens. I feel like them guys is watchin us, an I can' be calm. I know she is, she's always calm, but always alert, ready to whip round an stab anythin that tries to touch us.

We end up near a park jus before sunrise, huge an filled with trees. 'We could rest up there,' she says, pointin. We're both tired as fuck, an I can' feel my bum anymore. Gave up standin on the pedals, got too tired, an now I can barely keep my eyes open. We're out in the open but I'm also too tired to give a shit.

We leave our bikes in some bushes near the edge of the park an walk cross the grass to the trees, a few hundred metres. We're so exposed, I feel naked. Anyone could be in the houses over there, peekin through a gap in the curtains. We end up runnin the last few metres, not sayin anythin, jus knowin the other needs to get off this grass.

She goes up first, then I pass the backpacks. We climb up an up, as high as we can fore the branches get too thin. We rest with our backs to the trunk, so we've got views all round through the leaves. This is probly a good place to hide: the leaves mean we can see out but it's harder for people to see us. An who's gonna expect us to hide in these trees?

Still, we're so fucken exposed I can barely breathe.

'Should we take turns sleeping?' she says.

I nod, then realise she can' see me. 'Yeah, reckon so. You go first.' An she doesn' protest. I can go a bit longer without sleep, I'm good. 'I got a rope in me bag – tie yourself to the tree.' I pass it over an she does. The rope digs into my back as I sit there, doin nothin, an then I get used to it as the hours go past, like it's another knot on the tree's trunk.

The sun is high an hot. I'm glad we're in the shade, cause the grass round us is all brown; we woulda fried. The cicadas are hummin, an there must be one close cause the sound is deafenin. A coupla sugar ants cross over me arms, I can' feel their little legs. There's birds flyin round. But nothin really happens the whole time. Shoulda packed a book or somethin. I pick at the bracelet I took from Mum, twirl it around and around my wrist.

When she wakes I'll tell her we need somethin like that; it sounds petty when we gotta carry food an survival stuff in our backpacks, an there' not that much room in em, but we need some kinda distraction or we're gonna go fucken insane. Can' remember the last time I really wanted to read a book, but now it's all I can think about. It's like the only thing I can think of that don' need electricity and ain' a board game. Board game would be nice cept they're way bigger than books; can get tiny books that'll take ages to read. Maybe we can have one each, then jus keep swappin em as we get to houses. A travlin library.

As she sleeps, a car drives up the road an stops outside the houses on the edge of the park, near where we hid our bikes.

Fourteen

Jack doesn't look around as he drives, just keeps going with his jaw set, straight down the highway. No one's saying anything except Poppy, who keeps telling us how gross it was out there, like we didn't know. I want her to stop but I can't tell her to – if I do, she won't cope.

'How's the petrol looking?' Zufan asks, after a time. I feel like it's been hours but I don't know. I don't wear a watch, I usually just use my phone but I left it at the house. Maybe we should go back, but I don't know if I want to.

Jack doesn't reply.

We keep driving, passing more cars that have swerved off the road and crashed. As we go further, I see something up ahead.

'What's that?' I ask Jack, taking off my seatbelt and leaning forward to take a better look out the windscreen.

He shakes his head. 'Dunno. Think it's just more cars.'

Poppy, sitting in the front seat, nods. 'Looks it.'

'Anything moving out there, eagle eyes?' I say in a terrible American accent.

'Can't tell,' Poppy says. 'We should stop, see if anyone's there.'

Jack keeps driving until we get to the backlog of cars, and we don't see anyone alive. There's a whole lotta vehicles. A few zombies come shuffling towards us, but they're far enough away that we don't need to panic.

'No one's alive,' I say.

'This could be a trap,' Jack says.

'No one could make a trap this big,' I say. 'Look how many cars there are, Jack.' I gesture at the rows and rows continuing on as far as we can see. 'There must be a barricade up ahead; someone cut off the highway.'

All the people in these cars would have died here, hoping for someone to let them through, hoping to get to safety. Jack keeps having to drive off the road and onto the gravel shoulder, to get past the cars.

'This is just people panicking and dying,' Zufan says.

There's no noise as we look out at the cars; some have smashed windows. We can't smell anything yet, but it's only a matter of time if we keep sitting here.

'Someone could be watching us, though,' Jack says.

'We should get out and check,' Poppy says. 'There might be survivors.'

Jack's eyebrows draw together tight as he brakes and the van comes to a full stop. From here to as far as we can see, cars are stopped end to end. I can tell he wants someone to have a plan, a direction, a good one. But I don't know anything more than he does. I could say, *I have a plan, Jack, it's all right*, but I can't lie to him.

Finally I say, 'Maybe we should … see if we can get through, to get home – to check on people.'

'There's no way we could get through this mess,' he says.

There's silence in the van. The engine keeps thrumming and the window next to me is rattling in its frame. I know everyone we know is probably dead, but what if they're not? What if they're somewhere, waiting for us?

'Turn around, we'll find another way,' I say, when no one says anything. 'Keep moving, it's the best option.'

Jack drives down the way we came, and we try to get home another way. We don't really know where to go without our phones, and on this highway the paper map is too old to help much. After a few hours' driving, we reach another big barricade.

Zufan gets out of the car first. She walks right up to the barricade and the cars crashed into it. As Poppy and I follow her, watching for zombies, the smell hits. The barricade, big slabs of concrete, is intact, despite all the cars that rammed it. There's broken glass and blood everywhere.

'Zufan?' I say, putting a gentle hand on her shoulder.

A zombie starts to move towards us from between the smashed cars. When I scream, the zombie gets faster.

'There's so many cars,' Zufan says, and she sounds so far away. 'Why are there barricades?'

Another zombie joins the first, and they're not running but they're getting there. They're not people anymore, they wouldn't move like that if they were.

Poppy tugs on Zufan's sleeve. 'We have to go.'

More zombies join them. A lot of people died in these cars.

'Shit!' I say. One zombie is only a few cars away. 'Zufan, come on!'

Me and Poppy grab her arms, and we all start running back to the van. Jack has opened the passenger side door; I push Zufan inside, and me and Poppy clamber over each other to get into the back. She slides the side door over, but a reaching zombie hand gets stuck. She screams, lets go of the door.

'No, Poppy!' I yell, grabbing the door and pulling it. The zombie's head is inside now.

Everyone's yelling, and I don't know what to do except hold the door.

'Push it out with your foot!' Jack yells.

'I'm not fucken touching it!' I yell back.

'Drive!' Poppy tells Jack.

'There's heaps of them,' he replies. 'There's nowhere to go, the barricade is blocking the road.'

The zombie is snapping at me, so I kick its hand away. My hands are getting sweatier, and I dunno how long I can hang on to the door.

'Go backwards!' Poppy screams at Jack.

As he changes gears, she helps me with the door. 'We can pull it shut with the van's momentum. Come on.'

Jack reverses, the zombie peels away, we slide the door closed.

'Fucken hell,' Jack says.

'Like you can talk!' I snap at him. 'That thing almost

bit off my arm! If you're gonna drive make sure you can do it!'

'Dee,' Poppy says, putting a hand on my arm.

'Sorry. Jack. I'm scared.'

'No shit. You wanna drive? Be my bloody guest.'

I turn around and look at the ten or so zombies that had crowded around our van. We could've died just then. My heart is still beating too fast, and my arms are shaking.

We're all quiet, and then I hear Zufan crying. She's the only one who really, really loved her family. Judging from what we saw, no one could have got out.

We drive for I don't know how long. There's nothing, no cars, no zombies, just leaves and rubbish that's covered the roads now no cars are travelling by.

***

'Petrol.' Zufan is the first to speak. 'We can't use too much. How long do you think we'll last?'

'We've got a quarter of a tank, so maybe a hundred kays,' Jack says, checking the dashboard.

'How do petrol stations work?' Zufan asks. 'Can they work without power?'

'It's getting dark, though,' Poppy says. 'Maybe we should do it tomorrow.'

'Where are we gonna stay?' Zufan asks.

'We could sleep in the van,' I say. 'We won't have to break into someone's house or something. And we can lock all the doors, stay together and stuff.' The van has three sets of seats, so we should all have some kind of leg room.

'Plus we've got those blankets we found before.' Jack gestures vaguely towards the back. 'But it's still pretty warm out, and plus with all of us in here it's gonna get really hot.' He points to something shiny, distant on the road beyond us. 'We can park next to those cars. Maybe it'd be safer to, like, camouflage or whatever.'

He drives right up to some cars where there's a spot, and the sun starts to set, and the windscreen becomes orange and I can't see anything. Jack grabs his sunglasses from the dashboard, shoves them on his face and parks next to the cars made of the stench of death. Everything is quiet, quieter than when we were in the house in the small hours of the morning and nothing was around to make any noise. The engine hums as it cools, and I don't know if it's supposed to do that, I've never heard it do that, but maybe I'm only just noticing. Jack doesn't say anything, so I guess it's fine.

Then all I can hear is the breathing of the others. If one of us turned, we'd be dead in seconds, I'm sure. I'd panic, not open the door, trap everyone inside and then we'd be dead, we'd all be dead and it'd be my fault.

But we're not, so I don't think about it.

We're parked behind a bus. I don't want to know what happened inside that bus. How long has it been? That's the worst thing. I don't know the date, I don't know the time. I don't know how long it's been since everything turned to shit, and I want to, I so want to.

I want to see what my friends have been doing on the internet, I want a news broadcast, I want to read a blog, I want to listen to the radio.

I wonder if I'll ever listen to another song. Poppy never got to record the latest version of hers, and that's the worst thing of all, somehow.

'Can you open the door, Dee?' she asks from behind me. 'I want to get some fresh air.'

I nod, stepping out before her. The stench isn't as bad as I thought it would be, but maybe that's because we're getting used to it. Or maybe it's the wind, maybe it's changed. But it's not so bad, anyway.

'This is real, isn't it?' Poppy says. 'I don't understand.'

'I miss everyone,' I say, and we sit on the ground.

'Poor Zufan.' She draws a circle in the dirt with her fingertip.

We sit there not speaking, and I sigh. She leans her head on my shoulder and she smells like sweat and I know I do too.

I wonder if I'll ever have a warm shower again. Maybe. Who knows. Not me, that's for fuckin sure. This is shit, this is so shit. I feel lost with no information. Maybe everyone's been evacuated to safe places or taken overseas. Maybe we're left on a giant island filled with walking corpses. Maybe the government's going to gas the ones who are left.

'It'll be okay, Dee,' Poppy says.

My laughter bubbles up and bursts forth in slow motion, then there are tears in my eyes from how hard how I'm laughing. She can't know that, none of us can know that.

'Sorry, I'm not laughing at you,' I say, choking out the words. 'Sorry. I'm really not. I just … This is so shit. I don't see how it'll be all right.'

'Maybe it won't. But we can work with that, right?'

'We're gonna have to.'

In the van, we figure out where we're sleeping. Jack and Zufan have got in the middle, leaving the two front seats empty, I guess so they can't be seen. That leaves me and Poppy with the back. I find a blanket to curl up under.

The sun is almost set. There's nothing for us to do except talk, but what can we talk about? We know each other really well, and we can't exactly ask what everyone did during the day. We can't ask, *What are you doing on the weekend?* Everything is gone.

I sit up and stare out the window.

'I can't look out there,' Poppy says. 'I don't want to know if something is coming.'

'We could keep a lookout,' I say.

'Tonight, maybe we should just rest.' Poppy's voice is soft, low, tired. She's got bags under her eyes.

I lie back but can't sleep. The slow heavy breathing of sleep is everywhere around me, but even though my eyes are about to melt out of my head from tiredness, I can't sleep. I don't know if I'll ever sleep again. I stare at the roof and make pictures with the stains. Jack and I used to do that sometimes in his dad's garage when we got drunk after band practice; the others didn't think it was any fun. The stain just above the door was a rabbit, usually, but sometimes Jack would convince me it was a long-eared, weird-looking dog.

The stains in the car are just stains. And I don't even know what the stains are, or how they got up there. Don't think I made any.

I can hear a possum. It sounds close, too close, and its grunts and growls are right in my ear. It makes my bones shake. Why is the possum so close, anyway? It should be in a tree, shouldn't it? I try and block it out but I can't. Something changes, and then it sounds like the person from the lookout. It's that person, the one who tried to eat us; outside, trying to get in. I can't move. My body is made of sand, trickling down into the seat material, and no one's getting me out now. I am stuck here forever.

I don't know how much time passes, and sometimes the breathing outside stops. But it always comes back, and I don't know how any of the others are sleeping. Why aren't they waking up? Are they dead too? I swallow because I can feel the scream in my throat.

Eventually, I move the tiniest bit so I can get a glimpse of what's outside the window. Nothing, so I move up a little, and then I don't see the zombie from the lookout. Not there, not anywhere. It was a possum.

The thin moon shines on all the cars, and nothing's moving except a couple of zombies way in the distance that haven't figured out we're here. I look out the other side of the van – and then I see a pair of headlights approaching, not very fast.

I recoil instinctively, peering out from the bottom of the window. I know they won't be able to see me, but my teeth hurt from the shock of them. At least one more living person out here. I'm pretty sure I'm not dreaming.

It keeps driving past, and I want to get out of the van and run at it, yell at it, but I don't. Having survived this long, they could be dangerous. I wonder if they've killed people. I wonder how many of them there are, if there's just one person in that car. How terrifying, how peaceful. I would take my friends over being alone any day, but I don't know if I'll ever get time to myself again. I can't go off for a walk because I might die.

I close my eyes and they burn.

After a couple of minutes, I hear another car come down the road and open my eyes to watch the headlights approach. Are they together? Did they lose each other? How could they lose each other? I know I'm going to cling to my friends for dear life, there's no fucking way in hell I'm going to let one of them go. They're my family, now more than ever.

If I let them go, how am I going to find them again?

The driver flashes their headlights once, twice. Maybe it's looking for the other car. Maybe someone stormed off in a fight and regrets it, realises the argument was nothing.

The car keeps driving, and I look at Poppy sleeping. I can't lose her. I know I won't. We've always been together, and so everything will be fine. Just like she said. We're going to be okay.

I watch the red tail-lights disappear. I wonder if the other car kept going down the highway or turned off somewhere.

Do they know how petrol stations work? There's so much about the world I don't know, I realise. Without the internet, I don't know how to find out things.

I lie back down, I don't sleep, and everyone breathes around me, in, out, in, out. When the morning comes, there are no birds singing.

Fifteen

'Fuck.' I can still feel vomit bits in my mouth and I try to spit them out, but all I can think is that I'm gonna die covered in my own vomit and piss, in the middle of nowhere, after just killing a zombie. Well, Rhea killed it. I didn't even get to kill a zombie in the zombie apocalypse. There is no justice in the world.

'All right there?' one of the people says. They've all got like, machetes and shit. All of them are white but in, like, a pink sunburnt way. No guns that I can see.

I nod, and Rhea touches my shoulder as she crouches beside me.

'First zombie?' the same person says.

'Yeah,' I reply. I don't want to stand because my legs will be shaky and I don't want them to see how weak I am. Like, mentally, I could totally cut them to shreds with my wit, but I've got no muscles. Plus we haven't really been eating properly.

'First one's always the worst,' the person says. They start to walk over to us, and Rhea's nails dig into my shoulder. They stop in front of me, offer me their hand. I don't want to take it because I know it's more than just a help up, but if I don't they'll be offended. There's like ten of them and two of us, and they're all adults and they look much stronger than us. I reach out my hand, Rhea lets go, and I'm pulled onto my feet quick. They haven't looked at Rhea, so I turn and help her up.

'We got a camp not too far from here,' they say. 'Got food.'

I nod, I don't know what to do. Rhea's face is blank, frozen.

'You two should come along,' they say, and now they look at Rhea. 'Dangerous out here. Could get hurt.'

I want to punch them in the face for looking at her.

How do we get out of this? Two weedy little teenagers and all these people. Could we outrun them? Probably not.

'Pretty dangerous,' I say. I want Rhea to say something.

'Well, come on,' they say, giving me a blokey clap on the back as they sidle up beside me. 'Our camp's fit for a king.'

I'm not a king.

I reach out for Rhea's hand as the person steers me to their group, and Rhea grips me tight. Her fingernails are digging into my skin and I'm pretty sure mine are digging into hers, but we can't let go.

Our stuff, we need our stuff. But I don't say anything; I don't want them to know how much we have, and I definitely don't want them to know we have a car. I hope the keys aren't in Rhea's pocket, in case they search us. Keeping all our stuff under that bush where we slept was a good idea, I guess.

It feels like we're walking for hours, but it's probably only one. While we walk, the head person is identified by one of the others as a he – 'He's a good bloke, you can trust us' – and he says his name is Matt. His group was out on patrol when they heard our shouting.

'Gotta be careful who ya let hear ya,' he says. 'Real quiet in the bush. Far's we can tell, this all started out in the country somewhere, some meat factory. Anyway, tried to evacuate everyone an' that, but ended up killing off areas at risk of infection, or somethin.'

Jeezuz, tell me something I haven't guessed. So it's been zombies this whole time. Fuck *off.* Shittest apocalypse ever, can't even post about it. There is literally no doubt in my mind I would livetweet the end of days if I could. Instead of enjoying the apocalypse from the comfort of my living room, though, we're stuck out in the bush and our mum is fucking *dead.*

We get to the camp and other people are wandering about. Four-wheel drives are everywhere, five that I can see, and the camp's got heaps of tents, those khaki ones that looks pretty durable, not the cheapo ones you get from Kmart or whatever. They've got a fire pit, but it's not lit. Plastic tables and chairs and everything are laid out.

'We're back,' Matt announces loudly. 'Got some company.'

A few people come over to have a look, and from the closest tent a teenager with long blond hair emerges, maybe our age. The person is chubby, has red cheeks and is so cute I might just die. They see us and their expression brightens a little, but they don't come over or look us right in the eye.

'Caitlin,' Matt says to them, gesturing to us. 'Show em around.' Caitlin nods and then Matt turns to us, smiling. 'Caity's my daughter, she'll take care of ya.' Then he kinda pushes me in her direction, and it's like Rhea isn't even there.

I take Rhea's hand again and she's sweating even though it's not that hot. 'What are we gonna do?' she whispers, and hesitates before adding, 'I don't feel safe. Something's wrong.'

The tents are all lined up exactly; everything has a particular order. Someone's raked all the leaves and stuff away, cleared paths. Nothing's out of place. Everyone is wearing the same colours, somehow.

'I know,' I reply. 'We should talk about it when we're alone. They'll probably give us like a sleeping area, right?'

'Hey,' Caitlin says when we're in speaking distance. 'I'll show you where the toilet is first.' She turns and points, and I notice the knife strapped to her calf. 'This way, it's a bit of a walk. But it's not so bad, even though it's a drop toilet.'

'This is Jojo, by the way,' Rhea says, 'and I'm Rhea. We're twins.'

Caitlin grins. 'I couldn't tell from your faces.' She turns and starts stomping through the bush. 'Just being loud to scare off any snakes. Plus if any zombies are

out here, they'll hear and we'll be expecting them.'
Gumleaves crackle and twigs snap. 'You travel far to
get here?'

Rhea and I exchange glances. 'Yeah,' she says. 'Pretty
sure my legs are gonna fall off.'

'True that,' Caitlin says, nodding. She glances over
at the camp. 'Almost there.'

She might be leading us to a trap. We're going to die.
Fuck. I don't want to die. Mum's gone, like she was never
here in the first place. How can someone just be *gone*?

We get to the drop toilet, which is, like, an old-
fashioned dunny and it stinks. But I guess it's good for
pooping? What're we gonna do when we run out of
toilet paper? Do we *have* toilet paper? Gross.

Caitlin looks around like she's making sure no one is
in the toilet, and then ushers us closer. 'Youse've gotta
have a car, right?'

Rhea narrows her eyes. 'Why you asking?'

''Cause I wanna get out of here. My dad's gone weird
– well, he's always been weird but this is culty, I swear
to God. When this all started he was frantic, watched
the news for a bit, got all his camping gear he's been
hoarding cause he was a prepper. There's stacks of food
buried in this place. And now he's, like, the leader of this
camp and they keep finding people and bringing them
in, and it's like, I dunno. It's fucked. They separate the
men and women, and I think they're tying to pair us
all up. There's this boy Dad's trying to set up with me.'

I blink a couple of times, while Rhea laughs and says,

'Well. Wasn't expecting that. I thought you were gonna lead us to a trap and kill us. Bloody hell.'

'It's awful out here,' Caitlin says, 'and it's only been two months.'

'Two months?' Rhea says. '*Months?* Are you sure?'

Caitlin frowns. 'Yeah? I mean, like, give or take a few. But I've got my period twice and I'm, like, super regular.'

'Does that attract extra zombies?' Rhea asks.

Caitlin shrugs. 'There aren't a lot out here, so I can't really tell.'

'Anyway, back on point,' Rhea says. 'Two months. We've only known about this for, like, two weeks maybe?' She looks at me and I nod.

'What?' Caitlin asks, frowning again.

'We're from Bundoora-ish,' I say.

Caitlin starts at my voice, probably because I haven't said anything until now. 'I got no idea where that is,' she says, and grins at us. Pretty sure I just fell in love with her and, judging by Rhea's face, she did too.

'Shitty suburbia,' Rhea says. 'There was a curfew and whatever, then we weren't allowed to go outside. There was like a news blackout and the internet wouldn't work.'

'They evacuated the country-country towns, mostly,' Caitlin says. 'Then, like, they called them hub areas, or something? Places that were infected or at high risk, but then that fucked up because people tried to hide it, like their bites or whatever. Lots of the buses they were using to transport people crashed. Then when they tried to evacuate my area, my dad got all these cun–' She sees something behind me. 'Fuck off, again?' She gets out a switchblade from her shorts pocket and walks past me, hand brushing my shoulder, and my stomach flutters. Yep. Definitely in love.

There's a zombie, in one of those fishermen's vests I thought were only in old movies. He's even got the hat with the fishing flies on it – if they're called that? Anyway, he's got no arms but he's shambling towards us. Caitlin strides up, cool as anything, and sticks the knife up into his eye socket, angled so it goes to his brain. Should I be using he pronouns? I frown. Zombies probably don't have a concept of gender.

'You're really good at that,' Rhea says. 'At, er, at stabbing. Yeah.' She shifts, smiles.

Caitlin blushes but keeps eye contact. 'Thanks.'

Goddamn it, Rhea. This is the apocalypse. No time for awkward teenage romance. 'So, escape?' I say.

Those two dorks seem to jolt back to our shitty reality and look at me.

'So you and your brother –' Caitlin starts.

'They're not my brother,' Rhea says. 'Sibling.'

'Oh. Sorry.' Caitlin turns to me; I smile at her. 'Another queer, though! Thank goodness, it's so hard being around non-queers all the time. You probably don't want to tell my dad you're non-binary. He's not the … yeah. Like, I could never tell him I'm an asexual lesbian. Um.' She coughs.

'Rhea is bi, too,' I tell her.

They smile at each other again, and Caitlin blushes

faintly. 'Anyway, we should leave at daylight, probably. Like, Dad's pretty on it, he watches everything. He's got a few people who, like, report stuff to him. We have to be careful.'

'We'd have to go get our bags and stuff – the car keys and heaps of our food is still there,' Rhea says. 'Then we'd have to get to the car without anyone seeing us.'

'What if we leave at night?' I say.

'Might be too quiet,' Caitlin says, frowning as she bends to wipe the zombie blood off the knife. 'Cause all the dead leaves and sticks on the ground crunch heaps loud. They'd hear us going. Plus our torches would give us away easy.'

'Why are you trusting us?' I ask.

'To be honest, you don't look like murderers. And if I'm going to die in this zombie shit, I don't want to die with my dad and these dickheads.'

So we're the only option. Would she ditch us if someone better came along? Maybe. But right now she's our only option too.

'All right,' she says. 'Let's leave soon. Let's leave tomorrow.'

Sixteen

I try an reach round the tree trunk to wake her, but I don' wanna startle her or nothin, so I only poke her gently. She yawns an stretches, but doesn' make any noise until she whispers, 'What?' an looks around. I don' need to answer her. 'Shit. How long have they been there?'

'Jus got here.'

'Okay. Is it the same people from the house?'

They're too far away to tell proply. Two big people – might be the ones that was upstairs, but I don' think so. There's a smaller person with them, with long hair, wide hips, an I'm glad we didn' come across that one cause they look like they don' take any shit.

'They could fuck us up if they find us,' I whisper.

We wait an watch. They go into the house they parked in front of, come out with a whole bunch of stuff.

'They must have a pretty good set-up if they can take all that,' she says.

They got heapsa kitchen stuff: food, knives, cushions, wooden chairs, blankets, books. Hope they didn' take all the good ones. They pile all of it into the ute tray, then go into the next house. They jus leave open the doors of the houses they bin in.

'Do you need sleep?' she asks, after the people've bin inside for a bit. 'Here, take the rope while they're not lookin.' She undoes it from round herself an passes it over.

Before I can tie it, the people come outta the house. I freeze, arms hangin in the air like I dunno what they're for. A bit of the rope is danglin, but nothin they can see, I don' think.

They don' go into the next house, instead they pack up, lock the ute doors with a flash of orange lights. An then they start walkin towards the park.

'Fuck,' she says. 'Fuck, fuck, fuck.'

'What're we gonna do?' I say. The tree was a shitty idea; too much out in the open. But lucky we didn' go into a house, they mighta caught us in one.

'We've got the advantage, right?' she says. 'The high ground. They'll have to climb to get at us.' She swallows. 'Unless they have a gun, but they probably won't want to make too much noise.'

So we watch them walk down the path in the park, an they walk slow, but they're not lookin up at all. They're muckin around, shovin each other an that. I don' think they seen us. They pass almost under our tree, skirt round the edge of the bottom branches. If they look up, they're gonna see us. But they keep walkin, an soon they're outta the park, onto the road, hidden by the houses. Why're they leavin their car? Do they think no one's here anymore?

Only then do I feel my heart beatin like never before; these people look rough as guts.

'Tie the rope,' she whispers.

'Dunno if I can sleep, now.'

'At least tie it, just in case. You haven't slept in ages. You're gonna fall asleep soon anyway, probably.'

'Orright,' I say, cause she's right.

'I'll wake you if something happens.'

Good thing neither of us snore. I settle into the tree trunk, easier than I thought, an close my eyes. My heart's still thumpin an maybe it's a bad idea, them people are so close, but it's easy to be calm. The air is warm, drier than yesterday so it's not as muggy an that.

I listen to her heartbeat in my dream. Everythin is dark an warm an there are teeth everywhere. The heart wavers, changes, an then I can jus see my family. My zombie family, an even in the dream it seems silly.

***

A heap of time passes, I'm pretty sure, because when I wake up the sun is higher an the air is hotter. We're still pretty cool beneath our blanket of leaves, but I'm sweatin.

'I'm awake,' I say, jus so she knows. 'They come pass?'

'Yeah, a while ago. They had armloads of bottles, there must be a bottle-o somewhere around here. Did you sleep? I couldn't tell.'

'Yeah. Good sleep, weird dreams.'

'I think we're going to have weird dreams for a while. If you didn't have weird dreams when this is happening, I'd be a bit concerned, really.'

I wonder what her dreams are.

'We should get out of here,' she says. 'They look like they knew the route pretty well.'

An this place, more than my street, looks like it woulda bin full of zombies. Them three would have to be tough as nails to have survived that. They don' look like the kind that hides in treehouses, waitin for everythin to go to shit.

'Now?' I ask, though I know the answer already.

'They might come back. Probably not today, just cause they had a lot of wine with them. But like I said, they know what they're doing.'

I nod. 'We should get a tent.'

'That'd be good.'

We climb down from the tree an run to the bikes. We jump on, ride a couple of streets down, then stop. Don' wanna be seen by those three.

'A tent's gonna be fucken heavy,' I say, pantin already from jus the backpack.

She frowns. 'Maybe we can find a place to camp, first. Then get a tent there.'

'Somewhere near a river,' I say, realisin how thirsty I am. I get the bottle from the holder on my bike, take a few sips.

'Good one,' she says. 'All right. Know where to go?'

I shake my head. Dunno much about my town an its surroundins – cept my river, which is probly overrun with zombies by now. That fucken factory.

'We'll just keep going, then,' she says. 'Let's go.'

We ride into the outskirts of town. The sun's at its highest point, an it's gettin real hot, the trees seemin too far away. We ride on, our wheels clickin. I notice she's got a little tyre pump attached under her drink holder. I dunno how to pump tyres, but it'd be easy enough, I reckon. An she's got a little bag under the seat, maybe with tyre patches or somethin. Hopefully our tyres don' fucken get holes in em, cause I got no idea about changin em.

'You know about bikes?' I ask her.

'Not really,' she says. 'We can figure it out if a tube pops.'

Tube, tyre, whatever – long as it goes.

We keep ridin. Less houses, more trees. We reach a rise an pull over to the roadside. 'Well,' she says as we look out at the sea of trees. 'This looks promising.'

I look round an see it. 'Over there,' I say, pointin. 'See the gaps in the trees? That's the river. We're upstream from my river, so we shouldn' get contamination from the factory zombies.'

'Your river?'

'Yeah, the one we got water from near my house. Mostly I'd go there stead a school. I was down there when my dad was turnin. Came back an then he … y'know. Killed em.'

'Your mum?'

'An my brother.'

'I'm sorry.'

'Dunno where my other brother is. Think he's dead.'

'Did you …?'

I look at her, an I nod.

'Me too,' she says.

Were they zombies? Maybe it's better if I don' ask. I dunno if she woulda killed em, but I ain' gonna put anythin past her.

'All right, we should make the river in a couple hours,' she says, after a bit. 'Maybe we should take the tent now.' She brushes her hand gainst my arm. 'You ready?'

I nod, an we smash a window of the closest house. We look through all the closets an cupboards, then find a tent in the shed after I knock the lock off the door with my cricket bat.

'It's a bit dusty, but it should be okay,' she says, unzippin the tent bag to look inside. 'And they got bikes in here, so if we need to we can swap them out later.'

We carry the tent between us an try replacin the lock as best we can so it don' look like we broke in. It's heavy, too heavy, but we can' leave it or we'll be sleepin outside, an if it rains that's not gonna be fun.

'How we gonna do this?' I say. 'It's too heavy for one of us to carry alone.'

'We could sling it between the bikes, go slow?' She surveys the land ahead. 'Might be a bit hard.'

I nod. 'Right.'

It's hard holdin the bat an tryin to balance the tent bag between us while havin the packs on our backs.

'Can you go a bit slower?' she asks, face all red.

'Sorry,' I say, tryin to. It's hard – the road's flat an everythin is tellin me to fang it.

After a few more minutes, she asks again.

'We can' stay too long in the open,' I say. 'Those people might come back.'

'I know,' she snaps, 'but I'm tired. Can't go on like this. We've had no proper food and I'm thirsty.'

'So am I,' I say, then wish I could take it back.

She sighs an brakes, the tent fallin from between us.

I brake jus before losin my balance. 'Oi!' I say. 'Don' do that!'

'I need a break.' She gets off her bike, throws it down. 'For two seconds, all right?' She sits on the ground an puffs, head restin on her pulled-up knees.

'Sorry,' I say. 'Carn, let's leave the tent an go find a spot, then we'll come get it.'

She sighs one more time, an stands. We leave the tent bag in the closest garden, ditch the bikes a few hundred metres into the bush so they can' be seen from the road.

'We can follow the river,' I say, seein it up ahead through the trees. We're crunchin the dead twigs an leaves under our feet as we crash through the bush. There's a magpie feather, an I grab it from the ground, put it in my hair.

'I don't know if anyone's out here,' she says, lookin round. 'We're pretty much alone.'

She winks at me, an I laugh. She grins an starts laughin too, an the laughter bounces around the trees, upriver, an I haven' heard laughter in so long. She grabs me hand so I pull her close an kiss her, quick, then she darts away, runs into the river, water splashin up round her legs, unshaven, an she's so fucken beautiful. The sunlight's shinin on the water, like stars driftin past. I drop my bat an follow her, an as I get closer she splashes me, an I trip an get my bum wet. The water only goes up to my belly button when I'm sittin.

She walks over an joins me. 'We can wash our clothes, finally,' she says, lyin beside me. 'But it's too hot to do anythin right now.' I lie next to her, our heads propped above the water by our elbows. She smiles at me. 'We could live out here.'

An if someone had said that to me in ten years in the old world, I woulda laughed at em. But because it's her an we're here, this is the most perfect thing anyone's ever said.

'We could,' I say, an then her eyes go wide as she looks behin me.

Two zombies are comin for us, too quick. We struggle to our feet, the rocks under our shoes suddenly too slippery, more than they were before.

'Your bat,' she says, 'where is it?' She pulls a knife from the strap on her leg.

My bat's lyin on the ground from where she winked at me.

'Fuck!' I scramble to get it but the zombie'll reach me before I do.

She stands up, gettin ready to pounce on the closer zombie. 'I'll protect you.'

I find a big stick an hold it like a cricket bat, ready to swing.

She's like a cat. When the zombie's close enough she lunges, stabs it right in the eye socket, an it goes down. She stabs again an again, an the knife gets caught in the zombie. She backs away from the fallen body as the other zombie comes up. This one doesn' know who to go for first; after a tiny sway, it starts off after her. It's got both its legs so it walks fine, but it's only got one hand.

I whack my stick on the zombie's back. 'Don' you fucken dare.'

From behin the zombie she grins at me, an I can' help but laugh. The zombie ain' distracted though, an it keeps gettin closer to her.

'Oi!' I yell, tryina ram the stick into its skull.

Now the zombie turns round. It's stronger than I thought, harder to keep away. Its arms, reachin out to me, make me panic. I keep hittin it with the stick, but that doesn' do any good, the zombie just keeps comin. She gets out from behin it an I know she's goin for her knife.

'Can' do this much longer,' I say, dodgin back, hittin the zombie with my stick again. My arms're too weak.

But then she grabs her knife and kicks right into the back of the zombie; it falls towards me an I scream, backin up.

She crouches beside it an stabs it through the neck. Her breath's ragged as she uses all her strength, the weight of her body. An she keeps stabbin it an stabbin, an she won' stop.

An then she's cryin.

'It's all right,' I say. 'It's okay.'

She looks at me, face splattered with blood, tears runnin down her cheeks. I check for more zombies, then walk over an hug her from behin, curled round her like another skin. I can feel her heartbeat an rest my cheek gainst each *boom*, an we sit there, beatin in time, an we get slower, slower, relax, calm. She shifts, an then I realise my arms an legs are asleep. I uncurl from round her an lie down, my whole body tinglin. She lies next to me, on the side from the corpse, an as we lie there the blood pricks its way back into my limbs.

'You okay?' I ask.

She sits up an rests her head on her knees. 'Not really,' she says, an smiles sideways at me. 'But that's all right.'

An so we stand up finally.

The first corpse is close to the river. 'We should get that away from there,' I say. 'I can drag it if you like.'

'Should we burn them?' She pauses. 'The smoke. Never mind.' She sighs. 'Let's just leave them, go upstream a bit. At least they'll be markers so we know where to get the bikes.'

'All right.'

She washes the blood from her face an then we trudge upstream, feet in the river, an it's like before times except I'm not alone. We don' speak; we don' need to.

After maybe an hour we find a clearin that's perfect. It's got less dead leaves on the ground so it won' be so loud, an there's a giant rock we can pitch the tent beside. That way no one's gonna sneak up from behin us, and the shade will keep us cool.

Now the shadows are longer, an the evenin birds is singin. The fact the birds sing here makes me feel a bit better, along with the river being right beside us.

'We go back an get the stuff?' I ask.

She nods. 'This is such a good spot. We should be able to get some proper sleep.'

We head off. When we're back at the bikes, I say, 'I could try an make a sling for my bat. Keep it on my back.'

'Sounds good. Then you'll have a spare hand whenever we're out. And if I can get a couple more knives, that would be great.'

'Next time we go into town, should make a list of shit we need.'

'Maybe we could find some chickens,' she says. 'Get eggs.'

Food. My stomach rumbles. We've only got a coupla cans left, everythin else we left in the house.

We don' ride the bikes back, jus wheel em. Take it in turns to carry the tent; if we rest it on the handlebars it ain' so bad. Back at our clearing after settin up the tent, we don' do anythin for the rest of the day except eat. Then we crawl inside, an we're tangled.

Seventeen

Poppy admires the flock of galahs as she shields her eyes from the sun. 'Nice morning,' she says. 'If you ignore the highway covered in cars filled with dead bodies, it's almost perfect.'

The zombies still haven't started clawing at us. It seems like they've moved on down the highway, because we've been standing here in the trees on the side of the road for a while now and none have showed up. The wind blows through the trees, and from this angle there's no rotting stench. It's early enough that the sun isn't too hot yet, the breeze still a little cool.

'Look at that one,' Poppy says, pointing. One of the galahs is spinning on its branch, hanging upside down before flapping back around, not letting go of the branch as it squawks.

'Dork,' I say, as she laughs. There's something under her laugh. I tap her shoulder, motion for her to be quiet. 'Something.' There's a distant noise, not a rumbling, but …

'A car,' she says.

We run back to the van, underbrush cracking across my shins; I can feel the bruises and the cuts starting. We'd better have some first-aid shit in the van, because if I get a serious cut and die from infection, I will kill someone.

I run to the side door, slap my hand on the glass. 'Open up!' I say, half whispering.

Zufan peeks up into the window. She's bleary-eyed, hair tousled from sleep.

'Zufan!' Poppy shrieks. 'Now!'

She unlocks the door and I haul it open. Poppy jumps inside; I tumble in after her and almost close the door on my foot.

'What are you doing?' Jack asks from the driver's seat.

'Get in the back!' Poppy yells.

'On the floor,' I tell Zufan as Jack clambers over, and she does without asking why.

Jack shakes his head. 'What's going on?'

'We heard a car,' Poppy tells him, and his eyes go wide as anything.

When the two adults and toddler approached us before, that was different – we hardly knew anything about what was happening. It was so unsafe to wait for them like that in the open, but we needed information. We were lucky that time.

We all spread out to make room for each other on the floor. I end up on the back seat, bending my legs so they're under me, and I could see out the window if I just peeked up a little. I don't because I'll wet my pants and probably get us killed if we're seen.

The car gets closer, louder, rumbling. It's a noisy engine, maybe a four-wheel drive. There isn't any music playing, and I wonder if they have a CD player. If our van did I'm sure we'd have music on all the time.

The car stops, it sounds close. Doors open, I don't know how many. The air inside the van is heating up; we're in the sun now and everyone's breathing too hard. I close my eyes, ball my fists in front of my face, and breathe in deep. The cushion of the seat is dusty, there's a tinge of dirt every time I inhale. I exhale through my mouth, and my heart slows.

Then the voices start, and my heart's back to beating like mad.

'You were on watch, mate,' someone says. Their voice is gravelly, like scratches across stones.

Another person replies, but their voice is lost in the shouts of the others. I peek out through the window, just above the edge. They're not looking at me, further away than I thought, maybe a couple of hundred metres. They're standing next to a four-wheel drive.

There are four of them, tanned and middle-aged. Three against one.

The bald one shoves the person standing alone. 'It's your fault she's dead,' they say in that gravelly voice, 'you fucken –'

'Hey,' the lone one says, recovering from the shove.

'Get down,' Zufan hisses, and I miss what the four people are saying now. She tugs at my pants, motions with her hands, but I shake my head at her.

'They're not looking at me,' I whisper. 'They're further away than they sound.'

Bang.

A gunshot, louder than anything I've ever heard. Poppy yelps, the others swear, and I get another look outside. The person standing alone has fallen, all I see are legs sticking out from behind a car. The bald person is handing the gun to one of the others. It's got a long barrel; I don't know what kind it is. I've never seen a gun in real life before, except on the hip of a police officer.

I close my eyes, press my cheek against the car seat. It's dusty, smells like sweat.

'Did they see you?' Zufan whispers.

'No. They killed someone. No one make a sound. If they find us …'

The four-wheel drive starts again and soon drives off, leaving an alive stillness that's too heavy. Soon I hear noises. When I look out the window, I see ten or so zombies shuffling towards the body. I put my hand over my mouth so I don't cry out.

'What?' Poppy asks, touching my arm.

'Zombies. They must've been drawn from the noise.'

'Or the blood,' she says, and looks out the window too.

I don't want to watch them eat the corpse. I draw back, close my eyes again and listen to the others breathing. We don't move for at least an hour, legs cramping, car heating as the sun gets higher. The air is so thin. On our way out we don't look at the body, just keep on driving down the highway and hope we don't head right to where the people with the guns are.

Eighteen

The next day, Caitlin's dad keeps his eyes on us, especially me. There's no chance for us to escape. He doesn't like me talking to her anymore. Adam is the only boy who's supposed to talk to her, and I think he's the one Matt's trying to get to be Caitlin's partner. He's strong, white, tall and conventionally handsome.

Matt doesn't really speak to Rhea, but I see him watching her. She's sent out with Caitlin to collect more firewood, while he gets me to patrol with the men. The woman do the cooking and the cleaning, and the men do the hunting and the patrolling, and it's all a bit ridiculous. But at least I don't have time to think about Mum too much.

A few days after, I'm taken fishing. I've never been fishing before, but from what I've seen in movies it's very peaceful, relaxing. Fishing isn't about fishing, it's about the experience or whatever. Anyway, turns out fishing is the most fucking boring thing in the world. I miss talking to Rhea. I'm not allowed to talk to the women too much.

I don't catch anything, but one of the guys, Bruce – Brucey – shows me how he's made a fishing rod. He tells me where to look for worms, how he made a hook with bits of wire. It's pretty smart really, and I probably do actually need to know this. Can't live off of canned food forever. We mostly sit, and then he tells me about something that happened in 'the old days', as he calls them, and then we sit some more. He catches three pretty decent-sized fish, and when I pass them over to Rhea that evening the other women seem impressed.

The next two days I'm assigned to patrol a couple of times, and on the second day during the afternoon patrol we find, like, ten zombies. It's scary how good the men are at killing them. They could kill me, I know they could. Gary says he'll take me out to see the cows, and he can show me how to kill one. I don't want to learn, but I think I have to.

I'm so tired like I've never been before, my legs are covered in tiny cuts, and I've got blisters from holding a shovel all during patrol. Matt has a gun, but I've never seen him use it; it'd draw every zombie here from kilometres around. I'll have to get stronger to kill anything with a shovel, I think, so I mostly just try not to get eaten by zombies while the others take care of them.

But now, at least, we're all sitting around the campfire and it's warm, and Rhea and I totally have our own tent and it's pretty sweet. She and Caitlin are totally a thing now, kind of. With the work they're assigned they can chat, spend a lot of time together. I don't think Matt and Adam have noticed; they probably just seem like very good friends to them.

'I'd kill for some marshmallows,' I say, getting a stick and prodding around the base of the fire. It's slowly burning my face, I'm pretty sure, but the way the sparks fly up when the stick hits them keeps me going.

'I'd kill for internet,' Rhea says.

'I'd kill for a proper bed, a hot shower, actual walls.' Caitlin sighs, closes her eyes. 'Casual murder. I can't believe you were only put under curfew two weeks ago. How the hell does that even work? Wouldn't word have spread?'

'Maybe something to do with the internet,' Rhea says, scooching closer to Caitlin on the log so their knees are touching. 'And we're not good at paying attention to the news.'

'Except on Twitter,' I say.

'Even so, though, like, the news wasn't reporting anything properly,' says Rhea.

'Oi!' The shout sounds out through the bush. There's movement behind us.

I turn and see a zombie shambling into camp. Fucking hell. Bet the watch got pissed and have passed out; though after all the zombies we found today, you'd think they'd be a little more careful.

Rhea gets up and reaches for the machete Matt's mate gave her. She hasn't been without it since – even when we're sleeping, she's got it beside her. I'm kinda scared she'll grab it in her sleep one time and wreck her hand, but so far so good.

She gets the zombie in the spine, severs the spinal

cord in one go. She wipes a bit of blood onto the zombie's t-shirt and sits back down. 'Fuckin watch can't do shit,' she says.

She's always been made of steel, like Mum, but seeing her like this I want to cry. We're not supposed to be killers. We're kids. We're supposed to be avoiding homework and staying up too late. I'm proud of her, of course I am. But it shouldn't be like this. Mum should be here.

The men notice the dead zombie. One calls out, 'Good work, love!' to Rhea, and she mutters a string of swears under her breath. Caitlin touches her arm, and we all go back to staring at the fire.

'Tomorrow,' Caitlin says. 'We'll get out of here. We can make some excuse, anything.' She scratches at her arm, and I don't think she notices she's doing it. It's what it feels like here, itchy. Want to leave but can't, stuck.

There's more leaves crunching behind us. I turn first – Rhea's whispering something to Caitlin – and then I yelp, fall sideways off the log and whack Rhea's leg so she'll look. She turns around and sees the, like, five zombies near camp. I turn to call out to those guys, and see more zombies in other areas of the camp. I don't know where the fuck they came from because we're in the middle of fucking nowhere.

There's a shout – it's Brucey. He's to the left in the trees, must've been on his way to the toilet. A zombie's chewing on his leg.

'Oh my god,' I say, crawling backwards from the ones near us.

Caitlin bends down, puts a firm hand on my back. 'The fire.' Her voice is so calm. 'Please don't crawl into it.'

It's right behind me. 'Oh, right.' I stand up, dust myself off. 'Thanks for that.'

'Fuckin zombies!' Rhea says, hitting me on the arm. 'Pay attention.'

'They're everywhere,' I say. 'One of em just got Brucey.'

'Shit,' Rhea says.

There are more shouts from the guys; they're all drunk and the zombies are going for them. I start to go over to help, but then Rhea yelps, she trips over a branch, and those five zombies near us are getting closer. I'd rather save my sister than a bunch of drunken dickheads, to be honest.

I help her up and we fight together. I get one in the spine with a big knife that Caitlin gives me; Rhea gets two standing next to each other, both in the back of the neck; Caitlin kicks one to the ground and gets the fifth in the eye socket. While Caitlin's killing that one, Rhea goes to the one pushed on the ground, gets a knife I forgot she had from her pocket, and stabs it through the eye. Blood splatters all over her face, and she shuts her eyes and mouth quick as anything.

'Can we get blood in our eyes?' I ask Caitlin. 'Is she

infected?' I can't feel anything except my heart bashing against my rib cage.

'Nah, happened to me a while ago. You're all good, Rhea.'

Rhea opens her eyes after wiping her face with her sleeve. She sticks out her tongue and retches. Then we hear more crunching near us, two more zombies coming out of the bush. There's more screams from the guys – I look over, and about ten zombies are chewing.

'Fuck,' Caitlin says, and despite her words before about her dad, she's got tears in her eyes. 'We have to go.'

Rhea ducks into our tent, finds our torch and flicks it on. 'Get your stuff, Caitlin,' she says. 'We only have enough for two.'

Caitlin goes to her tent, next to ours, gets her stuff and shoves it in her sleeping-bag; she doesn't seem to have another bag. She comes out holding a torch, and then we're running.

My lungs are going to burst, hurting from the bottom up, and all I can hear is the pounding in my head as my feet connect with the ground. The blood pours down the veins in my arms, swelling my fingers. We run past another zombie, it starts shambling towards us but we're too fast. The frantic torch beams make everything seem like a video game, almost not real, and that comforts me a little.

We have to slow to a jog, then walk. It was about an hour's walk last time, and now I have no idea how much time has passed since we left the camp but I can barely breathe.

'It's around here somewhere,' Rhea says finally, slowing, stopping.

We walk another ten minutes and find the body of the first zombie we killed, rotting and covered in flies and gross shit, and I vomit again.

'I'm good,' I say, gasping when I've finished.

Rhea pats my back, then we nod at each other. Keep on keepin on.

'The bags are under some bushes,' she says. 'Probably over ...' She shines the torch. 'There.'

I go to them. Rhea's better at killing than I am, plus she's got the torch. It hasn't rained since we've been here, so everything is still dry. I put it all back in the bags and get out the car keys. 'Got em, let's go.'

We start walking because it's still ages til the car.

'We're making a lot of noise,' I say.

'Can't do much about it,' Rhea says. She's tired. I'm tired. Caitlin's probably tired. Plus we're by ourselves, in the dark, possibly being chased by zombies. Not the best fucking way to go about having a casual stroll.

Caitlin's torch keeps fading, soon it's only brown, doesn't even light up the ground before her feet, and she switches it off.

We stop talking and just walk, gumleaves crunching, and it's getting colder. It might rain soon; something's different in the air, not as dry as it was before.

More crunching. *Crunch, crunch, crunch*. I move to

the left, closer to Rhea to avoid a huge rock to my right.

'Caitlin?' Rhea says.

No answer.

Rhea shines her torch through the bush. There's just tree trunks, ferns, no Caitlin.

A scream rings out, from back the way we came.

'No?' Rhea whispers, and then we run to the source of the noise.

Caitlin, covered in blood. A zombie has her arm in its mouth.

'Fuck!' Rhea leaps over, her machete already out. 'Stay still,' she tells Caitlin, and chops down on the zombie's neck. The zombie detaches from Caitlin, her blood all over it, and Rhea keeps hacking at the neck. Its sounds are wet and choking as it tries to grab Rhea.

Caitlin delivers a final blow. She's so pale I can see her bones. She slips to the ground, looks up at us, tears in her eyes but they don't fall. She clutches her arm, blood's oozing out dark. Too dark. It's in between her fingers, and she's rocking back and forth. Her hair's greasy, stringy down the sides of her face, and her eyes are too wide.

'This is so shit,' she says, laughter that turns into a sob that's cut off. 'Fuck.'

'It might not be like the movies,' Rhea says. She crouches next to Caitlin, takes a blood-soaked hand.

'It is,' Caitlin says. 'I watched my mum turn. And our neighbours. When we took them here in the beginning, and we didn't know how to protect ourselves.'

Rhea laughs but she's crying. 'This is the worst.'

'It is.' Caitlin grips Rhea's hand harder. 'You're really cool, by the way.'

'You're a super dork,' Rhea says. 'But you're pretty neat.' And she kisses her on the forehead.

'Don't wait for me,' Caitlin says. 'It's not pretty.'

'Do you want us … to …?' Rhea tries to ask.

Caitlin shakes her head. 'It's okay.'

They hug, tight and fierce, and Rhea says something I can't hear properly. Caitlin laughs sadly, then nods. They break apart and I go over, hug Caitlin, and she tells me to take care of Rhea.

'I will,' I tell her, and smile while my insides cut each other up like razors. How can we leave another person so soon after leaving Mum?

But we leave Caitlin in the dark because that's what she wants. We start the car, turn on the radio and listen to static as we drive down the highway.

Nineteen

When I wake in the mornin, there's a magpie warblin real close to the tent. I sit up, run a hand through my hair as I yawn, stretchin me arms up to the tent roof.

She must feel me movin cause she opens an eye. 'Morning,' she says, fuzzy.

'I'm gonna have a look round,' I say, findin my pants.

Rollin onto her stomach, she groans in that mornin way, safe an warm when everythin's right. 'All right. Let me know if there's anything.'

Maybe our only company's gonna be the sounds of the river an the birds. There's no wind out here, an the air is fresh outside the tent as I take up my cricket bat an walk over to the big rock. It's cold, damp, slimy. I run a finger through the stuff growin on it an leave a trail; my fingers come away green.

There's no zombies or nothin around, an I go to the river an take a drink usin my hand as a cup. The tent zip sounds behin me an she steps out. 'Just going to pee,' she says. 'I've got my knife, won't go too far.'

An for the first time since she's outta my sight, I don' get the panic. She'll come back. We're safe out here.

I hear her footsteps crunch away through the bush, an I sit on a rock in the river an wash my feet. If I rub dirt over my skin then wash it off, it sorta works like soap. My toenails're gonna get long.

She comes back an sits beside me.

I point at me feet. 'Should get nail clippers when we're in town.'

'Good point.' She grins. 'Don't wanna get scratched by your witchy feet in the night.'

Our hair's pretty greasy an that, but it doesn' really matter. We can go without shampoo an conditioner. Sides, maybe it'd jus poison the river anyway.

'I wonder what river this is,' she says, when she sees me starin off into the runnin current. We watch in silence; the leaves floatin on top go rushin past. 'Maybe the Yarra.'

It's not, but it don' really matter. 'Goin all the way to the city.'

'Can you imagine what Melbourne would be like now?' She sighs. 'If I were still there I guess I'd be dead – or walkin around, dead.' She glances at me and asks, 'You been? To the city, I mean. You grew up in that house where we met, didn't you?'

'I ain' bin to the city in a long time,' I say. 'When I was little Mum took me couple times. Don' really remember much, but. Noisy.'

'Smoky. Smelly. Good old Melbourne.' Her mouth doesn' move but I know she's smilin far away. 'I miss everyone.'

'Sorry,' I say. Dunno that I miss anythin right now.

She turns to me. 'I'm glad I found you.'

'Me too.'

An she smiles, holds up her knife. 'So, ready to stick some zombies? I'm starving.'

I nod. I'd rather stay here all day, lie in the sun an fuck ten times, but guess we can' always get what we want. Maybe after some food, tomorrow'll be a good day to do nothin.

She holds out a hand an pulls me onto my feet. I shake off some water, pull on my socks an shoes, an then she holds out my cricket bat.

We'll never be as relaxed as we used to be. Any second we could get eaten by zombies or attacked by other survivors. Now there's no school, an we have so much time to do whatever. The days stretch out right in fronta my eyes, long, empty.

'Bit heavy,' she says as she hands the bat over. 'Want to find a lighter one?'

I shake my head. 'I like the weight. Feels good, an it's easier to kill em with this.'

'All right. So, we need food, knives, nail cutters … Maybe we can get some seeds and stuff to plant things.'

'Dunno how to garden,' I say. 'You got any idea?'

'Not really. We could find a book, maybe.'

'That's the other thing – we should get a coupla books so we got somethin to do.'

'Oh, good idea.' She smiles. 'I'll get the backpacks.' She ducks into the tent an brings out the empty bags.

'All righty,' she says, slingin one onto her shoulder, 'let's get this show on the road.'

We take it slow. The mornin air's still cool under the trees an I don' wanna tire meself out fore we even get outta the bush. We wheel our bikes beside us as we try not to make too much noise.

'These leaves are such a fire hazard,' she says.

I can' help it, I burst out laughin. Such an old-times thing to say. 'Sorry,' I say, chokin out my words, 'I never even thought a that.'

'Bushfire season is coming. And from what I've seen on the news, they're terrifying.'

'Yeah. We got evacuated last year. Wind changed at the last moment, but it's fucken scary as shit.'

We reach the edge of the bush an there's the dirt road in fronta us. I get on my bike before she does, an it takes a coupla seconds for her to catch up.

'What're we gonna do if there's a bushfire here?' she asks.

'Dunno.' Burn, maybe. 'We're jus gonna have to be real alert. Any sign of smoke or that an we'll go, all right?'

She nods, an I can see her tryina swallow all that panic.

'Reckon there's a supermarket up ahead?' I ask. The houses are gettin closer together, the roads are bitumen, an there's less trees, more silence.

A zombie wanders outta a backyard an starts moanin at us, but we're too fast on our bikes for it. 'We can get it on the way back,' she says.

The houses are dense now, an there are more zombies, so we pull over an rush to the closest house. It has a chest-height metal fence; we close the gate an then they can' see us.

'We can keep the bikes in this backyard, maybe?' I say. The fence is painted dusty orange, easy to remember. 'You reckon?'

She nods. 'I don't think we're far off, anyway. Let's go.'

We go round the side of the house an there's a couple zombies in the backyard. A picnic table's still set up, food all mouldy an picked at by animals. The zombies turn round slow, an I knock em back with my bat. She gets the one closest to her in the neck, an this time her knife don' get stuck. She yanks it out with a squelch an black gluggy blood pours out.

I have to whirl round to knock two zombies down. They scramble on their backs an I turn to her; she's knifed another one but one's creepin up behin her. Her knife's in the first one's eye socket, an she twists to see the other one an realises she can' do anythin.

I run up an get its face. It falls down, an I whack it with my bat, whack it again – there are teeth everywhere – again, again, again. *You ain' gonna hurt her*.

She nods at me, then we move onto the last two, the ones I knocked on their backs. They've stood up, an she kicks one in the chest. It stumbles back. She takes her knife an plunges it into the one closest to her, gruntin as she does.

Day's gettin hotter, an sweat drips outta my hair onto my face. I get the zombie that stumbled an hear its neck snap. I realise after, still grippin the bat, that I got muscles now – never used to. They're not bulgin or nothin, but they're there.

'Right,' she says, flickin hair from her face. 'That was unexpected.' She bends an cleans her knife on the closest zombie's pants. 'Maybe we should look in here for the stuff we need,' she says, pointin at the house. 'If we need anything else, we can have a look around.'

I slide open the glass door an we walk in.

'Don' think there's anything inside,' I say, but as I speak zombies come out. About ten, an they're all little kids.

'Shit,' she whispers next to me, her words crawlin into my ear.

There's a little one in a pink dress lookin at me now without really lookin, an its teeth snap. Got some baby ones missin.

'Fuck,' I breathe out.

She looks at me an I look at her, an I know we can' do this, no matter what's in the cupboards a this house. We back outta the door an the tiny zombies flock to us, pressin their faces gainst the glass. Some of their mouths are covered in blood an some ain'. There are so many of em; all the adults are outside.

'Let's go.' She pulls at my elbow til I look away finally.

When we're in the street, it's deserted.

'That was so fucked up,' she says, quiet. 'It's gonna

get worse the more houses we get into. Let's just … let's see if there's a supermarket.'

We come across more zombies on the roads, but we can either outwalk them or get em real quick. There's no real drama, an soon we come across a milk bar.

'You want some lollies?' she says. There's a bit of light in her eyes for the first time since this mornin, so I nod. The door's wide open, an we walk through fly curtains covered in dust an grime from a million hands.

I open the fridge to get a fizzy drink. 'You want one?' She nods, an I get her a lime bottle. I woulda thought it would have smelt real bad cause of the milk, but there's jus a bit of fridge-smell.

She grabs handfuls of lollies an puts em in a paper bag from the counter. We look through the shelves for other things we might need, an they've got more than I expected for a milk bar; the one near my house jus sold drinks, cigarettes, papers, lollies. We find heapsa stuff: scissors, razors, nail clippers, string, instant noodles.

'If we get a pot we can boil water over a fire,' she says, and grabs a few boxes of tea. 'Maybe in the trees the smoke won't be too noticeable.' Then she gets a packet of pads from another shelf. 'My period stopped,' she says, her eyes flickin to mine once before not lookin at me again. 'It, uh, might be from the stress.'

My skin's cold, I forget the heat. 'Haven' had a lotta food, either,' I say. We used protection but I guess they don' always work.

'That's probably it. Maybe we should just do other things, though … just in case.'

'How long's it bin?'

'Six weeks.'

'Kay.'

She's tremblin but I pretend not to notice.

'We can go lookin for your knives next,' I say. 'An then for some pots.'

'A camping shop would be really handy right about now,' she says, an gives me a tiny smile. 'We'd be decked out.'

We can' have a baby, not in this world.

'Yeah,' I start – then I hear voices.

'In here, I reckon,' one says, an there are footsteps.

Her eyes widen an we run through the staff-only door at the back, closin it behin us.

'We didn't hear em come up,' I whisper.

'I don't know how that happened.' She places our bag of stuff on the floor so gently, it barely makes a sound as she lets go.

'Pretty stressful convo,' I say. Her look tells me I shouldn' have said nothin.

The people's footsteps are getting closer, an one a them gives a huge laugh. I listen to the sounds of them comin through the fly curtains, the plastic bits flappin together …

I notice, jus then, movement behin the desk in the staff-only room.

An I cry out, cause I'm a fucken arsehole. She looks

at me, draws her knife, an looks over to see the zombie stuck behin the desk. It's slowly workin its way out.

'They woulda heard that,' I whisper. 'I'm sorry.'

She doesn' say anythin cause there's nothin to be done, jus knifes the zombie. It's still twitchin, though, so I get it with my bat.

'There's something in there,' a person in the milk bar says.

'That zombie,' another replies. 'That's why we closed the door.'

'Heard human voices, but,' a deeper voice says.

I swallow an she raises her knife. 'We got this, all right?' she whispers.

I nod. The room ain' very big an there's only one door. We might be able to take these people on, if they come at us one by one.

'Get ready,' the first voice says.

The door opens to three people pointin things at us. A machete, a shovel, a fire poker.

They stare at us for a couple a seconds, an we stare back.

'Where're you from?' asks the big one with the machete.

'You should answer him,' says another one. 'He's a mad bastard.'

We don' say anythin.

'I asked you something,' he says, bringin the machete a bit closer to her. 'Where you from, sweetheart?'

The machete's real near her cheek.

'Don' you fucken dare,' I say, steppin over.

The man grins at me, tobacco-yellow teeth showin between his chapped lips. 'You're tough for a weedy little boy.'

I look over to her an she's pulled back her lips, coiled ready to pounce, an then she raises her knife. 'You say that again and I'll fucking gut you.'

The three a them laugh. They're still blockin the exit, an I jus wanna leave. I don' want this. Let's jus go, let's leave.

The big man raises the machete again. 'So where you hidin? With how many others?'

Again, we don' say anythin.

The machete is now pressed gainst her cheek, an she gasps, lowers her knife. There's no cut on her yet, an I breathe in relief. Don' want any zombie blood in us, I'm sure that'd fuck things up real bad.

'You scared?' the machete man says.

She don' reply.

'Righto, if you won't tell us where you come from, we got people who can make you at camp.' He reaches for her shoulder.

She backs away, knocks into me, an raises her knife. 'We're not coming with you.'

He laughs. 'Yeah. Y'are.' An he raises his weapon.

Her knife plunges into his chest, an his eyes widen. He lets go of the machete an it nicks his arm as it falls; spots of blood appear.

The ones behin him don' seem to know what to do.

She pulls out the knife an stabs again, this time where his heart must be, missin the ribs. So perfect, I wonder if it's the first time she's done it to a livin person.

'You wanna go?' she yells at the ones that are left.

An I know she knows we can' let em leave. They'll tell the others at their camp, then they'll all come lookin. An maybe they won' find us, we're pretty deep in the bush – but still, havin people tryin to hunt us makes my skin itch. Wouldn' be able to come to town again.

One of them rises to the bait an comes at us with the fire poker; the other one's slower, heavier, with the shovel. The fire-poker one goes for her, so I sidestep from round her into the milk bar an go after Shovel – who grabs my arm, twists it behin my back, an I drop my bat.

'Oi,' Shovel says.

Fire Poker an her freeze. Her face doesn' change as she looks at me, held hostage. Fire Poker looks pretty pleased about it.

'Goddamn,' I say, then kick Shovel in the balls. 'Fucken arsehole.' Shovel cringes, goes down, an I step away, scramblin for my bat on the tiled floor.

She puts her knife through Fire Poker, who falls with a wet scream. Shovel holds up a hand as she walks over. She don' even cringe as she gets up real close, kneels beside Shovel, puts a hand on their back, an drives her knife though their throat. She rips it out an she's covered in blood, like the milk bar round us.

'We gotta go before the others find these bodies,' she says, tryina keep calm, standin back up.

I dunno what to think. Three dead jus cause they opened that door. They're dead, they've died. She killed them. They attacked first, but they're still dead. Why didn' they leave us alone? They're dead. Fucken Christ.

'Hey,' she says, holdin out a hand. 'We have to go.'

An so we do, the blood dryin in the hot air round us. We start off runnin, but the bag gets heavy, so we slow to a jog, then a walk. The zombies come at us quicker than last time cause a the fresh blood, but we're fast enough to only have to knock back a few.

'I stink of blood,' she says. 'We gotta move faster.'

We finally reach the house with the orange fence where we hid our bikes. After lookin round the yard a bit we find a metal bucket in a shed, along with some pointy tools that'll do instead of knives. We find a machete too, an she takes it without sayin anythin.

After her new weapons are strapped to her with rags pulled from the zombies' clothes, I take the shoppin bag an loop it over my handlebars. A few zombies see us as we ride off but we're too fast, an the blood has dried cause it's so fucken hot.

It's maybe what used to be three or four in the arvo when we get back to camp. We strip off our clothes, wash em an our bodies, the water pink around us. After, we dry off on the rocks a bit away from the tent. An when we're dry, we don' do anythin cept go into the tent an lie down in silence. I dunno how long we're lyin there. I wanna vomit but have no energy.

'I'm sorry he called you a boy,' she says when the night is close an the crickets are singin. 'I know you're a girl.'

I roll over to face her. 'I'm more worried bout you. Don' matter what they think of me.'

'It's still terrible.'

'It is. But ...' I go to say, *They're dead now*, but I can'. 'It's all right. We're all right.'

An she brushes her fingers gainst my cheek.

I ask, 'They're not the first people you've killed, are they?'

She looks at me for a long time. I can see her thinkin if she tells me, will it make me think less of her? Or scared of her?

'They're not,' she says.

'It was scary.'

'It's scary every time.'

Our lungs match up, an we fall asleep as the air cools.

Twenty

It's maybe twenty minutes til we come to the next exit, and Jack turns on the indicator out of habit. It clicks a couple of times before he flicks it off, shaking his head. The on-ramp is clear enough that we can drive through; littered along every road are crashed cars from where people have either turned off the road or run into other panicked drivers. Nearer to the town there's a petrol station. A few cars are there, and dozens of zombies wandering around. When Jack pulls up the van, the zombies start making their way towards us.

'We got any weapons or anything?' Zufan looks around. 'How are we gonna do this?'

'Hit them with the van, Jack,' I say, whacking the back of his headrest.

'Will that wreck the van?' he asks. 'What if it cracks the windscreen?'

'Right.' I think for a sec. 'Well, we could …'

'Oh, look!' Poppy points, tapping my shoulder. 'They've got a shovel over there.'

It's resting against the fence near a couple of those grey rentable trailers.

'I got it,' I say, and I open the door.

As soon as I'm out of the protection of the van, though, I realise what a shitty plan this is. Considering there's no plan at all.

I bolt to the shovel, grab it and almost trip over a trailer. I turn around to see a snapping face that's missing an ear and some scalp, and I scream. Jabbing out with the shovel's pointy end, I knock the zombie over but another comes at me, too fast. I step back, and try and poke it away, but this one is stronger.

'Can someone help?!' I yelp out.

I notice there's a second shovel on the ground, hidden behind a trailer. I point to it as Zufan jumps out of the van. The two of us manage to keep the zombies away, but I don't know how to kill them. Zufan knocks one to the ground on its stomach, then presses the shovel into its guts, pushing down with her foot. There's a *squelch*, deep and wet, as the shovel goes in. The zombie doesn't seem to mind though; it just flails, trying to get back up so it can bite us.

Zufan retches and tries to stay focused. I whack another zombie in the face, and it spins but keeps coming my way.

'Oi!' Poppy is at my side suddenly, and she's got a crowbar. She hits the same zombie, using both arms to swing the weapon like a baseball bat, right in the neck. There's a *snap*; the zombie goes down. 'That's disgusting,' she says, and tries not to vomit as well, which just sets Zufan off again.

Together we carve up the rest of the zombies til we're covered in blood and sweat. We stand there, lungs heaving, and Zufan grins at me and Poppy. 'We make a good team.'

I nudge her shoulder with mine. 'I did most of the work.'

'You're right. You are far superior, my mistake.' Zufan taps my nose with the hand that isn't blood-spattered.

'So gracious, not smearing blood all over me.' I pat her arm; both of my hands are covered in blood.

'You're gross.'

'*You're* gross,' I say. 'But I like your face.'

Something flickers in Zufan's eyes, uncertainty maybe, but then she recovers. 'Wish I could say the same to you.'

Poppy goes over to Jack, who's trying to figure out how to pump the petrol. She tries to take the hose from him but he insists he knows what he's doing.

'Isn't there like a switch that the guy in the thing has to press?' Zufan says.

'Eh?'

'Like, when someone in front of you gets petrol, then they pay, then the guy flicks a switch, and it resets the pump and you can go.'

Jack looks at her. 'Is that a thing?'

'That's totally a thing.' She nods. 'It'll be behind the counter somewhere.'

'It's not like, a switch on the computer?' I ask.

'Maybe.'

'Show me,' Jack says to Zufan, and they walk into the shop. A dead body is propping the doors open.

'Are you okay?' Poppy asks, and it takes me a second to remember the reason I'm covered in blood and guts.

'Yeah.' I shrug with the shovel waving about. 'I guess. I dunno. I'm glad I didn't freeze. Are you?'

'Yeah,' she says. She hugs my shoulders and giggles, pointing inside. 'They can't figure it out.'

'We shouldn't laugh,' I say. 'We do really need petrol.'

'What else am I going to laugh at?' Poppy says.

Jack and Zufan come back out and look a bit deflated. 'Can't figure it out,' Zufan says. 'I think the button is on the computer, like you said.'

'So, Zufan reckons we can siphon some petrol,' Jack says.

'What, like … from another car with a hose?' I say.

'Yeah. Like in the cartoons. That'll totally work.' Zufan grins at me, her teeth still stark white. I haven't brushed my teeth, I suddenly realise, and they're furry, especially at the back. We need to steal toothpaste from somewhere.

'Oh,' I say, 'I just remembered. Last night I saw cars. Like, cars that were driving.'

'What is it with you two forgetting important shit?' Jack says, glaring at me and Zufan. 'Like we could die, you know?'

'Aw, come on, Jack,' Zufan says, waving a hand.

'We could actually fucking die, come on!'

'Hey,' I say, 'I haven't slept, all right? Give me a break.'

'You didn't sleep?' Poppy says.

'We can't afford any breaks,' Jack says. 'We're in an apocalypse!'

'For reals,' I say, 'that sounds ridiculous.'

Jack purses his lips. 'So does you saying *reals*. That isn't a word.'

'Well, what're you gonna do?' I gesture around at the emptiness. 'Hand me in to the police?'

'Oh, fuck off.'

'Hey,' Poppy interjects, 'we need petrol.'

'I'll do it,' Zufan says. 'I got experience sucking hoses.' She winks, then walks over to the ute parked at the petrol pump. After digging for a bit in the back, she finds what she's looking for. 'Come on, Jack, let's get this show on the road.'

He rolls his eyes but gets in the van and drives it closer.

'You want me to teach you how?' Zufan says, grinning as he walks over to her.

'I'm very capable, thank you.'

'You sure?'

'Just do it, please.' Jack sighs, rolling his eyes.

'All right. Dee, could you pop open the cover, please?'

I go to the driver's door of the ute and open it. A body's in the seat, and I make sure it's actually dead before reaching to open the petrol-tank cover.

When I get back around, Zufan's got the hose in her mouth. This silly mucking around is the best thing that's happened this whole time – everyone's laughing, even Jack after a bit.

'So, full tank,' he says once everything's done. 'What are we doing next?'

'We should find some food,' I say, and everyone agrees.

Zufan wipes her hands on her jeans. 'Wouldn't mind a mint or something, my mouth tastes disgusting after that.' There are petrol stains on her t-shirt.

'We can leave the van here,' Poppy says. 'There should be a supermarket not too far off.'

'We shouldn't leave the van,' Jack says. 'It's all we've got.'

'We can just raid the servo.' I point to the petrol station shop.

'You wanna survive on lollies and chips?' Poppy asks.

'Honestly, a little bit.'

'Well, I'm not gonna let you.'

'It's all going to be processed food anyway,' I say. 'Everything else has gone off.'

'I'd rather survive on beans than sugar,' Poppy says. 'Come on, it'll be fun. We can go shopping like in the ye olde days.'

'Memories,' Zufan says, staring wistfully off. 'The laundry powder, the packet noodles. Good times.'

'I'm not leaving the van,' Jack says. 'We've got two shovels, so maybe two people go to the shops, two wait here.'

'We'll go to the shops,' Poppy says, indicating me and her. 'I don't trust you to not get veggies.'

'I dunno if there'll be any veggies left,' I tell her.

'There mightn't be *anything* left,' Jack says.

Poppy picks up the shovel, leaves one with Jack and Zufan. 'We have to at least try.'

'Just be careful,' Jack says. 'Make sure you don't get seen by anyone. Or anything.'

'If there's anyone there to be seen by,' I say. I hope Poppy is okay to take the shovel – maybe I should.

'Well, this place might actually have people in it,' Zufan says. 'People who don't shoot each other, I mean. Never know.'

'Yes,' I say. 'We should try and avoid murderers.'

'Right.'

Poppy hands me the shovel as we walk, and so we start off, keeping low. I can smell myself and I really stink, so much. Maybe I can smell Poppy; I'm not sure whose smell is whose anymore. I'm sure I'll get used to it soon, but right now my armpits fuckin reek. I haven't shaved my legs in so long, either. We're gonna need new clothes too, and supplies like batteries and stuff. Maybe even a CD player.

Poppy taps my shoulder, stops in her tracks. 'What?' I ask, immediately looking around for any zombies.

'Over there. People watching us.' Poppy nods towards a house. 'Two of em.'

I can't feel the top of my head. 'Where?'

'In that window, second level. The one with the hedge out the front.'

Sure enough, two people are there. 'Are they

zombies?' I ask, but I can tell they're not. If they were, they'd be clawing the glass.

Now we're looking at them, the heads withdraw from the window.

'Oh my god,' she says. 'What do we do? Oh god. Oh god.'

'It's cool.' I try to push down the panic that's rising in me. 'We should get off the road.' I lead her to the closest house's backyard. It's empty, the lawn is overgrown, and there are fallen fruits all under a tree. I take a closer look: apples. I pick one off the tree and give it to Poppy. We sit in silence, eating apples; they're not quite ripe, but the juice makes my stomach beg for more. Then we use her t-shirt like a pouch to carry some. We should move, I know we need to move, but I can't help it.

'What are we gonna do?' Poppy says. 'They've seen us, they've *seen* us.'

'Maybe we should just go back.'

'What if they need help?'

I remember the last time she said that – when we were nearly eaten by that zombie near the lookout. 'I dunno if we should risk it. It could be a trap.'

Another silence between us.

'We can just jump the fences,' I say. 'Get back to the petrol station.'

Poppy doesn't respond, but she follows when I step over the low fence between backyards.

My stomach aches from the promise of food. We duck into a couple of houses and find packets of biscuits and a jar of lychees. Most things are gone, and we don't stay for too long.

I scrape my leg on a bush that's thornier than it looks, but the cut's not deep enough to bleed. I rest the shovel on my shoulder as we finally get out of the last backyard and find the petrol station.

And then, when we get a proper view of the station, we see those same two people. One is standing next to a four-wheel drive, the other sitting on the bonnet.

Twenty-one

Rhea doesn't stop driving until we find a highway blocked off with abandoned cars. We're not that far from Kinglake. She drives around the blockage, and we stop, restless and without proper sleep. We wake from not-sleeping and keep going; my eyes are dry and my tongue is too big for my mouth. The petrol tank is half empty but we don't bring it up because we don't know how long a tank lasts, and we don't know where to get more petrol. It's early morning, the sun is bright, and when I roll down the window I hear birds singing. Bit fucked up.

'I need to stop,' Rhea says.

I look over, and her eyes are red but she hasn't been crying, just on the verge for the whole night. I'm sure if she wasn't holding the wheel then her hands would be shaking; her knuckles have been pale the whole time. If I wasn't here she'd be crying. And the feeling, not even hidden, inside me is that I'm glad Caitlin died and not her. I don't know if that makes me a shit person.

'I can't drive anymore,' she says, and stops without asking if it's okay. 'We can just park here. No one's around to find us.'

'If there are more people.'

She looks at me. 'If you're the only person left in the world, Jojo, I'm going to vomit.'

'Love you too.' I could be hurt, but she doesn't mean it like that. I just let my words out automatically, without any real feeling.

'I just mean –' She sighs. 'I don't know.' Too tired for sarcasm, definitely not a good sign. The car shudders when she turns the key, also probably not a good sign, but then how the fuck do cars work? Should've got my learner's but, like, didn't really expect the apocalypse to happen. Like, I thought there'd always be trains and shit. And I'd have more time.

More time for a whole bunch of things. I was half-planning on learning to drive before I turned fifty, and then the world would just combust from all the global warming or whatever. That or we'd all bomb each other, and Earth would just be a crispy wafer floating in space, which would be pretty shit but also, to be honest, a little convenient because then I wouldn't have to worry about taxes.

Rhea pops the boot, and we move all the stuff from the back seat into there and get out some blankets and a little food. I lie the passenger seat flat and Rhea gets into the back, away from the steering wheel and all that, and we try to sleep out in the open. There are so many windows in cars, how have I never noticed this properly? It's a giant window box.

We cover ourselves with blankets, try to make us look

just like bundles of clothes, and after a while Rhea falls asleep; I know because she starts to snore. She twitches in her sleep and I stop watching because I can't stand the look on her face anymore.

I wonder if any others got out of the camp alive. Maybe if they were paying more attention then Caitlin wouldn't be dead; maybe we'd have escaped together. But these maybes lead to nowhere so there's no fucking point thinking about them. I miss Mum.

We should have taken some fishing rods, or maybe stuck around a bit to learn how to properly kill and eat a cow. There are heaps of cows around. But they're so big, and though I was shown once how to do it, I don't think I could on my own. And I don't want to use a rifle for anything – apart from them being noisy and attracting zombies, they're scary.

It's strange being on the highway with no noise around. There's some birds singing, and the cicadas are going off.

We should find a house. If what Caitlin said is true about these areas being evacuated, then maybe there'll be empty houses with food inside. If we drive further, then we'll be in country-country instead of this almost-country area … Maybe then we could find people, too. Nice people who aren't complete fucking assholes who insist I am something I'm not.

I learned some useful things at the camp, but that whole trying-to-induct-me-into-a-cult-of-masculinity thing is a bit off. Sure, I have a masculine side, and a feminine side, but neither is going to be my complete self and they're definitely not halves of me. I just … I'm glad I had the internet to figure out why being called a boy felt so wrong. Just to know there were other people like me, that there was a name for all these feelings, was … really nice. Non-binary, genderqueer. Not broken, not even a little bit.

And now there's no goddamn internet, I could scream. Won't, though, in case it brings another group of assholes this way.

Eventually I fall asleep.

Then the sun's on my face and the air in the car is hot. I cough, rub my eyes. Dehydrated, everything feels like sand. I pushed off all the blankets in my sleep but looks like no one found us. Should be more careful next time.

'Sleepyhead,' Rhea says. She's still lying across the back seat. 'No one's driven past.'

'Heard anything?'

She shakes her head and turns to look at me. 'Only the birds.'

'It's weird that they're still singing.' I take the biscuit she hands me. 'We could look for a house, maybe.'

'Finally move out of the nest. I was thinking closer to the city. We could become beautiful trash artists living off student benefits.'

My chest tightens because that's what our plan was, except neither of us is very creative so I don't know what kind of art we'd be making.

'That's a good idea,' she says when I don't reply. 'We'll just keep driving, find a place out here. Hopefully the petrol won't run out.'

'It'll be fine. We can always steal another car. Looks pretty deserted here.'

She nods, then gets into the front seat. She hands me the packet of biscuits. 'I ate about half while you were asleep, so you eat the rest.'

They're plain biscuits, the kind Grandma used to put butter on sometimes. Mum would dunk them in her tea. They're pretty dry but filling. I do miss the food the women at the camp cooked up, rabbit stew and those fish me and Brucey caught. Tiny sneaky bones, though.

***

Not too long after the blockade of cars, we pull in at one of those highway stops with a toilet, picnic benches and a barbecue area. 'A proper toilet! I'm gonna go piss in it.' Rhea bolts off.

I cry after her. 'Wait.' Panic rises like bile, hot and quick. 'Take weapons, there might be zombies.'

'Fuck,' she says, paling. 'Can't believe I forgot.'

We go in together, her first with her machete, and there aren't any zombies but there's a corpse, half-eaten. I gag and Rhea shakes her head, covers her nose. 'Goddamn it,' she says. 'I just want to pee in comfort. Is this such a crime?'

I raise my eyebrows at her because I have never peed in public in comfort before. Always had to choose between the men's or the women's, except for that one time in Scienceworks when they had ungendered bathrooms.

'Sorry,' she says. 'That was a shitty thing to say.'

'Yeah. It's all right, I guess – it's not like people are gonna look at me weird now for using the wrong bathroom.'

'Well, I'm gonna go pee behind that bush over there. Be back soon.'

Too bad there isn't any meat to barbecue. We don't have any gear to start a fire, either, apart from a box of matches – but I don't want to waste them when the smoke might lead the cult people to us, if they're looking. They probably think we have Caitlin. Unless they found her, in the bush.

I rummage around our food in the boot and find a packet of chips, barbecue flavour. I'm not sure exactly why chip companies think 'barbecue' is a valid favour, but the saltiness is delicious. I remember how dehydrated I am when my lips sting because they're cracking.

We've got heaps of bottles of water, but I guess it wouldn't hurt to have more. The nearest parked car in the highway rest stop looks like it's packed with stuff. There's two bodies in the front seats, but it's unlocked. When Rhea comes back from peeing, she walks over to me and peers through the windows. 'That's gonna stink if we open it.'

'Yeah,' I say. 'I was just wondering if they have any water.'

'We can find some in the town we look for a house in,' she says. 'Can't be fucked dealing with bodies right now.'

'All right,' I say. 'Let's keep on keepin on, then.'

We make it to a town that looks almost like suburbia. It's got heaps of houses, neatly in rows. Zombies are milling about everywhere. Doesn't look like anyone living would stick around here.

'There's a petrol station,' I say, pointing. 'Dunno how it would work without power.'

'Let's find a house first,' Rhea says, 'then worry about petrol.'

I look around, swivelling in my seat. 'Try that way, I reckon. If you look further there's heaps of bush, more likely to be a river or a creek, maybe?'

'And less people, hopefully,' she says. 'Don't want to run into anyone.'

I nod, but I almost do want to run into people. There's too much emptiness.

Rhea takes the road leading towards the bush, takes another road, and another. The next one is just dirt that billows out under our tyres. We pass a few houses, one with its windows all smashed up. There aren't any cars on this road, just us and a whole heap of leaves. No fallen trees or anything, which is great.

And then, almost at the end of the road, there's a house. It's huge, it looks super modern, and there aren't any cars in the driveway or the carport. Jackpot.

'We should be careful,' I say. 'There might be people inside.' But we're barely careful.

We park in the carport, open the front door, scream out to anyone inside. No reactions, so we get all our shit and take it into the lounge room. We take all our food and put it in the kitchen cupboards that already have some cans and pasta in them.

We have a house! A huge house. Bigger than anything we've ever lived in, and it's just us. I want to ring Mum, tell her the good news. We could have a housewarming.

There are, like, five bedrooms and so we pick two next to each other. Mine has a view of the bush, more rainforest than dry here. Rhea's can see the driveway. Although we couldn't tell from the front, the house is placed on the edge of the valley, looking out.

'Gonna go pee in the real toilet,' she says, and wanders off. She comes back, her face screwed up. 'It's not working. I hate everything. I'm gonna pee outside.' She takes her machete and leaves.

I wander around the house. A big room connects the kitchen, dining area and lounge. The lounge is filled with shiny new tech and the comfiest couch I've ever sat on, and the walls of the whole room are made of windows that look into the greenest place I've ever seen, filled with tree ferns and gum trees. There's a balcony with a couple of banana lounges on it.

Rhea eventually comes back in, and we spend the rest of the day sleeping in our separate bedrooms. It's a little terrifying at first, but after a couple of hours' lying awake, afraid that being alone means total and irreversible isolation, it's nice to have my own space. I stare out of the window, the leaves swaying in the breeze. Birds fly past; a kookaburra calls out.

I miss Mum.

***

Three days pass before we even consider leaving the house, and it's not til we've been there a week that we decide to check out the town. We take our weapons and leave the car. We're more out in the open this way, but we're quieter and less likely to draw attention. We don't find any people, and we avoid a lot of zombies by sneaking past. Rhea kills heaps too, and I get a couple. She's so good at it. I'm proud; I'm also sorry she has to be like this.

We're in town for a few hours filling two backpacks with food. A great thing about canned goods is the expiration dates are super far away. Our pantry is full.

'I have no idea what day it is,' I tell Rhea the next day when we're sitting on the couch, reading. 'Or month even. When's Christmas?'

'It's kinda nice,' she says, sinking deeper into the cushions. 'No need to rush around, go to school, do assignments.'

'I wonder if we'll forget, like, when our birthday is.'

'There's no way to tell, so probably.'

I nod, go back to my book – glad the owners of this house weren't ebook people, because they have a literal library and it's amazing.

***

It's another while til we go back into town. It's getting harder to tell how much time has passed, but Rhea's period hasn't come even though it should've, she says. Probably a combination of stress, the lack of being fed properly or whatever, otherwise that would be a great way to see how many months pass. But it's good too, because we don't have any pads or tampons.

We're walking down the middle of the road, wondering if we can find some new clothes because the people whose house we're living in don't share my fashion sense.

'Fuck.' Rhea drags me by the elbow to the side of the road, into the trees. 'Look!'

At the petrol station coming up, there's people. Actual people, teenagers. Three of them, wandering around, bashing a couple of zombies with shovels and a crowbar. When the zombies are all fallen, they clutch at each other while they laugh. Another gets out of the van, and it looks like they're trying to figure out how to get petrol. It takes a while, but then one finds a hose; they show one of the others how to siphon it out of a ute.

'We should invite them to our house,' I whisper.

'That could be dangerous,' she says, but I can tell her heart's not in it. Maybe other people can distract us from this grief; it's too heavy for two people. But then, more people would mean we'd have more people to lose.

'It could be,' I say, 'I just think it'd be good to have

some company. Especially because they all seem like dorks, and I don't think dorks would be murderers.'

She nods. 'Dorks are our people, after all.'

So we go up the road a little bit, because they'll probably want to go into town. We find a two-storey house, make sure it's empty, and peer out from the second floor.

I scratch at my beard, and I want it gone. It just increases my dysphoria even though my beard attempts are more bumfluff because I'm still a baby. My face looks awful. I try to remind myself that just because I have a beard doesn't mean I'm a boy, but it's hard sometimes.

'I'm going to the bathroom and getting a shave,' I tell Rhea. 'If there's any water.'

'Fucking Christ, you're vainer than anyone I've ever met.'

'Not because of the people we saw,' I say, but it might be a little. 'I'm sick of this facial catastrophe.' I really only shaved my face once a fortnight in before times because it grows so slow and patchy.

The taps don't work, but there's a little water left in the bath so I use that. Soon my chin is clean, and Rhea hisses to me that she can see them. I stop examining myself in the mirror and crouch beside her in front of the window.

Two of them are walking this way up the road, glancing around cautiously. They see us peeking through the window and scramble into the backyard of a nearby house.

'Goddamn it,' Rhea says. 'We've scared em off. Come on.' She stands. 'Let's go meet them at the petrol station – the other two must still be there.'

'That might scare them off even more.'

'Yeah, but at least we can talk to them. Plus they'll see our attractive faces and never want to leave.'

'You raise a very fair point.'

We race down the main road to the station. No one is there, and so I sit on the bonnet of a nearby four-wheel drive, and Rhea's standing. She nudges me when she sees them coming, and I sit up. She leans over and says, 'They look even prettier from down here,' and I can't help but laugh.

Twenty-two

We're runnin outta food an fucken starvin, but it's only now, maybe two weeks later, that we can even think about goin to town without bein plagued by images of them people we killed. Well, she killed. Sometimes still when I think about it I get all shaky, but we jus acted outta self-preservation or whatever.

Never realised how strong that instinct was til now, an it's fucken strong.

We're both gettin real skinny, an with the bikes it's really fucken easy to see how weak we are. When we're jus lyin round the bush we don' really do anythin, jus lazy as fuck cause really, what is there to do? I gotta find some books. On our way to town she's ridin in fronta me. When we round a corner we find a group of maybe seven zombies in the middle of the street, jus shufflin. She jumps off her bike – we're gettin good at that – an rams her knife into the first one's spine, whirlin round as she rips out the knife, plunges it into another one. Blood spurts more than usual; she yelps, ducks away from it, only gets some on her legs. I wonder again who she was, before.

Now I'm close enough that I jump off my bike, a bit harder for me cause of the bat, an then I clock one in the face an it goes down. I'm gettin better at breakin the spine on the first go. It's a fucken hot day, so they're startin to smell even worse. We clear the street fast as anythin. There's a couple zombies in the distance but they're not a threat yet, one's lost a foot.

We're takin the back streets cause we don wanna run into the group those three were talkin about, the ones we … Them three seemed pretty tough an that, an if they was jus gettin the grog then what the others'll be like I got no clue.

The milk bar'd probly be all gross now, covered in flies an blood. That place woulda bin real fucken useful, had heapsa weird shit in it.

'We could find you a pocket knife,' she tells me, bendin to wipe hers on one a the zombie's clothes. 'Might come in handy. And they have can-openers on them, don't they?'

'Army knives, got em. Sounds good.' It'll come in handy too; the bat's good gainst zombies but won' kill a person. Maybe I could kill someone with the bat, but I dunno, I feel like that's too brutal. Killin a person is too diffrent to makin a zombie real dead. Even if they do look like people.

'Shall we?' She picks up her bike. 'Maybe we can get into a supermarket,' she says once we're ridin.

'That'd be good. Probly be a few zombies in there but, should be right. Jus gotta watch out for that group.

If we run into them, they're gonna kill us for killin their friends.'

'You didn't do anything wrong,' she says.

'Yeah, but they ain' gonna give a fuck,' I say, an that makes her silent cause I agreed with her. 'You didn' do nothin wrong, either. They was gonna kill us.'

'That doesn't make it okay.'

'Maybe.'

An she looks at me, an I dunno what she's tryina say in that look.

We pedal past zombies, an there are a few winding streets we get lost down a coupla times, so many houses in this bit a town. As we round a bend, we see a pack of about thirty zombies jus wanderin around. 'Fuck,' she says, an turns her bike. I brake in my panic an she flies past me. 'Come on!' she yells.

I never seen so many all at once since we had to leave me house, an they're all lookin at me. Walkin right at me. Gettin faster, closer.

She grabs my arm. 'What the fuck! Let's go!'

When I don' say anythin, she taps my forehead. I zone in, my eyes focus, I look at her, an we pedal back the way we came. It's maybe bin an hour or two since we left home an I need food, real bad.

'Can we stop?' she says, after a while. We're at the edge of the estate now, near where we go to get home. Dunno how we found the right way. 'I'm so fucking hungry.'

I nod. 'Me too.'

An so we duck into the first house we find. The back door's bin ripped off, an the screen door flaps around. When we try an close the door it won' stay in its thing, so it keeps flappin when we're inside. There's no noise cept for the flappin. We walk into the kitchen an the house is dusty as shit, there's animal crap everywhere, there's even plants startin to grow in the patches of sunlight. Looks like someone raided this house, cause the pantry is almost empty. What's left is a couple of cans, jars an packets that've bin nibbled at by animals.

'Canned food again.' She picks up the closest one. 'Ooh, gherkins.'

'Jarred food. Which might be better, dunno.'

'Best before is January twelfth,' she says, lookin at the lid. 'Next year. They must've had these for a long time if they expire soon.'

'What date is it?' I ask.

She shakes her head. 'No idea.'

An that's when I realise in a coupla years I'm not goin to know how old I am. Maybe can count by the winters, but I'll forget, I know I will. I dunno how old she is.

She opens the lid with a pop, an straight away I smell the salt an the tanginess shoves itself up my nose an my mouth waters. She offers me the jar an I take one. It's a little slimy an a bit of juice runs down my arm to my elbow, but I bite in with a crunch. I never liked gherkins in before times, not really, but this is the most delicious thing I've ever tasted. So strong, crisp, an then it's gone. I reach for another.

We eat the whole jar in what feels like ten seconds, reachin again an again without speakin a word.

'Is drinking the juice gross?' she asks.

I shake my head. 'You wanna go first?'

She drinks less than half, so I tell her to drink more.

'If I have any more I'll drink it all.' She passes the jar to me. I drink the juice an it trickles down my chin. My stomach craves more, an I wanna sit down an crunch into a ball.

'Come on, let's explore the rest of the house,' she says when I've finished the juice.

There's a door that goes from the kitchen to the rest a the house, an I make to open it.

'Wait,' she says. 'Get ready.'

She pulls out a knife, I got me cricket bat. After she counts to three, she opens the door. A zombie spills out, musta bin leanin on the door. She screams, jumps forward, an the zombie's reachin for us, fingernails cracked an bloody. It opens its mouth but no noise comes out. It used to be an old person, it's wearin a dressin-gown; green, lacy pattern on the sleeves an collar. I whack it with the cricket bat as hard as I can, an the noise is sad, dull, an then the zombie stops movin. It's too fragile to do anythin but die.

'Fucking Christ,' she says, puttin a hand on her chest. 'Sorry. I don't know why I was so scared.' She shakes herself, puts the knife back in the holder on her belt. 'Come on, let's find the fucking supermarket.'

'Wait,' I say, an walk over to the bookcase behind the corpse in the hallway, grabbin some thin books.

'Maybe if we leave the bikes here,' she says, 'we can just take the way we did last time, to the milk bar, stick to the houses. That huge pack of zombies is still in the estate, so it might be safer risking the group of people.'

She doesn' really believe that an neither do I, but we don' say anything. Soon we're hidin our bikes in the bushes near the fence an we're walkin. We go a bit of a different way to avoid the milk bar.

She shields her eyes from the sun. 'There's a couple of big stores ahead.' She turns to me an grins. 'And it looks like there's a Mitre 10.'

Mitre 10 – that means tools. I haven' bin there since my dad took me when I was little an he was less of a fuckhead. Maybe not less, but I was too little to notice, maybe.

Maybe.

There are a few zombies, but nothin like the horde we missed; I get some of the closer ones, though, jus in case. The Mitre 10's front doors are open, an we have to step through all the shit on the floor. Everythin's bin pulled off the shelves. Paint cans spilled all down the aisles, the floor stark white.

'There's so much,' she says. 'Lucky we brought the backpacks.' That was my idea, an she smiles at me. 'Maybe we should take a few little tins of paint. In case we need to leave marks, or messages to each other.'

In case we get separated, she means. My blood runs

cold, icicles jabbin my organs. If we ever do, we're not gonna find each other again.

So we grab a tiny can each; they clack together in the bag. 'To open em we're gonna need screwdrivers.'

'They're good weapons, too,' she says. 'Good one. We should get a toolkit – maybe we'll need it later on, not just for the paint.'

In the tool section are bodies an a zombie. The zombie musta killed em an jus stood aroun since. She picks up a screwdriver an rams the pointy end into its head fore it notices how close we are, thick blood gluggin out as it falls to the ground. 'For example,' she says.

She takes two new screwdrivers, gives one to me. We get an allen key set, a coupla different-sized screwdrivers, an some other stuff.

'A hammer,' I say. 'An nails.'

'Maybe some screws as well,' she says, an we go an pick them up. 'This is too good,' she says, grinnin like it's Christmas. 'Maybe we should go further into town, see what we find.'

So when we're done with the Mitre 10, after pickin up some spray-paints too, we walk round an we find a Kmart. We look through the doors, chained shut. It's fucken full of zombies, more than I've ever seen at once. The sight sends me blood cold. Someone's spray-painted across the windows DO NOT ENTER but really, you'd have to be a dickhead to try an get in there. We do need new clothes, but the ones we got'll last longer, an it's still pretty hot even though it's bin rainin a bit.

After the Kmart, it's a bit hard to get through all the cars on the road. There are heapsa zombies but the cars block a lotta em. I knock a couple down an we run, dodgin the dead, an she laughs. I grin at her, then gasp. 'Look behin ya,' I say, pointin. A campin shop.

She grabs my arm. 'This *is* too good.' An we run the rest of the way there, not even carin if that group see us. They're jus a dull thought at the back of my head cause we got this goldmine right here. The front door is sealed tight, so we go lookin for the back door. It's locked too, but there's a window up high she might be able to squish through. We're so thin now it'll probly work. I hand her the bat an boost her up; she smashes the window an we shield our eyes, glass rainin down.

'Can you get in?' I say. Can' look, or she'll lose her balance.

'I think so.'

'Don' cut yourself on the glass.'

She moves from her knees onto her feet, an her shoes dig into my shoulders. I shuffle on my feet but say nothin, an then there's extra pressure, then none. There's a yelp fore she yells out, 'I'm okay!'

'Careful,' I say. 'Might be somethin in there.'

I hear the door unlock. 'Doubt it,' she says. 'This place seems sealed up pretty good. We might be the first people in here since, y'know.'

We relock the door when we get in, an there's no noise. That don' mean nothin, cause of what jus happened in that house, but this time it seems like there's really nothin. The air is cold. We walk through a tiny corridor an there's a few doors; one is open an the room is filled with cleanin stuff. When we reach the door at the end of the corridor, we pause.

'Just in case there's somethin out there,' she says, 'get ready.'

An then we open the door, an the shop is empty, an it's so big I don' know where to start. We walk around at first jus tryin to take everythin in. But there's a lot, an we end up sittin on some campin chairs.

'These are good,' she says. 'But maybe a bit too heavy.'

'Yeah,' I say, closin my eyes an leanin back. 'We could get some on a second trip.'

'We'd need a truck to fit everything I want,' she says.

My bones sink into the chair, an while we sit we hear nothin cept our breathin, an soon I can barely even hear that. I'm half asleep by the time she stirs, an then she taps my foot with hers. 'Come on, lady,' she says. 'We got shopping to do.'

The first thing we get is backpacks, them big ones hikers wear that hold everythin. We get new sleepin-bags, real warm ones that roll up real small. We find her knives, we find straps for the knives; we find somethin we can make into a strap for my bat. We get heapsa batteries, an two of them really long torches you can also hit people with. We get a lantern an a bunch of tea lights, matches, lighters. Next to the counter is a box of heat packs, ones that don' get hot til ya crack em an then stay like that for a few hours; we empty the box into her backpack.

'Ooh, bikes!' she says. 'Let's get new ones! Mine is too big, anyway.' She half skips over, the huge backpack jumpin from side to side. 'Look, we can put bags on them!' There's ones for under the seat, for the sides of the back wheel, an for the handlebars. 'This is so great.' She picks a red bike with fatter tyres. 'Why don't you have a look at that green one?'

Soon we're puttin every bag onto the new bikes, an some water-bottle holders. Once we've got everythin packed, we're ready to go. We back out the way we came, an stop at the first house we find. They've got canned sardines an onions, things I woulda scrunched me nose up at but now I'll take anythin. Our bags are heavy after we leave the third house. We go back to our old bikes, get the books an food there. See a few zombies, but we don' stop. One of em moans, wheezy an long, as we ride past, an the noise so close makes my bike wobble a bit. I don' wanna freeze if I run into a whole bunch of em again, an now I dunno if I'm all right.

At home we leave everythin in the backpacks an lie in the tent, sharin a packet of chips. It's too hot to do anythin cept start to read a book an get drinks from the river. I find a coupla blue feathers an bring em back to the tent. When it gets too dark to read, the night starts to make its noises around us, an we fall asleep to the sounds of water an frogs.

Twenty-three

The two are chatting when we come up to the van, lounging round like a couple of teenagers. Which they are, and which *we* are too, but I feel like I'm a hundred.

'What do we do?' Poppy says under her breath.

'Where are Jack and Zufan?' I ask, looking around. We've been seen twice now by these people, how slack are we? Nowhere is safe, we have to remember that.

We keep walking, trying to make the pace as normal as possible. We have a shovel, a crowbar, but who knows what they have? Who knows how many people they've got, hiding? Maybe they've got weapons, real weapons. Guns?

'Hey,' one says when we get closer.

Their faces are almost identical. They've both got short hair: one has a pixie cut, the other has hair down to their chin. They're probably our age, maybe a couple of years younger. Sixteen? The one with the pixie cut has full lips, the other one is shorter. One of their hands only has two fingers; the one with the pixie cut's got a scar across their face, just missing their left eye.

'Hello,' I say, and give a little wave. I've never said *hello* to a real person apart from now; it's always on the

233

telephone I say *hello*. I had honestly thought awkward social encounters would cease to exist after the zombie apocalypse, but I guess not.

'I'm Rhea,' says the one with the pixie cut. 'R-H-E-A.' The skin around their scar stretches, shiny. 'And this is Jojo. I'm a she, Jojo is a they.'

Jojo nods at us, lifts a finger from their complete hand.

'Where are our friends?' I ask.

'I think they might be hiding from us in the petrol station.' Rhea points at its window; sure enough, I see Jack and Zufan's heads poking out over the sill. 'What are your names?' Rhea asks as Jack and Zufan emerge. He's holding the shovel, ready to go.

Poppy and I exchange looks, and she nods the tiniest bit. What can it hurt to give them our names? I introduce everyone, giving names and pronouns.

'We might forget,' Rhea says and grins wider. 'But I'm sure with time, we'll get along like a house on fire.'

Jojo nudges her and grins, shaking their head.

'With time?' Jack says. 'What do you mean?'

Rhea and Jojo exchange looks. 'We thought you'd wanna stick together.'

'Don't you wanna team up?' Jojo says. Their voice is light, quiet.

Team up. That makes it sound like a game, and you can win games. 'Jack,' I say, because I feel like he's not going to agree, 'maybe they can help us, we can get some information and whatever.'

'We don't even have enough food to feed ourselves,' he says, hissing.

'We've got plenty of food,' I say. 'And they might have more.' They don't look particularly underfed; maybe as stressed and tired as we do, but not as hungry.

'We have supplies,' Rhea says. 'You can stay at our house.'

I turn to make significant eye contact with the others. 'They have a house.'

'Exactly.' He leans in so only I can hear his words. 'They could trap us.' His breath shivers across my neck. 'They could be anyone.'

'Why would they do that?' I whisper back. 'We've got nothing. There are heaps of cars, they don't need ours.'

'Maybe they're fucked up.' It makes sense really, his reluctance. He's got lots of reasons not to trust people, and I think the only people in the world he really trusts are us. 'Remember how we just saw that person get shot?'

'Jack, come on, they're our age.' I wonder if I'm being too dismissive. But the thought of a bed to sleep in is too tempting. 'The more people we have, the safer we'll be.'

'Fine.' He holds up his hands. 'Fine. I don't care.'

I look at Zufan and Poppy, and they both nod. I'm glad; I don't want to sleep in the van again.

The twins are whispering as they watch us, and Jojo's trying not to laugh. Rhea jabs them in the ribs and they straighten, their legs jiggling, hitting the tyre with their heel.

'So, where's your house?' I say.

Jojo jumps down. 'Follow us. It's a bit out of the way, but it's nice up there.'

'We should drive,' Jack says. 'We're not leaving our car here.'

'Okay.' Rhea nods. 'For sure. I'll direct you.'

In the van Rhea and Jack sit up front while the rest of us pile in at the back.

'Is this your house from before?' I ask the twins.

'No,' Rhea replies. 'Our house was very ... different.'

And I remember her scar, her sibling's missing fingers. Those scars are old; she grew up with that across her face.

'This house, though,' she says, 'it's amazing. You'll love it.'

'Why were you in town?' I ask.

'More clothes. The people here didn't exactly have the best dress sense.'

I laugh for the second time today. None of the others are saying anything, and Jack keeps looking around for other survivors who may or may not be ambushing us.

The drive isn't too long. The house seems about the size of the one we were renting before but way prettier and more expensive, and its surroundings are green and lush, not dried out from the summer sun. There are tree ferns and so much undergrowth it won't burn easily, not like with the layer of dead gumleaves that surrounded the rental house.

'This is great,' I say as we walk up. Jojo opens the door and we go inside. Where our rental house was old and simple, theirs is new, with heaps of windows, and it's modern. Everything's sleek and shiny, and the place is huge, much bigger than it looked from where we entered, stretching out on stilts into the valley.

'Wow,' Poppy says, breaking the silence. 'This is awesome.'

'It's a bit tricky to cover the rent, but we manage,' Rhea says.

I snort and she grins.

'We've got lots of bedrooms,' she says. 'But some of us will have to share.'

'Can we just, er,' Zufan says, looking at us, 'talk about it? Like, I mean just us. It's not that I don't trust you,' and here she gestures at Rhea, 'but we haven't seen many people who weren't, um. Y'know, dead.'

The sound of the gunshot lingers in my ears, the idea that someone would shoot someone else. It's all too much. Rhea and Jojo seem just like normal teenagers, like us – I can't imagine they would hurt us. But how do I know?

She coughs. 'Since before.'

Rhea nods. 'Yeah, we can talk.'

'How did you find us?' I ask her.

'Chance. Jojo's pretty quick on their feet.'

Jojo smiles at her but doesn't say anything.

'We … we really just wanted some company,' Rhea says.

Jack narrows his eyes.

'We can leave you to rest,' Rhea says, seeing Jack's face. When we nod, she and Jojo go out on the balcony that looks over the valley and sit on banana lounges. Because the doors are glass, we can see everything they're doing. Their backs are towards us.

'Why are they being so nice?' Jack asks.

'Maybe they wanted us to see the house first,' I say. 'It is nice. It'd be good not sleeping in a van ever again.'

'It's nice here,' Zufan says, 'but I don't know that I trust them.'

'We can at least stay one night,' Poppy says. 'We can get a few beds and put them all in the same room, and take turns to keep watch.'

Sleeping in a real bed sounds better than anything anyone's said all day, so I nod. 'I agree with Poppy.'

So does Zufan, and then Jack nods grudgingly after she does.

'Tomorrow,' he crosses his arms, 'we should talk more about this.' His mouth is straight, bunched into a line.

'What kind of food do you reckon they've got?' Zufan asks. 'I'm starving.'

When we ask the twins, Jojo brings out a few packets of chips and some canned beans. It's not much, but it's amazing and it's food. They show us their drinking-water bucket on the kitchen bench; in the backyard there's a water tank.

We scoff all the food, and soon we're sitting in the

lounge room, spread out on the couches. I'm sharing one with Zufan, our knees touching as we lie on opposite ends.

'So, how did you get here, anyway?' Rhea asks. 'You're a big group and you all know each other from before.'

'We're in a band,' Poppy says. 'We'd rented a house in the middle of nowhere, kinda like this one except, y'know, shit. And we just … didn't know anything. When the power went out, we drove to the nearest town and, well,' she sighs, 'then we found everything.'

'Or nothing,' I say.

'Right.' Poppy pauses. 'What about you two?'

'We were closer to the city,' Rhea says. 'The news started reporting all this weird stuff, then we weren't allowed to go to school. We stayed put, until Mum went missing, then we had to sneak around to figure out where she was.'

Jojo shifts beside her but doesn't speak.

'We stole a car.' She pauses again, looks at her sibling and takes a deep breath. 'We found our way to this town, then this house, and we've been here maybe, what, two weeks?'

Jojo nods.

'So yeah. Just still trying to settle in.'

'So what's the deal with the zombies?' Jack says. 'Are people calling them zombies, or is that silly?'

Rhea grins. 'It does sound a little silly. But I guess, yeah, that's what we're calling them. I dunno what they're called, like, officially. By the time we started paying attention, the media was being censored as all hell and the government blocked the internet.'

'They blocked it?' Poppy asks.

She nods. 'Or maybe the towers went down or something. Dunno how they did it.'

'How long has it been?' I ask. I have no idea how to measure time now.

Rhea shrugs. 'Maybe a month? Two? I'm not sure anymore. I don't know if it's even December yet.'

'Guess it must be, or almost,' Jojo says, scratching their head. 'It was November tenth when we weren't allowed to go to school for the first time.'

Through the window behind the twins I see angry clouds at the edge of the sky, coming over the hills covered in dark green gums. There's lightning in those clouds, a flash, then a huge belt of thunder rips through the house. We all jump, and Poppy squeaks.

'It's weird not knowing the time,' Rhea says. 'Everything used to be so dependent on time, and now I've just got no clue.'

Jojo puts a hand on her back.

'Well,' I say, 'we can kinda guess. Birds get along fine, so we can too.'

And she nods, her eyes look far away, and she doesn't say anything.

The storm rolls forwards, and eventually we disperse. I sit on the balcony with Jack and Poppy in the cooling air. The wind is picking up, the trees around us swaying.

'I hope this wind doesn't pick up too much,' Jack says. 'Trees could fall on the house.'

'Let's add that to the list of things to worry about,' I say.

'I was just saying,' he says, rolling his eyes, 'so we can prepare if it happens.'

'What are we gonna do?' I reply. 'Reinforce the trunks around us? We can't do shit.'

'Sorry,' Jack says, and he looks at Poppy, who shrugs.

'Sorry,' I say too. 'I just … I feel useless, and, like, I feel like I can't *see* anything at all. I want so much information and I can't get any of it.'

'I feel the same,' Poppy says, nudging her foot with mine. She's got red nail polish on; it's mostly chipped away, and her toenails need trimming, but there's still some paint there. 'Maybe Jojo and Rhea know more than they think they do.'

'Maybe they're withholding stuff.'

'Maybe,' she says, 'but I don't think so. They seem just like us.'

'I don't think they're holding anything back,' I say. 'I just think they don't know what they know.'

'Maybe we could go back to the place we were renting,' Poppy says. 'If something happened to this house.'

'Like if a tree fell on it?' Jack says.

I don't say anything, and Poppy pauses but doesn't acknowledge his input. 'All our stuff should still be there. We'd be pretty safe.'

'Unless someone followed us there,' I say.

'Unless someone followed us *here*,' says Jack.

My stomach feels cold. 'Someone could've. Those two found us, when we thought we were being careful.'

'We weren't being that careful,' says Poppy. 'We could've been trying harder.'

'We didn't really expect anyone to be here, except zombies.' I bite my lip. 'What if someone did follow us here?'

'Jojo and Rhea seem pretty on the ball,' she replies. 'I don't think they would have let anyone follow us. I mean, they got out of being imprisoned in their home in the first place.'

'I wonder what happened to their mum,' I say.

There's a silent moment, and I know we're thinking about our families, and the friends who didn't come with us. Even Harry, the dickhead at school who would always tease me, I wonder what he's doing right now. Can't think about it.

'She might've got out,' Poppy says.

'She was smart,' Rhea says from behind Poppy, and the three of us jump. Rhea slides the glass door shut, and it makes no noise. I make a mental note to check everything in the house for noise, escape routes. 'She's a zombie. Us getting out wasn't skill, it was luck.'

'I don't believe in luck,' I say. 'You should give yourself more credit.'

She doesn't reply, but something shifts in her face.

We don't say anything more, just watch as the storm

rolls in. The sky darkens, and the wind blasts us; Poppy grabs her hair so it stops flying around her face. The clouds aren't above us yet as we see the rain fall down, make its way across the valley. When it hits the house, it's cold. I close my eyes, and it's like tears running down my cheeks, salt-free, cool.

***

I wake up in the same room as Poppy, Zufan and Jack, and the air is musty. 'This is better than being in the van,' I say. 'It doesn't feel like I'm breathing in everyone's sweat.'

We've set up three double beds so there isn't any floor space, but at least we all have room enough to sleep comfortably. I'm in between Poppy and Jack, deliberately because I know neither of them kick during the night. Zufan, not so much.

'Shh,' Zufan mutters into her pillow. Poppy's already awake – her sitting up must have been what woke me – and Jack is stirring beside me.

'We'll bake you a glorious breakfast,' Poppy says. 'Of beans … cold beans. And maybe some stale bread if you're lucky. I could heat it up if I wasn't scared the smoke would attract things and/or people that will kill us.'

'So kind,' Zufan says, her words muffled by the pillow.

Me and Poppy drag Jack's half-asleep self to the kitchen because Zufan won't be moved. He sits on a stool at the counter, hair mussed and in his eyes. The counter's marble, or maybe fake marble, and not too dusty. There's a few cans of beetroot and tuna, so I grab those and the can-opener. I plonk them on the bench, startling Jack further awake, and look through the cupboards for plates and glasses. 'Can you fill these?' I ask Poppy, and she scoops them into the drinking-water bucket, sits beside Jack and hands him his glass.

'So what's for breakfast this morning, Chef?' Poppy asks, swinging her legs.

'Well, today we have a lovely selection of beetroot and tuna. Served … well, probably not together, as I don't believe that would be very tasty. But we carry on.'

'Wow, a feast,' Rhea says, emerging from her room. She's wearing a long, loose t-shirt and her hair is rumpled. 'I didn't know you could cook, Dee.'

'Yeah, she's the talk of Melbourne these days,' Jack says. There's an edge to his voice I don't like. It's mean.

Rhea smiles at him anyway. 'How did you all sleep?' she asks before biting into a piece of beetroot.

'Awful,' Jack mutters.

'Good,' I say, nodding. 'Really good. We've been stuck in the van for ages. It's nice not waking up to pins and needles in my legs.' Poppy's nodding along, and I notice she's already finished her beetroot; drinking her water quickly, trying not to, taking too many sips.

My stomach still feels empty when I'm done with the beetroot. I dish out the tuna. The salt makes my mouth water, and it takes everything not to eat the whole can by myself.

'I was thinking,' Rhea says when everyone's finished eating. We look at her, and she pauses at the angry expression Jacks's still got on his face. 'I was thinking, maybe if you guys want to go get supplies today, then Jojo and I can come with you? And we can leave a couple of people here, just to guard the place or whatever.'

I look out into the valley. There's mist this early in the morning, down the very bottom. There are dark greens, and everything has a hint of blue over the top. The leaves are still damp.

'Reckon it'll get hotter again?' Poppy says, when she sees me gazing out.

I shrug. 'Might.'

'Me and Pop can look after the house,' I say to Rhea. 'You can use my shovel, if you want – it's good fer killin' zombies with.' I put on a super-fake American accent, smiling.

'Well, thank ya kindly,' Rhea replies in kind. 'That sounds all right. Jojo and I were talking about it, and it seems like a good idea for us both to go. We know the route and how to keep quiet.'

We wake the others. Jojo springs up; Zufan isn't so bad but takes the longest. They're fed, and then I give Zufan my shovel and they all walk off.

'We can trust the twins, right?' Poppy says, watching them go. 'Like, this isn't the last time we're gonna see the others?'

As I watch their backs, I shake my head. 'It'll all be good, Pop.'

Twenty-four

Rhea said I could stay at the house if I wanted, but I don't want to be separated from her with these randoms. They're probably not gonna hurt us, but I don't want to be away from her. I could lose her, like we lost Mum, and Caitlin.

Jack is walking up front with Rhea, and Zufan walks beside me. I don't know what to say to her. I'm keeping an eye on Jack while he walks with Rhea because he clearly doesn't like us, what about Zufan? The other two girls seem okay. Though what do we even talk about?

'Uh, how are you?' I ask her.

She looks at me, her face all tight. 'Small talk doesn't really work now, does it?'

'Um.' I swallow. 'No.'

'I miss my family,' she says. 'I'm sorry about your mum.'

'I'm sorry about your family.'

Her eyes well up and she turns away for a bit to wipe away tears. I pretend I haven't noticed.

The buzzing of the cicadas is getting louder as we walk. We must've left at about seven or so in the morning, judging by the coolness of the air, but it's getting really hot super quick. My armpits are starting to sweat but, like, as long as I don't smell like a decaying corpse then I'm good. These zombies are setting a great example.

'All we get is gross food and this heat,' Zufan says after a bit. 'Like, we don't even know where this is happening, or if it's just us, or ...'

'Or the whole country. The whole planet.'

We emerge from the bush-lined roads onto a bitumen one.

'So, what else do we need aside from food?' Jack asks.

'Sunscreen,' I say. I don't burn as easily as some people, but it'd be useful to have.

'Okay.' Jack looks a bit confused at this before-times product.

We start walking down the main road, trying to avoid the zombies. When we can't, we get rid of them. After the second one I put down, I'm shaking. I wish we could stay at home and never do this again; I can't get used to it. We don't talk now we're in the suburbs, if this sparse collection of buildings can be called the suburbs – well, more than anywhere near here, I guess. Anyway, being surrounded by buildings and zombie noises is creepy as hell. There are so many windows; people could be watching us like Rhea and I spied on the others before. No wonder they were so freaked out. Definitely not our best plan, but I guess it paid off.

'Maybe let's cut through people's backyards,' Rhea says, drawing us to a stop.

We move without discussing it further. Mostly the

houses have small, waist-high fences or just shrubs and hedges. Only two fences are too high to jump over; we cut through the front yards. In the second yard, Jack holds up a hand and whispers for us to stop. He crouches and we follow. 'You hear that?'

I strain my ears, wait. There's the sound of ... metallic-something.

Jack peeks over the fence. 'Someone's kicking a can down the street. I only got a little glimpse, but there were heaps of them.'

'What'd they look like?' Rhea asks. She's trying to peer through the bushes but the angle's wrong.

'I dunno. People.' He shrugs. 'They don't look friendly.'

Blood drains from my face, and I shrink as small as I can. What if it's Matt? Are the cult people looking for us?

'Rhea.' I tug on her sleeve. 'What if it's them?'

'Who?' Zufan asks.

'There's, uh, a cult? That we got away from?' I don't know how to make it sound less ridiculous.

'Jesus.' Zufan grimaces.

Rhea goes and gets a look through the fence that's covered in a vine. When she comes back, she's shaky. 'I dunno who it is but I recognise their faces. I think they're from the cult.'

'Do you think they're looking for us?' I ask.

'Let's just stay here,' Jack says. 'Keep quiet.'

My legs soon start to cramp, and I end up sitting in the dirt. It's getting hotter; the cicadas are buzzing away. We don't hear any more noise from the people, so they're probably gone, but it's better to be safe than dead. It's got to have been at least an hour, I reckon, and we've played about a hundred games of naughts and crosses. We take turns using sticks as crosses and leaves as naughts, and I lose almost every time; I never could get the hang of it.

'Do you think it's safe now?' Zufan asks.

My feet have fallen asleep numerous times but right now they're both normal. Good timing.

'I guess,' Rhea says. 'We have to be super careful, though. What do you reckon?' she asks me and Jack.

He nods. I nod too, mainly because I don't want to be sitting here anymore.

We stick to the backyards again, and this time when a fence is too high to jump we scale it.

The first shop we find is a gardening one, and through the frosted glass we see the plants are all overgrown, looks like a tiny jungle. The next shop has a sign out front, pants sale, and the windows are all smashed. The next is what we're looking for, one of those mini-marts that doesn't have everything. Rhea and I had started to explore town, but we hadn't made it this far yet. We went the other way and found a tiny strip of shops that had a newsagent and an old Korean restaurant that had been raided.

We walk through the aisles, weapons raised, but there's not any noise. There's heaps of cleaning liquids, mouldy bread, soap. A few cartons of eggs are smashed in one aisle, and it's all fungus-y and gross. Rhea reaches over the mess for the three packets of tea bags left over, but apart from that we skip the aisle. After searching everywhere, we find post-its, pens, heaps of baby food, and one can of pea and ham soup hidden under the middle of an aisle. It's a big can, so if we split it six ways we'll each get a good serve. The thought turns my stomach into a cavern – warm soup, my god. Maybe we can cook it inside somewhere.

It's not as much as we wanted, but we can still raid the houses when we need to.

'We could get some seeds,' Zufan says when we pass the garden shop. It's built like a glass greenhouse and the windows all have bars behind them. The door hasn't been broken into yet; its locks look pretty impressive.

'Back door?' Rhea suggests, and we walk through the car park to find the slightly splintery wooden door. Jack pries it with his shovel, and Rhea hacks a little around the lock with her machete. When it gives, the two of them go sprawling. My heart beats a bit too hard at the thought of the machete's sharp edge, but Rhea just takes my offered hand and stands up, dusting off her butt. 'Ouch,' she says, but she grins.

'Good one,' I tell her, picking her machete off the ground. 'Please don't die by flying machete.'

'I will try my darndest.'

'Keep a lookout in the car park while we find some stuff?' Jack asks, and we nod.

***

The seeds must be really fuckin interesting because Jack and Zufan are taking forever. I kick a rock down the car park, Rhea kicks one too. We take it in turns but mine generally go further.

'I am the rock ruler!' I tell her. 'I will –'

There's the sound of a car engine.

'Fuck,' we say together. Crouching low, we can't see anything … until we look across the car park and the oval next to it, and see a dirt cloud on the road behind.

'They've found us?' I ask.

'Maybe.'

We bolt inside the garden shop's back door and close it behind us.

'Guys, hide!' I tell the others.

They look at me and they're covered in blood. I scream.

'What?' Zufan says.

'The blood! On your face!'

'There were zombies in here,' Jack says.

'What! Why didn't you let us know?' Rhea asks. 'You could've died, or turned and then come out and bit one of us!'

'Why didn't you tell us you escaped from a cult?' Jack shoots back.

'Come on,' I say, 'those people are outside so get away from the windows.'

About a minute later we hear the car drive past – actually, two cars. There are heaps of voices when the cars park and people get out, more than five. They don't come here, though, just head into the mini-mart.

'Do we wait or go now?' Jack says. 'If we leave now, we should be okay.'

'What if they notice us?' Rhea whispers. 'We should wait.'

'We came in from the back,' Jack replies.

'Yes, but they'll hear us, or they'll see us – we don't know where they are exactly.'

'But,' Jack says, then makes a noise of frustration. 'Guess you're right.'

So we're sitting in the garden shop and there's a zombie corpse right next to me, still in the shop's uniform. Its teeth are all crooked; maybe it tried to eat us through the window. The air is stuffy, and sweat is forming on my forehead. A bead runs down into my eyebrow, against the side of my face.

While we wait I grab as many seed packets as I can fit on my person, and I give some to Rhea as well. I don't really know anything about gardening, but I can learn.

Maybe ten minutes pass before we hear the chorus of voices outside again. They're complaining about the lack of food in the mini-mart, then they're complaining about each other. Soon, they drive off and everything is silent again.

'Let's get out of here,' Rhea says, and when she stands I can see sweat on her too.

It's great when we finally get back outside to the fresh air. It's fuckin hot but way less humid. The walk back home seems to take forever, maybe because feeling like you're being watched is pretty damn stressful. But no one comes out to grab us.

'Maybe we shouldn't tell the others about those people,' Jack says. 'They'll just worry.'

'That's a real shitty idea, Jack,' Rhea says, and her voice is stone.

Nothing more is said on the subject.

When we get home, Poppy and Dee come out the front to meet us. We tell them about the group of people and they're worried, but they're more interested in the soup. Dee has the idea of making a tiny fire in the sink. It takes ages and we have to disconnect all the smoke alarms, but it's worth having hot food.

Twenty-five

I wake up cold an my body is tense as; I crawl into my sleepin-bag an try an figure out why I'm awake. There ain' any frog or possum noises, or anythin cept the sound of the river. An then I wait longer, an there's the crunchin a leaves. Rhythmic, one foot after the other. Dunno how I heard it in me sleep. Maybe the silence is what woke me, knew somethin was up.

I nudge her awake, whisper to her to be quiet. 'Can hear someone,' I say. 'Don' think it's a zombie.'

She swallows. 'Shit. How long?' I can' see anythin of her, it's way too fucken dark.

'Dunno, jus woke up.'

We listen, an then there's more crunchin, louder this time. Then there's more, too many for one person.

'Pretty sure it was somewhere round here,' one says, a deep voice.

'Yeah, near the river. If we keep walkin we'll find it,' another says.

'Fuck, we have to go,' she says. 'Everything's on the bikes, yeah?'

'Except for the food,' I say, pointin at the tiny pile in the corner.

'We take them, and then we get on the bikes and ride the fuck out of here.'

'Must be round here, I remember that tree,' the first voice says. They're getting closer. More footsteps, an when I unzip the tent I see a torchlight not too far off.

'They're real close,' I say. 'We have to go now or they'll see.'

'All right,' she says. 'They're going to hear the bikes as soon as we take off, though.'

'They're on foot. We can get a head start.'

We look at each other. She kisses me, fierce, then nods. 'Let's go,' she whispers.

Boltin to the bikes, we slide on our backpacks, I shove the cans in the top a mine, an we ride off. Don' wanna leave the tent behind but we don' got a choice.

The torchlight gets brighter as we hear shouts from the people.

'Follow me!' I yell at her. I've more used to the bush than her, an the moon is three quarters full so I can mostly see. We crash through the leaves litterin the ground an I'm takin us further into the bush, away from the river, away from the men, away from our home that wasn' practical or fancy but still a home, an now the men are gonna trample all over it.

We could stop but I dunno how, my legs have forgotten. This bike's better for me than the last one but, an ridin is easier. I hope hers is better too.

When the birds start to sing again we stop. We're deep in the bush an I got no fucken clue where the fuck anythin is anymore. We're not near the river, an everythin is jus trees.

'Sorry,' I tell her.

'It's okay. They're not gonna come this far looking for us.'

'You're foolin yourself. We killed their mates, they went that far before.'

She looks away. 'Guess you're right.'

Damn fucken oath I am.

'So what do we do?' she asks.

'Sleep in shifts. It was fucken wrong to think we were safe. We're never gonna be safe again.'

'With no tent.'

I shrug. It's summer, we can work it out. 'We got the food, though.'

'How will we survive? We've only got two cans.'

I put a hand on her shoulder. 'We can do this.'

She looks at me, her mouth drawn back so I can barely see her lips. 'All right.'

'All right.'

Twenty-six

Poppy found a guitar in our room and she's been playing it all day. It's been about a week since we got here, and we've been to town a few times. No sign of those cult people that the others saw the other day, and so Jack and Rhea took the van to get supplies from town this morning. I requested pizza but somehow doubt that's going to happen. Jojo's in their room, they tend to keep to themselves unless Rhea's around.

The worst thing about this house has been putting on the clothes, because they still smell like the owners. Sometimes I wonder about the people who lived here. There are a lot of bedrooms, one more after we converted the study, though I'm still sharing with Poppy. None of the rooms are children's, and there's enough clutter to make me think this wasn't a holiday house. A few framed photos sit on the mantelpiece, and I've noticed albums jammed into the bottom of the bookcase, but I don't want to look at them. The lived-in smell's gone away now, or I'm used to it. One of the people was the same size as me, but none of their shoes fit me very well. For now I'm keeping my own.

Finite resources. That's another thing I don't want

to think about. Jojo mentioned they know how to fish; I guess if we find a fishing rod we can all learn.

Zufan walks past the couch I'm sitting on, post-its in hand. She clicks her pen as she taps her chin. She's taken to leaving post-its around the house in replacement of Twitter. I don't read them, they make me too sad. I miss the internet.

Poppy's still distracting herself with the guitar. She gave up trying to remember her song and instead sings other people's. She hasn't even played one of ours. Right now she's strumming something I know but can't place.

I like music, I like playing drums, but I'm not like Poppy. Poppy needs music, it's a part of her. I don't think she's all right without it, but she wouldn't say that out loud.

Zufan keeps clicking her pen, so I take the book I'm trying to read and move onto the balcony. It's my favourite part of the house; if I ignore the railing it's like I'm just sitting up in the trees. I lie on a banana lounge and the sun makes my skin sing. I could fall asleep, and we've got all the time in the whole world, so why not? I rest the book on my stomach and close my eyes. There's nothing that needs doing; Jack and Rhea are taking care of that. Still haven't got used to being alone, though, so I can't fall asleep in case something happens.

The balcony door slides across, and I open an eye to see it's Zufan.

'Hey,' she says. 'You sleeping?'

I shake my head, too comfortable to do anything else, and close my eye. The trees rustle in the breeze, and though we've been here a while now I can still smell the eucalyptus. There's a kookaburra somewhere, and a few whipbirds.

'I found a book I think you might like,' Zufan says. 'I left it on your bed.'

'Thanks,' I say, and smile into the sun. I hear her take the banana lounge next to mine. 'This one's shit.' I gesture at the book on my stomach.

We listen to the faint guitar music. 'Poppy's so good,' Zufan says.

'It's hard,' I say. 'I miss band practice.'

'Yeah.' There's a pause. 'Maybe we could go back to that house.'

'I don't even remember the address, Zufan. Don't think we could find it if we tried.'

'I remember,' she says, and then she names a street, but it doesn't sound familiar to me and I wonder if she made it up. Her pen clicks; I flinch at the noise. 'Well, anyway, it would be good to play again,' she says. I hear the pen scribble on the post-it. 'I don't know that we ever will. Properly, I mean. Because of the whole no-electricity thing.' She clicks the pen again.

'We'll have to have some kind of group identity crisis, probably. Then I'll go off and do my side project, which will consist of me using gumleaves as harmonicas.'

'Beautiful,' she says.

I open my eyes and turn to her. She's resting her arms

under her head and her shirt's riding up her tummy a little. I close my eyes again, too distracting.

'It's great out here,' she says. 'I can see why you're always on the balcony, reading or whatever.' Her pen clicks yet again.

'Stop clicking that and you can stay.'

'Maybe I will,' she says. '*Maaaaybe* I will. Sorry. But, like, tell me if I'm intruding or whatever.'

'All good. It's … less comfortable being alone now, after all this.'

I hear her shift in her lounge. 'Yeah. Guess you're right.'

'Yeah,' I say, and then we lie silently in the sun. Having her there feels safe; I fall asleep. My dreams are of blue trees and running, blood, and then silence, so much of it.

***

I wake up to Poppy shaking my shoulder.

'Wha–?' I say, trying to unstick myself from the banana lounge.

'They're not back yet.' Her eyes are wide, I can see too much white.

I sit up and realise the sun is setting. Zufan's inside.

'Jack and Rhea,' Poppy says. 'They're still out there.'

'How long have I been asleep?'

'They were just going to get some lollies from the servo. Jack didn't trust Rhea to go with Jojo.'

I look inside. Zufan and Jojo are sitting on a couch, talking – well, Jojo's talking, and doing a lot of it. We go inside and Jojo looks at me. 'What do you think we should do?' Their face is pale as they jab their finger at me.

'I … I think we should wait. We don't know where they went. We don't have a car.'

'That's what I thought, too,' Zufan says. 'Jojo says we should go after them, and Poppy doesn't know.'

Poppy shifts beside me.

'But my sister's out there!' Jojo says. 'We need to rescue them.'

'Where would we rescue them *from*?' Poppy says, harsher than I expected from her. I wonder how long they've been having this conversation while I slept.

'Poppy's right,' I say. 'We might put them in danger. What if they're hidden and we just go in and reveal them? We don't know enough. And it will get dark soon.'

'We can't just leave them,' Zufan says.

'What if it was us?' Jojo says from where they're sitting on the couch. 'We'd want to be rescued, right?'

'They might have just taken longer than they thought,' Poppy says, 'and decided to stay overnight so they wouldn't have to travel in the dark.'

'Of course you side with Dee,' Zufan says. 'You always do.'

'Hey.' Poppy walks to her, towering over her. 'I can make my own decisions.'

Zufan shakes her head and doesn't say anything as she looks away.

'Well, I'm not going anywhere,' I say. 'We'd only be putting ourselves in danger for no reason.'

'It's not no reason!' Jojo says.

'Sorry,' I say, 'I just mean they're probably fine, and we're fine right where we are.'

Poppy nods along.

'Fine,' Zufan says.

I don't look away from Jojo, and they don't blink.

'If they're not back by lunch tomorrow,' I say, 'we'll go look for them.'

Jojo finally blinks. 'All right,' they say. 'Tomorrow.'

***

That night I don't think any of us sleep. After a while I hear someone walk in the corridor, and then Zufan's bedroom door opens. A couple of seconds, then Jojo's voice. Zufan replies, the door closes, and there's no more noise.

I lie awake and listen to the insects. The van doesn't return. In the morning the birds sing, and there's a heaviness in my lungs that won't go away. As soon as the sun starts to rise, I get up. There's a can of asparagus and I take a couple of pieces, and find Zufan on a couch in the lounge. I sit next to her and she seems as about awake as I am.

'Hey,' I say.

'Hey.'

I lean my head on her shoulder. She puts an arm around me and I move my head to rest on her chest, and her body is warm. It's nice, in the cool morning air.

'What did Jojo want last night?' I ask, though I'm not sure if I should.

'They just didn't want to be alone. They sleep talk, by the way.'

'Did you sleep?'

'A little. On and off.' I can hear her heart beat and I feel like a person again. 'I'm surprised Jojo slept. I couldn't wake them. I thought they might want to be awake, just in case the others came home.'

'I couldn't sleep at all.'

'He's someone you always just expect to have around,' Zufan says.

'Kind of,' I say. They're almost the right words for Jack.

We wait on the couch, but the others don't come out. My stomach is screaming and I can hear Zufan's rumbling, but we make no move to feed ourselves.

Poppy comes out a bit later, gives us each a biscuit and sits on the chair nearby.

'Do you think Jojo's awake?' I ask. I could fall asleep at any second. My eyelids are itching, everything is blurring, and I don't know what fucking time it is. I just want to know that simple thing. Why didn't I think to buy a watch before? Goddamn it.

And then we hear the engine and the tyres. My heart stops. I jump off the couch and race to the front door.

'Wait,' Zufan says, grabbing my elbow. 'It might not be them.'

I swallow. 'Shit.'

Jojo appears in the hallway. 'Do you hear that?'

'We're not sure it's them,' Zufan says, and Jojo's face cracks. Zufan crouches beside the window next to the front door and looks through the curtains. We wait; the car sounds get louder. If it's not them, I don't know what we're going to do. If it's not them, that means something's happened to them. If it's not them, that means we're not safe anymore.

'It's the van,' Jojo says. 'It's too far to see the faces … Rhea!' they yelp, and then bolt out the front door. Zufan, Poppy and I follow them.

The van reaches us, and Rhea's driving.

'What's going on?' I ask as they get out of the van.

Jack's got blood all down his leg.

'He's fucking bitten!' Rhea shouts over whatever Jack was going to say as we all start to go inside.

I laugh. That can't be right. Jack is Jack. We don't always get along, but he's Jack. He's supposed to always be there. I've known him my whole life. I hold his hair back when he needs to spew in the toilet; he's my lookout when I have to pee in an alleyway or a park.

'I don't know if it's a bite,' he says. 'I think it's from the window.'

Jojo locks the door after we're all inside.

'No. You said that zombie didn't get you, but I *know* you're being shifty as hell.'

'I'm not.' He's trying to speak louder than Rhea, but I think that might be impossible. He sits down, dried blood rubbing off onto the couch.

'You fucken are.' She jabs a finger at him, moving to push past Poppy.

'Don't you dare hurt him,' she says. 'Don't!'

'He could kill us all!' Rhea says. 'What the fuck, Poppy?'

Poppy doesn't move.

'Jack?' I say, trying not to yell.

'I wasn't bitten, Dee, trust me.'

I look into his eyes, this boy I've known for years. He's always been there. Ever since Poppy brought him to the music room one lunchtime when they'd made friends in choir. He was just as tall, a bit quieter.

'We can't risk it,' I say. 'Jack, go out on the balcony.'

'What?' He tries to stand up, but Poppy keeps a firm arm on his shoulder.

'Let me bandage you up first, Jack,' she snaps. I'm surprised at her, but I don't say anything.

'If you hurt Jojo, I swear to god,' Rhea says.

'I'm not bitten,' he says. 'You've never liked me. You just want me out of the way.'

He's looking pretty sweaty; I don't know if it's from the disease or if he's just lost a lot of blood. He's really pale.

'This is so dangerous,' Rhea says. 'This puts us all in so much danger. If you hadn't cut your leg on the window yesterday, we would have got home safe.'

'It was your idea to stop at that house in the first place, to see if they had any food.'

'Your blood attracted all those zombies – someone could have seen us. Those cult people who were looking for us, they probably know we're here. They might've followed us home!'

'Sure, I did that on purpose. Right.'

'Stay still!' Poppy says, her voice shrill. 'And shut up, both of you. This isn't helping.'

'We could all –' Rhea starts.

' – stop it, Rhea, we're all tired,' Jojo says.

'Wait and see if I die?' Jack replies.

'Shut up, just shut up!' Poppy says. I haven't seen her like this since exam prep. 'There's your bandage, now go outside and prove you're safe.' She points to the balcony.

Jack stares up at her. 'Are you serious?'

'We can't take any chances, Jack, and you know if it were one of us you'd make us do the same.' She crosses her arms. 'Go outside.'

'You all can't trust me? That's fucked.' He looks around at us; no one says anything. He crosses his arms and doesn't move from the couch. 'No.'

'Jack, it's just a balcony, it's nice weather, if you're not bitten just go out and relax. It's not a big deal.'

'My closest friends don't trust me, it sounds like a big deal.'

'Fine,' Rhea says, throwing up her hands. 'But if you turn I'm killing you right here, and we'll get blood all over the nice carpet.'

Jojo says, 'Rhea –'
'If he turns we have to kill him!'
Silence again. We know she's right.

***

For the rest of the day, none of us can relax. We each pack a bag, and we put all our food and important stuff in the van, in case the people come. I know I can't take everything, but I want to; now I've got material possessions again, I don't want to give them up.

Jack packs a bag too, and Rhea has her machete out the whole time. We're all not quite looking him in the eye as he storms around the house. He's getting paler, sweatier, and he doesn't seem to be keeping track of his thoughts.

Dee moves the van a bit down the road. The plan is to sneak out of the house on foot and make our escape, if we need to.

Me and Zufan are finished packing first, so we watch the driveway. We sit beside the front door, and sometimes one of us will get up and look out the back and side windows, but because of all the trees there isn't a way to get to the house except through the driveway.

'Do you think they'll come?' I ask Zufan. The insects outside are humming.

'Jack and Rhea are pretty clever. I don't think they'd have led people to us.'

'I don't want to have to join a cult and marry some dude to repopulate the Earth.'

'Do you really think they would make us?'

'That's what Rhea said was happening with that girl they met.'

'That's so fucked,' Zufan says. The whole time she speaks she doesn't take her eyes off the driveway. 'What about you?' she asks. 'What do you think about Jack?'

'I think they're coming.' I know they're coming. Once we packed the van, I just knew. I took a last look at the view from the balcony as the sun was setting, and I knew. This place could have been something perfect, and it's going to be taken away. I want to cry but I don't have the energy.

Maybe if we had better weapons, we could stay. Maybe if we weren't kids. Maybe if we knew what the fuck we were doing.

'I think we'll be okay,' says Zufan.

Twenty-seven

I pass through the lounge room and look out to the driveway and I can see headlights. *Holy shit.* I don't move, can't move. *Where's Rhea? Shit. Shit, shit, shit.*

Tears leak from Poppy's eyes though she tries not to let anyone see. Rhea comes in from the back door – she must've just gone to the toilet outside – and I relax. She comes in and looks at us all in the lounge, not saying anything.

'We have to get out now,' Dee says, because none of us are doing anything. 'Before they get here.'

We should've left ages ago. The way everyone's shoulders slump, mouths set, I know they're thinking the same thing: will Jack come with us? He's looking so pale.

I've never had my own room before and this space was all mine, for however many days we were here. But there's no time to feel bad about that. Our stuff is in the van already, no time for anything that isn't useful, so I leave the volcanic rock I found, I leave the giant gumleaf, the smooth piece of green glass. I desperately want to take the books, my chest tightening as I think of how I never finished any of them, but we have to leave them.

'We'll go out the side,' Dee tells us, 'through the laundry door. That's our best bet.' Poppy lets out an almost-sob, and Dee turns to her. 'You can't,' Dee says, and her voice shakes, 'you can't make any noise, okay? I promise there will be time for that, but right now we just have to stay alive. We gotta be quiet, okay?' She grips Poppy's shoulder, and Poppy nods, earthbound. 'All right?' Dee turns to the rest of us. We don't say anything, so I guess that's a yes. She glares at Jack, and he doesn't respond. He's having trouble standing.

Dee goes through the laundry door first; she thinks quick, is a good lookout. I go after her, and we peer around the side of the house and see two of the four-wheel drives from the camp, each stuffed with around seven people. I see Gary who was going to teach me how to kill a cow; he's got a wicked-looking knife. We have no chance at all. And there might be other people in the trees, ready to shoot us if they see us running.

'Hey!' one of the people calls, a big one with a deep voice, walking up to the front door and out of our line of sight. 'Anybody home? Joe? Rhea?'

'Fucking hell,' I whisper, and Dee looks at me. I can tell she's as scared as I am but she's got it hidden real deep, only barely on her face. I'm ready to piss my pants.

'Okay,' she says, 'so they're the cult people.' She goes back to the others while I keep watch on the cars.

The people aren't looking this way, all watching the one who's still shouting at the front door. Across from us are a couple of square metres of cleared ground, and then the bush starts.

'On my signal,' Dee says to everyone.

The bush in front of us is thick, so they shouldn't see us if we keep low. The plan is to be as quick as we can, because they'll probably hear us.

'All right,' I whisper back. My heart's in my throat. I swallow but it stays there.

'Ready,' Dee says, 'and … go.'

They leave one by one, and I don't see anyone glance our way; most are starting to move away from the cars and into the house. I hear a *crash* from inside.

'Jojo,' Dee calls out.

I turn around – everyone's in the bush except me. I take one last look at the cult people, and none see us. It's getting darker, and the ones at the cars have a couple of torches on.

We start through the bush loud as anything, but maybe they're distracted by their own noise in the house. They're still shouting at us, but they think we're inside.

Once the house is almost out of sight, Dee stops us and we do a head check and we've still got everyone.

'Shh,' Poppy says, though no one is talking. She points towards the house, and when I turn I see a torchlight poking through the laundry door. I forgot to close it, fucking *shit Christ*.

'All right, we gotta go,' Dee says. 'Rhea, you've got the machete, you go first.'

The sunlight's fading and we don't have torches.

Rhea takes off anyway, leads us, and my shins are getting cut up from the underbrush, but we can't stop.

'Quicker,' Dee says. Though we don't look around, we know the torchlight is getting brighter, in the trees to our right not too far off.

Jack is dragging us slower. He stops, has to lean against a tree. 'I don't … feel too … good.'

'Jack,' Dee says. She's gone completely white and her eyes are welling up.

'See,' Rhea hisses to me, 'we have to kill him.'

'Jack?' Dee says. He isn't responding. 'Jack, are you okay?'

He snaps at her with his teeth – he's all grey. Rhea moves fast, kicking him in the chest so he falls down.

'Rhea, what the hell?!' Zufan cries out.

'He's gotta go,' my sister says, and she's got her machete out. She puts a boot on his chest. The others all stare down at him: Zufan looks mad at Rhea, Dee is ashen, Poppy is crying. My arms have goosebumps.

'We can't,' Zufan says.

'We have to,' Rhea replies.

Dee nods; Poppy looks away.

I can't watch as Rhea finishes him off. The *squelch* is too awful. I can't believe she's done it. Jack's gone. He's dead. I swallow. How many more people do we have to lose?

'Come on,' Rhea says. 'We have to go.'

She takes the lead again, and we start to bash through the bush; there's no way to do it quietly. No one's talking;

Poppy won't stop crying. Zufan starts too, but she's silent.

'Wait,' Rhea says.

I freeze, grip her arm. The others stop. Dee crouches.

'Someone's up ahead,' Dee says.

There's a loud rattle, then groaning starts as we get closer, and I know that's not a person. Shuffling, the zombie keeps leaning against trees. It sees us and comes closer. It's got blood around its mouth, but it's dark and brown. This one hasn't fed in a while. The noise must have brought it this way.

'Rhea,' Dee says, 'you got it?'

Everyone else has had the energy sucked out of them.

Rhea nods, raises her machete and walks up, calm. But the zombie's not firm on its feet. It sways, then it lurches forward. Rhea has to dodge it, steps back and slams her back into a tree trunk.

'Rhea!' I yelp, and the others shush me because those people are still looking for us.

I can't lose her.

'I'm okay,' Rhea says as she picks up a thick stick with one hand. She stabs it into the zombie's chest, holding it at bay while she raises her knife again. It's grappling at her, its nails all cracked or gone, dirty, the fingers bent out of shape. She drops the stick and whacks her machete into the side of the zombie's face, grunting. She yanks out the machete, spins the zombie and gets it in the back of the neck. This all happens so quick I don't think I breathe. How did she become this killing machine?

The zombie falls to the ground. I grab Rhea and hug her, make sure she's alive.

Without saying anything, we keep going. I step over the zombie, see the wound Rhea made in its neck and have this weird sense of pride. She's great with a machete.

A minute or so later we find the road. Rhea asks Dee if we've passed the van, but she shakes her head. 'Further up.'

Now Dee's in the lead, Rhea and I in the middle, while Zufan takes the back and keeps an eye on the road. The gumleaves crunch under our feet. We round a little bend and there's the van, and the keys are still in it, which is great – I'd have forgotten them, and I'm pretty sure everyone else would have.

Dee's going to drive, and she makes for the front seat. I look down at my legs, covered in fresh scratches from the bush, my arms too. Dee and Zufan have scratches on their faces, and Rhea's got a little blood on her arm from where she stabbed the zombie.

As Dee opens the van door, she says, 'All right, let's –'

A scream, too close and too familiar.

With the crowbar, Zufan hits the lunging zombie in the side of the head. But it keeps coming. It grabs her, crunching on her shoulder. She screams.

No. This isn't fair. It's too soon.

'Shit!' Dee says, the only one who moves. She steps out of the van, gets out her shovel and almost gently pushes the tip against the zombie's neck, pushes it back, but it's still got a hold on Zufan. Rhea snaps to attention and stabs the zombie in the neck. It crumples backwards.

Zufan falls to her knees.

Dee goes over and smashes in the zombie's head with the flat of the shovel, smashes it again, rams the sharp edge into its face, puts her foot on the shovel to give herself more power. The zombie's stopped moving but she keeps going, tears running down her cheeks.

'Dee,' Poppy says, and she comes up and takes the shovel. 'It's enough.' Poppy's crying too.

'They would've heard me,' Zufan says from the ground. She's sitting up, one hand holding her wound. 'Leave.'

Poppy and Dee crouch beside her.

'No,' Dee says, which is really fucking bad, though I get it. But we can't.

'Please,' Zufan says. She's going pale from blood loss, stress, I don't know. 'I'm a danger now. I shouldn't have screamed. Please go. I don't want to kill you. You saw Jack – he could've hurt any of you.'

'We're not leaving, Zufan,' Poppy says.

'We have to,' Rhea says. 'They're going to be here soon, we can't stay any longer.'

'Get in the van,' Dee says to Zufan.

'She is *not* getting in the van,' Rhea says.

'Please,' Dee says.

'We just saw what happens,' Rhea replies. 'She's dangerous.'

'Yeah, Dee, we can't,' I say, moving in front of Rhea, who still has her knife out. It's covered in fresh red blood. 'Zufan, I'm sorry, we have to leave you here.'

She nods at me, tears streaming down her face. I can't look away from her. She's dying. She was the one who made me feel the most comfortable, she stayed with me when Rhea was missing, and now she's dying.

Poppy can't stop wailing; she's covered her mouth with her hands. I really hope she doesn't pass out.

'Leave,' Zufan says, 'and … don't say goodbye. Just go.'

We get into the van, Dee starts it up, and we go off down the road, leaving huge dust clouds behind us. I turn to check if the cult people are following, but I can't see any torches. They have the house, but they don't have us; they don't have what they want.

Twenty-eight

There's a fuck ton of mozzies round, but by now we're gettin used to em. There are heapsa bites on my arms but cause I'm sunburnt as shit they don' really itch.

'Reckon we could get infected by mozzies?' I ask her. We're ridin on the highway, slow. It's bin a couple days since them people found us, an I reckon they're still bush. Maybe they didn' expect us to go on the highway, cause they ain' found us yet.

'What?' She looks at me, her hair gettin in her face cause a the wind.

'Like if one bit a zombie, an then bit one of us.'

'A mosquito?'

'Yeah.'

'Hmm.' We ride forwards, an then she answers. 'I don't think so. We would've been infected by now, right? We've been bitten plenty of times, even in areas where we know there's zombies. So … I guess the virus or whatever must die if it's not in a human?'

'That's good,' I say. 'I'd bin worried we'd be sleepin an then wake up zombified.'

'Yeah.' She laughs. 'That'd be pretty shit.'

'Do you reckon they were lookin for us cause we killed their mates?'

'I heard one talk about guns. I think they thought we had guns.'

Dunno why they thought two chicks ridin bikes with a fucken cricket bat would have guns. We don' even have a fucken car.

'Maybe all them movies bout zombies made em think guns jus popped outta the ground or some shit, I dunno.'

She snorts. 'Maybe.'

It's night an we're ridin, which I woulda felt uncomfortable doin before. But now with them people followin us, travellin at any time seems a good idea. Sides, the moon's full so we can still see pretty good.

'You wanna stop for tonight?' she asks. 'Maybe we could sleep over there.' She points to the bush next to the highway. Last night we slept in an old car; it was creepy as shit an I couldn' stop thinkin about who owned the car. Did they die in it? Maybe they turned in it.

'Yeah,' I say, so we go off the highway an ride through the tall grass whippin our legs til we get to the bush an the grass stops.

'You sleep first,' she tells me as she rests her bike gainst the nearest tree. 'I know you didn't sleep last night.'

'Thanks.' I get my sleepin-bag out. 'We're gonna have to find water tomorrow, reckon. Don' got a lot left.'

'Running out of food, too.' She grins. 'Maybe we could go out to a restaurant.'

I lie on top of my sleepin-bag, too hot to get in. 'That'd be nice.'

'All right. You sleep, I'll make reservations, then we'll head out later.'

I close my eyes an everythin hits me. Before I even know it, I'm asleep.

***

She doesn' wake me but I somehow wake meself when it's the middle of the night. 'Time for me to take over?' I whisper.

'Thought you were sleeping,' she says. 'Did you?'

'Yeah. Jus good at wakin meself up, I reckon.'

'Well, I guess it's your turn. Wake me if there's anything.' She kisses me, an we swap so I'm sittin on the leaves an she's lyin on the sleepin-bag, still warm from my body. The moonlight filters through the trees as her small breathin starts.

There's not really any noises around, cept for the night wind. A breeze picks up an so I get up, take the other sleepin-bag an drape it round my shoulders. With my legs bare it's still not too warm.

When me bum starts to go all numb, there's a cracklin noise like leaves under feet not too far off. Could be a possum, but I reach for my cricket bat anyway. I crouch low an peer into the bush. The light from the moon plays through the gumleaves but I can' see anythin.

Crack. It sounds closer but I can' tell where it's comin from. If it's a dead one I should wake her, but if it's one a them people I shouldn' move. Them zombies got real good hearin sometimes. Or maybe it can smell us. I lick a finger an put it in the air but though the wind's comin from that way I can' tell where the sound's comin from, so we could be upwind.

If it's a person then her knives'd be better. A cricket bat to the face is gonna slow ya down but a knife in the ribs'll do wonders. Draw blood, but. Could bring dead ones.

Now she's got about five knives on her, strapped to her body. One on her wrist, her upper arm, each ankle, an then one strapped round the side of her chest, lyin next to her ribs. She's not had to use that one, yet.

The sound happens again, louder, like in a pattern. Like someone's walkin up to us. Too even to be a dead one.

It's one a them people. Shit.

They know where we are, otherwise why would they be walkin that fast? *Crunch, crunch, crunch*, the dead leaves cracklin under their boots.

I nudge her, an her eyes flick open. She takes one look at my face an sits up quietly, slippin outta the sleepin-bag. There's a flash of the moon on her wrist as she gets out her knife.

'It's one a them people,' I say. 'Not a dead one.'

She peers through the trees, crouched, muscles tight like a cat. An she moves her fingers round the handle of her knife, gettin ready. I grip my cricket bat with two hands an raise it as I stand. The person knows where we are, anyway.

The stompin gets louder an then I hear their breath an they're behin me. I whirl round an give em a smack to their face with my bat. Don' phase em, they jus stumble an come back. I raise my bat again.

Then I notice the *drip-drip-drip* from the stomach.

An there is no fucken stomach. Ripped clean out, blood everywhere. The zombie gets closer as I back away, an the moon's on its face. Not a person face anymore.

This one's so fresh, turned not far from here. Shoulda heard somethin. Screams, shouts, anythin.

She springs from behin me an shoves the knife up into its eye socket. Black blood slugs out. She lets go a the knife an watches the zombie fall.

There's silence cept for the wind.

'We have to leave – it's still got fresh blood.' She doesn' look at me when she says it but leans to get her knife outta the face. 'And we weren't that quiet, others probably heard us.'

I nod an stuff my sleepin-bag into my pack. She stuffs hers in, an we grab our bikes.

We ride til dawn, when our legs feel like they're gonna fall off. I call her Dawn sometimes, never to her face. She never told me her real name an I didn' ask. I don' have one. One I like, anyway.

***

She starts coughin.

We think it'll go away. Her lungs are tired from the ride. But in the night she starts shiverin an it's not cold, an I start to worry. She says it's fine but she won' look at me when she says it. An then a fever starts.

I hold her hand the whole time; she don' let go. We need more food, she's gonna die because we're so starvin, god-fucken-damnit. I dunno anythin bout health, not really. Dunno nothin bout gettin food that ain' from a kitchen or a shop. We dunno this stuff. Who knows this stuff?

I keep watch again an I'm fucken tired but I can' make her do it. She tosses in her sleepin-bag, rips it off, puts it back on. I dunno what to do. She rolls in the night an I don' think she sleeps.

'I'll get better,' she says. 'It's summer and I've just got a cold. It'll go away soon.'

But the next day she jus gets worse an she's shakin like mad. Knives might make you get too close. Zombies must've got some sick shit in their blood, an maybe she's got somethin from that one.

This day we don' go anywhere. She sleeps most of it an I don' at all. At sunset, my eyelids stop bein heavy an I'm alert again. The night is silent. Dunno how long this is gonna last but I'm grateful.

***

The next arvo we hear voices. I wanna call out to em; maybe they can help with whatever she has. But she gives me a look, an I remember what world this is.

The voices are far off but jus hearin em means they're too close. I leave her with our stuff an go have a look.

I lay on my belly an watch em. They're bit noisy, even jokin an stuff. Coupla them have smokes, an though I never smoked in my life I want one – they smell rank but like the world before. I grip the dirt under my hands an tell meself to stop bein such an arsehole. Old world's not comin back, this is all we got now.

In the old world I mighta asked her to marry me. Figure even though we've not known each other long, we've bin through a lot an not tried to kill each other so we'd be all right married.

The three people look like they're settlin in for the night, so I go back to her. She's sweatin.

'You need meds,' I say. 'We gotta find a chemist.'

'I don't think I'm pregnant.'

I sigh in relief, cause I dunno what we woulda done.

'My period's just stopped. If that's what you're worried about.' She shakes her head. 'And towns are too dangerous.'

'I'm worried bout you. You could die.'

'I won't,' she says an coughs, real loud.

We freeze. But the people's voices keep on like they didn' notice.

'Let's go,' she says. 'They're going to find us.'

Twenty-nine

Jack and Zufan are gone, and I can't understand. I keep going to tell them something but they're not here; there's only four of us in the van. No one's said anything. Poppy's breathing pretty heavy to try and keep in her sobs. Rhea won't look around at anyone, keeps her eyes completely focused on the road like she's driving in busy traffic in the old times. Jaw set, arms stiff.

Jojo sits up front with Rhea, and they just stare out the window.

'Rhea,' I say eventually, when I feel like my mouth isn't going to fall off. My voice cracks on her name, but I keep going. 'We should stop. It's too dark.'

She nods, and pulls in at the next rest stop along the highway. There's an old fire pit surrounded by logs; she parks near that.

'Maybe we should light a fire,' I say. 'It's a bit cold, and maybe having something warm might be … nice.'

She just nods.

'We're going to build a fire,' I announce, 'unless anyone has any objections?'

'It's night-time, so no one's really gonna notice a

287

plume of smoke, right?' Jojo says. 'We're so far from the house, we should be out of sight.'

Maybe they're wrong, but Poppy and Rhea don't argue. The twins go get some wood and kindling, and I dig out the matches in the van. It'd be nice if we had marshmallows. I look for ages, though I know there aren't any among the cans of tuna and pickled veggies.

Rhea and Jojo start the fire. It pops and crackles, and the warmth on my face just makes me feel worse. I sit next to Poppy in the dirt and she puts her head on my shoulder. After a while she takes my hand and it's nice, just sitting there with her. She's stopped crying.

She starts singing, barely over a whisper. At first I don't recognise it, but then I remember the flow of the words; it's the song she was working on, trying to get right. Her voice is quiet enough that Rhea and Jojo might not hear us, and I join in with a lower harmony. I know I can't sing very well but it doesn't really matter anymore. Our voices loop around each other. Then I hear the bits where Jack's voice should go and they stick out, holes in the song.

The fire is starting to overheat my toes but I don't want to move; I nudge off my shoes but that doesn't help. 'Sorry,' I say, when I have to move to keep myself from burning.

Poppy sits up straight so she's not leaning on me anymore. Her face is so tired; she looks a hundred years older. 'I might … go to bed, or, I …' She runs a hand through her hair. 'Something. I'll go to sleep.'

'We may as well sleep out here with the warmth,' I say. 'Bring your stuff if you like. I'll keep an eye on you.'

She smiles, almost, and gets her bedding. Her hand brushes against my shoulders as she walks past on her way back. When she lies down, she wraps herself up like a caterpillar; I can only see the top of her head, a few of her fingers tightly grasping the edge of the blanket.

After she goes to sleep, Rhea does the same. Jojo and I sit there, cruelly awake, staring at the flames.

'Maybe we could find a better house,' Jojo says. 'One that's easier to protect.'

'Yeah, but what if this just happens again?' I say, and pick up a stick, poke it into the fire's base. I get a better view of the embers, they glow, pulse. 'I don't want to have a home taken away again.' It's not that I want to shoot down all their ideas. 'And anyway, what're we going to do for food?'

'There are those seeds we got,' Jojo says.

'What?'

'The seeds, from the gardening shop in town. When those cult people turned up for the first time, I guess we got distracted by –' They pause. 'Um, stuff.'

Death.

I swallow, trying to forget how to feel anything. 'What are they seeds of? Do you know how to garden?'

They go over to the car and get out their bag, and when they sit back down beside me, they're a little closer. Inside the bag are tiny packets of promise. 'Snow peas, tomatoes, chillies, thyme, sage … We have heaps. Pumpkin!' They pull out more, and we spread them on the ground, marvelling at the future.

'This is amazing, Jojo. I can't wait to tell Poppy in the morning.'

'Our mum loved the garden. I have no idea how to do anything, but we can learn if we have some land.'

'Yes.' We stare at the fire, and eventually I have to close my eyes. 'I think I might go to sleep. Do you want to keep watch, or should we wake up someone else? It's been a couple hours.'

'I'll be okay.'

But as I make to get up, they grab my wrist.

'Wha–?'

'There's someone out there. I saw their face.'

Thirty

'All right, okay. I'll get weapons, you wake the others,' Dee says.

I wake Rhea and I wish she could just have five more minutes to rest, then I get Poppy up. I grab my knife from my bag and stand, my insides made of concrete. Dee gives Poppy a shovel. Rhea has the machete that she hasn't let go of since … I don't know when.

Dee has the other shovel ready. 'There's someone watching us,' she breathes to the others when Poppy asks what's happening.

I pack up all our shit because I guess someone has to, plus I'm pretty useless in a fight.

We stand in a circle, backs to the fire. The flickering light bounces off everything I can see – no faces, no human anything.

'Was it a zombie?' Dee asks me. 'Or a person?'

'Definitely a person.' I tighten my grip around the knife but I don't think I'll know how to use it properly.

'Do you reckon there's just one?' Dee asks.

'Dunno. Maybe?'

'Oi!' Rhea shouts. 'Who's there? Come out and fight us if you're gonna.'

That almost makes me piss my pants, and goddamn it if I wasn't already on edge.

Poppy's starting to say something, but the words choke in her mouth as a figure appears out of the darkness.

The person is white, tall, got ragged but clean clothes on, but they're smiling at us and holding out their open palms. 'I just wanted to talk to you all,' they say with a soft voice. 'I was going to wait until morning, but I wanted to make sure you weren't going to run away.'

Like finding someone hiding in the bushes wouldn't make us want to run away. Like, put two seconds' thought into these things.

'What do you want?' Dee asks.

'Just to talk.'

Dee crosses her arms. 'Yes, you said that.'

Poppy looks at Dee with an alarmed expression. 'There might be others,' she says. 'Be careful,' she adds, quieter.

We shouldn't have lit a fire.

Dee doesn't move, just keeps her eyes fixed on the new person. Rhea shifts her weight beside me, her feet far enough apart that she's balanced.

'I saw you drive up while I was gathering some food, and so I stuck around.' The person's face is calm, composed. I don't think they're alone. 'We want to invite you to join our community.'

'We?' Dee asks. 'Community? How many people?'

Rhea swears under her breath.

'I can't tell you that, I'm sorry.' They pause, looks around at us. 'We have food.'

'What if it's …?' I mutter to Rhea, who narrows her eyes.

'I want to know,' Dee goes on, hard as anything, 'why you want us to come with you.'

'We can discuss that on the way.'

Dee pauses, looks round at us, and she's shaking, her mouth drawn back tight. 'We need time.'

The person nods, doesn't blink. 'That's understandable. We can discuss it further in the morning, if that suits all of you.'

'We want a good night's sleep,' Dee says. 'You can come back at noon.'

'That would work.'

'Good.'

And then the person sits on one of the logs beside the fire. Rhea is vibrating with rage, balling her fists.

We huddle into the van with our weapons and bags, and with the side door open so we can watch the person. They haven't moved from the log. Everyone's breathing too hard.

This person's an adult; they could look after us. I don't want to look after myself because the world is too big and we're tired and hungry and too much has been taken away.

'So, what do we want to do?' Rhea asks. There are bags under her eyes, she keeps rubbing them.

'I don't want to keep going,' Dee says, and I breathe

in relief because someone wants to do the same thing as me. 'I'm tired. They could protect us.'

'Why the fuck does she want to help us?' Rhea asks. 'What if she's with Matt? Those cult people? Maybe we should ask some questions. I don't feel comfortable.'

'You seemed pretty comfortable murdering our friend, Rhea,' Dee snaps.

Rhea shrinks away. 'I had to do that.' Her voice is small. I put a hand on her arm.

'I know, I know, fuck, sorry.' Dee presses her palms into her eyes. 'I'm sorry.'

'Let's ask some stuff,' Poppy says. 'Pretty sure none of us are going to sleep, now.'

And so we file out of the van. I keep glancing at the trees around us, but it's too dark to see anyone.

Dee sits the closest to the person and asks, 'So where do you wanna take us?'

'We've found a fenced-off property we've built on a little bit,' they say. 'There was a house and a couple of sheds, and we've turned the sheds into bedrooms and put up a few tents. It used to be a dairy farm, so there are a lot of cows. So far we only milk them, but we're trying to figure out how to make cheese. There's a few chickens and a huge veggie patch. We've got water tanks, at the very back of the property there's a river, and there are a few dams scattered through the paddocks. The cows follow you, it can be a bit weird.'

The person's smile shows too much teeth, but I can't tell if they're just too earnest or if they're going to slit all our throats. Do they have a weapon? They're so relaxed.

'So, you've got food?' Poppy says.

'Yes. And we can grow our own. We're hoping to be self-reliant when winter comes.'

I think of our seeds; they would definitely know how to grow them.

'What is that, six months?' Dee says. 'Is that enough time?'

'It's all the time we've got.'

'Right.'

'I know it seems like a big leap of faith,' they say. 'I am asking you to trust me a whole lot. But we could use people like you.'

'Like us?' Dee says.

'Young, able-bodied.'

'What would we be doing?' Rhea asks.

'You might be doing what I'm doing right now, going out looking for food. Or you might be tending the veggies or the cows, doing handy work.'

'And you've got enough food?' says Dee.

They nod. 'We feed everyone who helps.'

'Do you have, like, a form of government?' Poppy asks.

'Not exactly. We're deciding everything on majority votes, for now.'

'Right,' Poppy says, and she doesn't speak again, just sits there with pursed lips.

'So, what do you say?' the person asks. 'Do you need more time?'

Dee looks around at us all. 'Noon.'

'All right.' They smile.

'You can sleep over there.' Dee points to a spot that's not too far off, but out of the circle.

'Thanks,' the person says, a little too eagerly.

We set up in the van, because we have to protect it with the person here. Rhea offers to do first watch with Dee, the van's sliding door open a little so they can see out but the person can't really see in. I wish we weren't sleeping in the van; at least there's more room for us now that ... now there are fewer people.

'I think we should leave,' I say. 'They could be with Matt.'

'It sounds like a different set-up,' Rhea says.

'Yeah, but it's too convenient. They must've followed us from the house. Someone just turns up and offers us free food? Come on.'

'It does sound good,' Poppy says.

Dee watches the woman, and Rhea watches the surrounds.

'What do you think?' Dee asks her.

Rhea takes her time, which means she's really unsure. 'I ... I don't really know. It seems too good to be true, y'know? But when we saw you ... We were lonely, and scared. We'd been alone for so long.' And we missed our mother so much. 'You just looked like you were lost, and that's how we were. It was reckless, but it paid off.'

'Maybe this will pay off,' Dee says.

I want to agree, really, but something in my guts isn't sitting right.

'Maybe. What option do we have?' Poppy says. 'We can keep going, living in the van, or we can try here.'

'We might find another house,' Dee says, echoing what I told her beside the fire before, what she denied. 'We might be all right on our own.'

'Maybe,' Rhea says. 'But then that one might be taken away. And then the next, and the next. At least this way we'll have protection in numbers.'

'Unless they want to harvest our organs,' I say.

Rhea laughs low. 'Well, that too.'

'I do want to sleep in a proper bed again.' Dee sighs. 'Even if they're camp beds in tents, that would be like paradise right now.'

'Yeah,' Rhea says. 'There'll be a toilet, too.'

'And milk. I haven't had milk in so long. Cooked eggs, I can't even imagine. And roasted veggies …'

My mouth waters.

'Something other than canned tuna and beetroot. Is this a miracle?' Poppy says.

'It still seems dangerous,' I say.

'But we can't stay out here, I can't stay out here,' Rhea says. 'Not again. Finding the house after wandering around with Jojo for god knows how long, that was like … And now, back in the wild, with no security or anything, I don't know if I can take it. I want to go there, I really do.'

'We can have a vote in the morning,' Dee says.

'All right.'

'Okay,' Dee says, a desperation there. 'Okay. I don't want us to split up. We'd never find each other again.'

Thirty-one

We follow the highway for a bit, til it's dark again. Coupla dead ones get in our way but I jump off my bike an bash in their heads with me bat. It's gettin easier, an I know the right place to hit em now. Plus we're not goin all that fast, cause she can'.

We take an exit ramp an pull up on the side of the road. She's breathin real hard but tries not to let me see too much.

'We should rest,' I say. 'Can' fight like this.'

She nods, coughs once.

Ridin round the outskirts an through the bush, our tyres crunch the old gumleaves but we don' stop. Ain' another way to get through that'll make less noise; all the roads are dirt but they're covered in shit cause no one's drivin on em.

We find an unlocked shed. She holds open the door an I hold up me bat, ready to kill anythin that comes out. There's nothin so we go in, block up the door real good, an it's nice jus to be in a place where we don' have to watch our backs every second. I take off my shirt an pin it over the window, find a tea light in my bag an scramble round for some matches. The candle doesn' give off much light but don' really matter.

'Not bad,' I say.

We spread out our sleepin-bags on the floor an we're tangled through the night. Dunno where my legs end an hers begin. It'd be claustrophobic as in the old world, but now havin her so close an real is better than anythin.

We wake at dawn an she doesn' look better but she doesn' look worse. I pull down my shirt an put it back on, pack everythin up. It takes her a while to wake up proper an she smiles at me in the mornin light. The shed's gettin hot already from the sun so we get our bikes ready. She finds a stick an uses it to keep the shed door shut. 'So dead ones can't get in.'

I look at the shed. It'd be nice to sleep somewhere like that again, almost kinda like a house, cept shittier. Tent was good, til we realised it wasn' as safe as we thought. That's the worst thing.

She don' look back as we ride off but I do, an I wonder if maybe we can go back. I'll ask her later. Sure she wouldn' mind a coupla more nights' rest in a safe spot. Only problem is it's too close to the town. Here's hopin there's somethin we can use to fix her.

The road is dead quiet cept for our wheels an breath.

We see the first buildin of the town, an she signals me to get off the road. I follow her an we ditch our bikes, hide em in someone's overgrown front yard. 'Keep your bat ready.' She gets out two knives, one in each hand. 'Come on.'

Before we set off she has another coughin fit an I rub her back. We look at each other when she's done but don' say nothin. If she coughs in the town, could mean we die if somethin hears her. But we don' say.

I go first, skirtin round the edges of the buildins. It's empty an everythin's dusty, good cause there's not too many leaves making noise. There's a dead one but I get it in the back of the head fore it realises we're there.

I grunt as I swing – quiet, but loud enough for someone to hear.

'Get down,' she says, pullin the back of my shirt. We're behin a bush in front of a buildin, a scrapbookin place. The window is smashed. Dunno what you'd raid from there.

Mouth full a dust, I try not to choke as I look round for the reason we're low.

It's one a them people, a man. Back when I was spyin on em an they was smokin an drinkin, I heard one a the others point at him, laughin, 'Look at him, he's gone off his rocker!' Now his clothes're more ragged, shirt torn, an there's blood spray all over him. He's walkin crooked but not in a dead way. He looks round, head swivellin like a bird's, dartin this way an that, huntin for the source of the noise.

'I know youse is there,' he says, an he's got a spanner in his hand. 'Heard yas.'

'He's gonna find us,' I whisper.

She nods. 'Be ready for it.' Her knives twitch in her fingers.

He's gettin closer an closer an then he walks straight past us, rounds a corner a coupla buildins down, an then he's gone.

We keep low an keep lookin for the chemist. It's to the left. The windows are all smashed an there's a coupla dead ones in there. She goes in first, knifes one in the eye. I follow an knock a couple down. I get one an smash its head in, she knifes the other one I knocked over. Goin through the rest a the shop there's no more.

'Know what ya need?' I say, lookin round at the perfume an nail polish, bandages an baby formula.

She shakes her head. 'Something out the back, I'm guessing.'

There's a coupla bottles of cough syrup on the shelves out front so I put down my bat, grab all the bottles that's left, an put em in a bag. They're noisy but havin these'll help.

She coughs, her throat tearin as she gasps for breath.

'Let's have a look, then,' I say, an head to the room behin the pharmacists' counter up the back. I wonder how many studied thinkin they'd end up in a lab fightin disease but ended up here, a chemist in a small town in fucken Woop Woop that no one gives a shit about.

There's a noise of a door openin. We look at each other. My cricket bat's at the fronta the shop an all I've got is a fucken bag of fucken cough syrup an vitamins. Goddamn it, mistake that's gonna get me killed. Jesus.

She's collapsed in a coughin fit so now there's no

point in hidin. The guy comes out behind the counter, come in through the back door.

'You,' he says.

I say nothin. I wonder if he killed the others he was with. I wonder if they turned first, if that fresh zombie was one of them.

My bat's too far away. He'd get me before I could get there, even if he's still limpin. I look at her but she can' barely breathe cause a the coughin so she can' help me. I'm standin next to a rack a teddy bears, not gonna be any good.

'Youse've got weapons, yeah?' he says. His eyes are fucken everywhere. 'Carnta survived this long thout em, can ya?'

Dickhead. 'We got a cricket bat an that's all.'

'That all?' he says. 'Ya think I dunno?'

'That's all, swear.'

She's bin makin her way to me, crawlin when he's not lookin. Only a coupla metres away.

I can see he don' believe me, not a little bit. Maybe he's wonderin best how to kill me with the spanner. Or could snap me neck. I wasn' skinny before an now I'm almost nothin. Never bin this fit before, an this unhealthy.

'Just you two?' he says.

I don' answer.

'With a cricket bat?' He shakes his head an mutters.

'Where'd your friends go, then?' I say an nod to the blood on his shirt. 'Jus went for a walk, did they?'

An he looks at me an I know I'm about to die. His eyes ain' a person's eyes anymore.

He comes at me like one time when I was a kid an a dog tried to bite off me face; missed, an I had to get stitches in me arm. Only this guy's much bigger than a dog. Looks like he's only made a muscle an skin an anger. He comes at me an I dodge, fallin into the rack of teddy bears. Should be soft but still hurts like fucken hell. Wind gets knocked outta me, an I roll away from him.

She's sayin something, takes me a sec to hear she's sayin, 'Catch!' She throws the knife near my feet. I reach over, still on me belly, an grip the wrong end of it. Blood pricks outta me fingers, an I grip the handle proper.

He grunts comin at me again. I turn jus in time so I'm on me back. He's above, trips over my feet an falls on me, still got them manic eyes. The knife's gone in through his ribs.

I can feel that, can feel it, through the handle.

He gasps in me ear, cries out. Warmness stains my hands an I can' look at it. Can' even yank out the knife.

I jus roll from under him an stand, dust off my pants like nothin happened.

She don' say anythin.

I go behin the counter an pick up heapsa boxes of pills. Open em all, chuckin useless ones to the floor. Think I know which ones I'm lookin for cause last time I was coughin sick, the doctor gave me green ones; half was dark green an the other bit lime. They smelled like shit but they worked. Didn' know pills had a smell til them ones. *Take two twice a day an you'll be right*, he said. *Cough'll go away*.

She's sittin now, head in her hands. The guy's blood is seepin out from under him, gonna reach her if I don' find the right ones soon.

Then I find em, the right-lookin pills, an grab four boxes. Dunno if these'll help but that's all I can think to do an she says she trusts me.

Can' look at him. He wasn' a dead one an I killed him. Fucken hell. Me hands are still warm. There's an old lab coat hangin up an I wipe the red off. Can' get all of it, but. The red's showin up brighter than it should on the white. Me hands are shakin.

She's cleanin the knife. The guy's rolled on his back, dead eyes starin at the ceilin. He's surrounded by fucken teddy bears for fuck's sake.

'I got em, come on,' I say, an walk past him, put the meds in the bag with the vitamins an cough syrup, an grab my bat.

She don' look at him, jus steps round the blood an follows me. I hand her some a the pills an she swallows em dry.

When we get back to our bikes we still haven' said anythin. Mum's bracelet's gone. I slap me wrist as if that'd bring it back, but it musta got lost when I killed that guy. For a sec, I wanna tell her to turn round, we gotta go get it, but I don'. An then we jus keep ridin.

Thirty-two

In the morning we huddle away from the fire pit where the person is sitting. They seemed to sleep okay, and that makes me even more convinced there are other people out there, watching us. None of us slept – well, there was no snoring, nothing that sounded like sleep.

I lay awake looking up at the sky, amazed by how many stars there were, bright and cold, away from the city. But I guess now there aren't any city lights.

'I don't know what to do,' Poppy says. She looks around at the rest of us.

'I ... think we should,' Rhea says, and Jojo nods along with her. 'What about you, Dee?' Rhea asks me.

'I don't want to go.'

'Zufan and Jack *died*, Dee,' Poppy says. 'I don't want to be out here.'

I swallow. 'I know.' I feel their loss like a hole in my chest. 'But how do we know these people are safe? It seems too good. We don't know who they are. But we have to stick together,' I look at Rhea now, 'because we won't find each other again.'

Poppy glances at Jojo and Rhea before looking back at me. 'If I go, you'd choose them over me?' Her voice is shrill, panicky.

'No, Poppy,' I say, touching her arm. 'But we can't get separated.'

'We lost Jack and Zufan.'

Jojo's face hardens, their frown deep. Rhea looks away.

'Exactly,' I say.

I was perfectly capable of living my life without these two before we met them, but now if they're gone … I don't know what I'll do. There's only so much pain I can block out of my brain before it'll be too much and I won't be able to block out any of it.

Poppy is looking between me and the twins. I feel my face tightening. She has to understand. We stare at each other in silence.

'I think it could be a good idea,' Poppy says, trying so hard to keep her voice even. She's breathing slow, deep, while her hands shake.

'Poppy,' I say, 'we have to stick together. Please.'

She swallows. 'It could be safe.'

'We won't be safe anywhere.' I don't want to fight anymore.

'Maybe Dee's right,' Rhea says, 'and these people won't be able to protect us from anything.'

'But I disagree,' Poppy says. 'This way we can have some security. We won't have to run like we did from the old house.'

'But what if it's them?' Rhea says. 'What if it's the same people?'

Poppy falls silent.

'No, you're right, Rhea – we have to leave,' Jojo says, crossing their arms. 'It could be really bad, and we're okay on our own. We have the seeds I found, we can grow our own food.'

The person comes over and smiles at us, that smile with too many teeth in it. Maybe they were a newsreader in the old times, something like that. Receptionist, maybe. Primary school teacher.

'So what have we decided?' they say, and their persistent smile makes my skin itch.

Rhea nods. 'We're just packing the car.' She draws herself up. 'We have to go.'

'You don't need to do that,' the person says. 'We can walk from here.'

Poppy frowns.

'We're not coming with you,' Rhea says.

'Why not? Don't you want to be safe?'

'Dee,' Poppy says quietly, reaching out to hold my arm, 'this is bad.'

'My name is Joy, by the way,' the person says, and holds out a hand to Rhea.

Rhea stares at Joy's hand for a second, doesn't shake it and leaves them waiting. Was that a dangerous thing to do?

Joy taps the side of the van a couple times, then clasps their hands together. 'Now look, it would be a lot easier if you just came with me, right now.'

Nobody says anything or moves. The bush has been quiet around us, but now I hear something moving.

It could be anything, just the animals going about their business. But I don't think it is.

'Sure?' Joy says, waiting again for one of us to change our minds. 'Well, all right.' Joy claps a hand back on the van.

The noises get louder, and I know it's people. Soon we can see them properly: four people, all taller and musclier than us, are coming over. They have a younger person with them, maybe a teenager, who looks as scared as I feel. Otherwise they all look relaxed, and one of them is even laughing at something another one said.

Joy turns to us and says, 'I'll be back in a moment,' then walks to the others.

'Plan?' I whisper to Poppy.

'Go back in time and convince ourselves to drive off last night,' she says.

'Pop –'

Rhea butts in, putting her hand on Poppy's shoulder. 'If they have cars, I dunno how much point there is in driving away.'

'What if they hurt us?' Jojo says.

'Joy wouldn't have hung around if they were just going to kill us,' Rhea says. 'They'd just, like … make us slaves, or something.'

'Or eat us,' Jojo says.

Rhea grins tightly. 'Maybe Joy was waiting til they got here.'

I see Rhea checking to make sure her big knife is still hidden. Is her machete still in the van? I don't have a weapon on me and realise how dangerous this is. Why did I pack my shovel in the van? I should have found a little pocket knife or something. I think Rhea's the only one of us who's armed. She's got her eyes everywhere, scanning the trees for anyone else who might show up.

Joy brings over the group and introduces them, names I forget instantly because I'm too busy trying to decide whether they look like they want to kill us. Their faces are passive now. 'They're just going to make sure we get home safely,' Joy says.

'We're not coming,' I say. 'We told you.'

'I think you should,' Joy replies, smooth. 'Nothing to worry about.'

I feel panic in my throat, clutching tight at my windpipe. The teen with them looks at me for too long. I wonder if they're trying to tell me something.

The rest of them look so calm. The person on the left's jacket is big enough to be hiding something – a weapon? They move closer; one of them gets too close to me. The hairs all over my body rise, my heart picks up, my face flushes, my hands shake. I hear the person breathe in, then they start to grip my elbow.

I yank it away wordlessly and the eyes staring down make me cold.

Jojo sees me flinch and yells out to the person, and then the one next to Jojo grabs them by the elbows, holds them steady. Jojo struggles against the person's grip, and then the person beside me grabs and holds me in the same way.

'What the fuck?' I call out, kicking the one holding me in the shins.

Their grip just tightens.

I watch as Rhea pulls out her knife and lashes out at the nearest person – Joy.

Poppy's in the same grip as Jojo and me; she's kicking the shit out of that person's shins and I see pain on their face. I hope the one holding me has the same expression.

The teen who's with the group isn't holding anyone, or any weapon. I wonder what their deal is. They look pretty well fed.

Rhea lashes out again, and Joy has a cut on their upper arm, blood trickling down.

Jojo keeps yelling, and I kick the person holding me extra hard, they wince in my ear.

Rhea starts to come help Jojo but the teen shouts at her to stop, then Joy grabs her by the back of her t-shirt. Joy's tall, wide, and Rhea looks so small.

Rhea whirls around. 'Don't touch my friends!' She elbows Joy's nose, and Joy goes down, clutching their face. Rhea starts towards Jojo again.

Joy looks up from the ground and says, 'Fuck, no you don't,' and pulls a knife that shines in the sun.

'Be careful!' the teen says, and starts towards Rhea.

Joy kicks out at Rhea's legs, and she knocks into the teen. They both stumble, fall into a heap. Joy gets closer to them. Then the shine of her knife is gone, buried in someone.

It can't be Rhea. I can't breathe. She can't go.

Thirty-three

It's like my skull has exploded; I don't know what that noise is. Rhea, Joy and the teen are all in a knot. I don't know who's screaming. What's happened? Rhea? I cry out her name.

Then I realise it's not her who's been stabbed, who's making one of the most awful sounds I've ever heard. It's the teen. Joy's stabbed their own teammate.

Everyone has stopped.

Poppy wriggles an arm free and elbows the person holding her in the face. She lands on her hands and knees as she's released, jumps up, and then Rhea snaps into action, gets me loose. I turn around, knocking the one who was holding me to the ground. Rhea picks up a rock and doesn't pause before she brings it down on the person's face. A spurt of blood and a *crack*, a muffled scream. I have to turn around, give my attention to Dee, who's still struggling.

Joy and the others are coming at us.

Rhea points her knife at them. 'Come near us and I will end you,' she snarls, her body tense, her legs looking ready to spring.

Joy has pulled the knife from the stabbed teen and raises it, hand shaking.

'You wanna hurt anyone else?' Rhea spits out. She's got blood flecks on her face, shirt, arms. She's breathing so hard. 'Do it.'

Joy doesn't stop pointing the knife, but slowly, slowly, her arm starts to fall.

I step forward and check the teen's vital signs, just in case. We'd never be able to treat a wound with this much blood, but ... Their skin is soft, warm, their beard hair scratchy under my fingers. I move aside their hair to check the pulse in their neck, right above the wound. Nothing. They're not breathing. I wonder who they were.

'They're ...' is all I can say as I look at everyone, but they all seem to get it.

I stand up and Rhea takes my hand.

The zombies will smell the blood; they'll be here soon.

Behind us Dee kicks the person holding her away, and we gun it back to the van, clambering in. Rhea's behind the wheel. She jams the van forwards, and then we're off down the highway again. There's a stitch in my side, my heart is pounding in my skull, and I can't breathe, I can't. Nothing looks familiar.

'We don't know where we're going,' Dee says.

'We've never known,' Rhea shoots back, spinning to face Dee, and my sister's still got the blood on her face, she's still got these eyes that won't stop moving. She throws up a hand. 'We can't stop moving.'

'Come on,' I say, putting my hand on her shoulder. 'It'll be okay, we'll be okay.'

I know she doesn't believe me, but it's okay because I don't know if I believe me either. The relief of knowing she wasn't stabbed is all I can feel right now.

Poppy looks out the back window. 'No one's following us.'

We reach a turn-off on the highway and find a dirt road. It doesn't look familiar, but we start along it because at least it's something. Cicadas are buzzing all around us, getting louder and louder as the road goes on.

'Rhea,' Poppy says, 'why don't you take a rest?'

Rhea pulls the van to the side, right near an old bus stop that looks like it hasn't been used for years. We get out to stretch, and there's room enough for all of us on the bus stop bench. Rhea doesn't sit down, though, and she starts pacing. The blood on her face has long dried, and it's unsettling to watch her pace around and not blink.

'Why don't you take a rest?' Poppy says again.

Rhea doesn't glance at her, just keeps walking. 'We should've left earlier.'

'Yeah, all right,' I snap. 'You keep saying that and it's not gonna make a fucking difference.'

'It's our fault.' Rhea turns to me. 'If we'd just gone, or stayed with Caitlin's cult dad, or –'

'Stop blaming yourself,' I say. 'And me.'

'We shouldn't have let Mum go, she should have escaped with us!' Rhea's crying. 'She should be here.'

'Rhea.' I don't know what to say to that. I start towards her, to give her a hug.

'Fuck off,' she says, shoving me backwards a step.

Poppy's voice cuts through. 'Rhea.' She stands up. 'Apologise right now. This is no one's fault.'

Rhea stares at me, her eyes still wide and empty. Her jaw set.

Then her face softens, and she looks at her feet, back up at me. 'Sorry. That was shit.'

I nod at her, and we all sit at the bus stop, silent.

'We've been too loud,' Dee says. 'We should keep moving.'

So we do.

Thirty-four

She won' stop coughin an I can' think what to do to help her. Should she take more meds? We don' even know if it's the right shit I gave her. Maybe I'm gonna kill her with em.

'Can we just –?' she says, then gets off her bike an sits on the nearest fallen tree.

Roads, we try an not go near em when we can. Killin that guy … I never wanna do that again. The way his breath sounded right in my ear. Need to stay away from towns.

'You right?' I'm standin with the bike between me legs. Can' both of us be restin when there's shit out here that can kill us, maybe more of them people. That one I got looked like he was the last one, but. He was all broken.

'Yeah,' she says, then starts hackin up a lung. She puts a hand over her mouth, tries to muffle the sound. 'Don't wanna –' more coughin '– make too much noise.' Tears leak out as she tries to keep the coughs in.

'We need good food,' I say. 'Fruit an veggies. Better for ya than them vitamin pills.'

'Oh, great idea. Let's just go to Woolies and pick

317

some up.' She glares at me before lookin away. 'Sorry.'

She mutters somethin under her breath. Guess I'd be angry in the old days but now, when all we've got is each other, there ain' a lotta room for alone time. I get it.

She stands, takes her handlebars an jus … looks at em for a bit. Pumpin herself up, I guess. A deep breath, an she gets back on. 'I think the road's that way,' she says, noddin to where the trees are thinnest.

She's right, an when we get out onto a dirt road we can' see any houses. There's a telephone pole to the right, so we take off that way, swervin round a few potholes; I hit one an the shudder goes through my bones. A bit after the telephone pole there's a driveway. Must be a big property, cause we can' see any other houses. The driveway winds down an loops through trees, an when we round a corner we see paddocks, a big house.

Ridin past the nearest paddock we see the fence is broken, the paddock's empty. The others have skinny horses in em. Their ribcages pokin through sends cold into my body.

I skid to a stop at the nearest gate. 'Jus gonna open it for em,' I tell her as I get off me bike. She goes to the next gate. The horses don' seem to notice what we're doin, jus eye us off an don' move. At least now they can leave if they want.

The driveway up to the house is too steep to ride, so we walk our bikes. The muscles in me legs are hard, an I feel em workin as I push my feet into the ground.

I'm not as thin as I used to be, only muscle. Always hungry. Dunno if I'm ever gonna stop bein hungry again.

We leave our bikes on the lawn. The wooden verandah sounds like home under my feet, an the dust coverin everythin makes my eyes hard.

Smack.

Someone's hittin gainst the window an I yell, jump back, almost knock her over. 'Fucken hell.' It's a dead one, a teen maybe our age, at the window with half a face. Shit. Glad they dunno how to use doors.

'There might be more,' she says, gettin one of her knives out. 'Come on, let's see if there are any fruit trees.'

Round the back is a dog yard connected to the door. The zombie follows us when it sees us through the windows, an another two come out through the open back door – mighta bin its parents when it was alive. The fence is shoulder height, so they can' get through. That low empty moanin comes outta their throats. When we get closer it changes to a snarl, spit trails drippin out.

The youngest one, its eyes are so empty. I can' stop starin at the way it keeps snappin its teeth. I wonder who it was. Maybe it was gonna take over its parents' property; maybe it was desperate to get out. It's so hard to think of it as an it an not a person.

This is the worst fucken train of thought so I cut it off, turn back to her, an we keep walkin to where fruit trees might be. We climb up through a rose garden an dodge a few bees, find no trees. What we do find is a water tank with a lil tap, musta bin for the garden. We drink the water, fresh an clean, wash our faces an arms. The sun's jus warm enough under the shade, an she falls asleep in the grass.

***

We set up in the shed, an things are all right. We'll run outta food if we stay here, but as we rest for a coupla days her cough ain' gettin worse. Maybe even gettin better. We've still got heapsa vitamins. We gotta eat, but.

'You ready?' She pulls on her backpack.

'Yeah,' I say, gettin on me bike.

We find our way to a paved road then onto the highway. Maybe this is a bad move, but dunno where we're goin. Could be nowhere. Seems we'll never leave the highway, endless roads will always fucken lead here. I feel too out in the open, but dunno if I care anymore.

We stop after a coupla hours, don' eat anythin, an sit in the shade of a truck. Rattles an groans come from inside it. We ride on, dodgin cars an a few dead ones.

An then we hear voices. Young voices.

We sneak a bit closer an there's a group of four teens, maybe a couple years older than me. They're next to a four-wheel drive and a big white van.

'They're only our age,' she whispers to me.

'What're they doin?'

'Dunno. But they're not dead.'

'There's, like, a wire you can use,' one says, hair close to the skull, jagged. 'Here.'

'Which wire, though?' another says. A sweet face. 'I can't see anything.'

Two who look mostly the same – twins or just siblings? – stand off to the side, shoulders touchin. Only watchin.

'This is hopeless,' the short-haired one says. Throws up their hands, turns an walks from the van. 'I told you the van needed oil or something, and now it's carked it.'

An then sees us.

'Fuck.' Their eyes widen, an they pat their belt for a weapon but there's nothin there. 'Everyone!' they yell, an everyone cept one of the twins turns around.

The sweet-faced one picks up a huge shovel lyin at her feet, an one of the twins draws knives quick as a flash.

Me and her don' move. I hold up me hands. 'We don' wanna hurt youse,' I say. 'We need food.'

'Please,' she says beside me, her voice quiet. She gets out her knives one by one, all five of em plus one I didn' know bout, an lays em on the ground. The extra one surprises me, I dunno how I missed it.

We must look weird, muscly but so thin with sunken skin tight round our bones.

'I'm Eve,' I say. It comes to me, the name, like somethin outta the fog. Clear an right. I gesture to her. 'An Dawn.'

She meets my eyes an almost smiles. I did good with the name, I reckon.

Dawn is the end of eve, always. Hope it don' go down that way.

'We use she pronouns,' says Dawn.

The others nod at us, an Dee introduces herself and Jojo, Poppy, Rhea. Jojo says to call em they. The others are all she.

Dawn – it's weird callin her by a name – Dawn moves a bit closer to me, I feel her body's warmth on my arm.

'We have vitamins,' I say, slingin my backpack off. 'Do you have any food?'

'Wait,' Dee says, pointin at me. She turns to Poppy an nods with her head towards us. 'Check an see if there's something in that bag.'

Poppy walks forward an opens it up; a coupla bottles roll out.

'You can have some if you like,' I say.

'We have to keep moving,' she says. 'We need to get as far from those people as we can before they find us.'

'Once we get a car that still works, it'll be fine,' Rhea says.

'Didya look under the sunflap?' I ask em, pointin to the four-wheel drive. Dawn raises her eyebrows at me. 'Me dad used to put his keys there sometimes.'

Dee goes over, checks both the flaps an there's nothin. But in the glove box, a spare key's stuffed into the manual. 'Here we go,' she says.

Rhea takes the key. She looks at us. 'Wait. We still don't know if we can trust them.'

'Please help us,' I choke out.

'Rhea, come on,' Poppy says. 'They're like us.'

'There's four of us,' Dee says. 'We can take em – look how thin they are.'

'What if we lose someone else?' Rhea says, runnin a hand through her hair. Looks like she hasn' slept in ages.

'We don't know what'll happen,' Dee says. 'What about when we found you? We'd be dead if it weren't for you.'

'She's right,' Jojo says.

'Sorry, yeah.' Rhea sighs. 'Let's go. We need to get out of here.'

'It'd be great if you didn't kill us,' Dee says to me an Dawn.

'Sorry about your friends,' Dawn says.

Dee tightens her lips, shuts her face off. 'We should get going, come on.' She climbs into the passenger seat but doesn' close the door. Rhea gets in the driver's seat, then the other two climb in the back door.

'Leave the bikes?' I ask Dawn.

'They won't fit. Can always get more.'

Might not be true, but ridin in a real car again sounds so bloody good, well fuck me. 'All right.'

We get in the four-wheel drive, a real proper car, an Rhea starts it. Never proply realised how quick the world goes by when you're drivin.

Thirty-five

The new girls don't talk. Sometimes they exchange glances, but that's all. Only say something when questioned, and even then the answers are short.

The highway is smooth under the setting sun, and it isn't so bad with me and Rhea swapping driving position every now and then. The four-wheel drive we found only has five seats, with Rhea driving and me beside her, so the others are sitting on the seats behind us or in the very back. No need to worry about seatbelts.

It's getting dark when Rhea slows to a crawl and turns on the high beams.

'This looks familiar,' Poppy says.

'I think this is where we stopped a while ago, when we saw that person get shot,' I say. 'We can park here maybe, hide with the other cars. It worked last time.'

'That's really smart,' Eve says.

'It was Zufan's idea,' Poppy replies, and she stops smiling.

'Let's do that,' Rhea says. 'I want to stretch my legs a little too.' She turns off the high beams and the car comes to a stop. She's been a bit calmer since a few nights ago at the bus stop, but I don't think she's sleeping well.

I get out of the car and Poppy gets out too. After watching out for zombies, we start looking through the other cars here for more food, blankets, whatever. She grabs a torch and lights it up. 'Aw, shit,' she hisses, peering into the nearest car. 'They've got a whole heap of lollies stashed in there.' She points and I see the glove box lying open. I also see the car is home to a seatbelted zombie, and I almost pee my pants.

'I'll kill this one,' I whisper, 'and you go round and keep watch, and get the lollies. Then we'll pop the boot and have a look.'

I've got a small knife Dawn gave me, but it'll be enough. The zombie snaps at me, the seatbelt holding it back. It reaches out for me and there's dried blood on its fingers, crusted under its nails. The door isn't locked – luckily, because smashing the window might attract more zombies. This one is gnashing its teeth at me. At least I'm more used to the smell now. I jab my knife into the side of its neck. It twitches, and I stab it again, trying not to feel as the blade slips between the bones, finds a resistance. I push harder and, swallowing a yell, finally kill the thing. It slumps against the steering wheel – and the horn.

Beeeeeep.

'Fuck,' I mutter, poking the zombie's head with the knife until it's not resting on the horn anymore. So much for trying to keep quiet.

To reach down to pop the boot, I need to get too close to the zombie I just killed. And I need to move as quick as possible in case others show up. I feel its cold arm against mine, clammy and ... fuck. I close my mouth and keep down the urge to vomit. Although I know it's proper dead, I'm imagining it biting me, right in the back of my neck. A shiver passes through me as I reach around for the lever, but the zombie's legs are in the way.

I close my eyes, breathe in slowly – and there's the lever, finally. I pull it. The boot opens and I wrench myself out of the car.

Inside the boot, we find everything. Two pillows, two sleeping-bags, food, a big container of water. Some of the food's off, but the smell's nothing compared to the zombie stench.

A couple of zombies turn up because of the noise from the horn; they're scrawny and bent over, easily killed.

Back at the car, we share out the sleeping bags, lie the seats flat, and it's almost comfortable. We open a few cans of food and take it in shifts to pee, and soon it's too dark to see much.

***

Poppy shakes me awake when it's my turn for watch, and I see Jojo waking Rhea. The moon is bright in the window, and me and Rhea sit together up the front. We're slumping in our seats, though, in case someone sees us.

'Did you sleep?' Rhea asks.

'Yeah. I guess I ...' I didn't want to be awake, because

then I'd have to think about Jack and about Zufan. I have Poppy still, but because we were always a unit, always together, whenever I look at her I know the others are gone.

Rhea nods and gazes out the window to the highway. 'It's nice when we're driving,' she says. 'Everything's easier to take in.'

'So much has happened, it's nice to kind of forget.'

'I feel like I'm forgetting my mum, sometimes.'

'How'd your mum die?' I probably shouldn't have asked.

'We lived near a hospital where she worked as a nurse. She kept going to check on stuff, then she was turned. When we went to look for her the hospital was all zombies. We found her. I wanted to bury her, but we couldn't.'

I wonder about who else she might've lost. Friends? Did she have other siblings?

'Did you lose anyone?' she asks. 'I mean, before we met?'

'We didn't find anyone. We started to go back home, but then we couldn't get there. I dunno if I wanted them to be alive. I don't think I did.'

'Yeah, I don't care that my dad is probably dead,' she says. 'We lost someone later, a girl we met. Caitlin. She was really sweet. The culty people, she was with them.'

We sit in silence, listen to the bugs around us.

'Do you think the new people are okay?' Rhea

says, quiet and low. Less piercing than a whisper. She's nodding towards Dawn and Eve. 'I don't want anyone else to die. I can't handle it. Feel like my brain's on fire.'

I shrug. 'Dunno. They've been on their own this whole time so they can take care of themselves, if they wanted to they would have hurt us by now.'

'Would they?'

'Easier to think that,' I say, before breathing out long and slow.

We don't talk after that, just make sure there's no one outside. And there isn't, only the cicadas and the possums.

***

'I don't want a cicada up my butt,' Poppy says as we walk through the bush beside the highway.

'Dunno if anyone wants that.' I turn around so she can pee, and to keep watch. As we walk, we head away from the barricade. The zombies here seem to be on the other side, but the ones we come across we dispose of pretty quick. Still. Constant vigilance.

Poppy finishes and walks up beside me, and we stand there breathing in the fresh air for a few moments. Going back to the car seems like too much effort. It's hot and I don't even remember what deodorant smells like.

'Oh hey,' Poppy says, 'there's a rabbit over there.'

It takes me a few seconds to see where she's pointing. The rabbit's one of the ones like in cartoons, with the white tails.

'We could eat it,' I say, and without really thinking I throw my knife.

We both stare, silent, as we watch the knife go right into the rabbit's little furry body.

'Holy shit,' I whisper. 'Did you see that? Am I dead? Are we dead? Did that just happen?'

Poppy laughs and clutches my arms. 'We can cook it!'

The body's warm and limp when we go over. It's so small. I don't want to look at it, but also I'm starving for fresh food.

'Do you know how to skin a rabbit?' I ask Poppy.

'Sure. I go hunting all the time.' She gives me a deadpan look, then breaks into a smile. 'We can figure it out, probably.'

We take the rabbit back to the car and no one knows how to cook it. Not surprising, really.

Jojo laughs, shaking their head. 'How are we gonna eat it?'

'Light a fire and we could draw people to us,' Rhea says.

'The fire doesn't have to be big,' Dawn says. Her voice always surprises me because I never expect her to say anything. 'If we keep it small maybe there won't be so much smoke.'

Rhea just shrugs.

'Do you know how to do that?' I ask Dawn.

She shakes her head.

So me and Poppy decide to wing it and go back to the bush and lay down a flattened cardboard box we'd been storing stuff in, and I try to prepare the rabbit. There's not really a lot of meat on it, and I don't know if there are certain bits we can't eat. This isn't exactly hygienic, but I'm just so hungry.

'This is fuckin gross,' Poppy says as she keeps watch while I figure out how to do this. There's so much blood and everything's so slimy. Fuck.

'What if it's diseased?' Poppy asks, peering over my shoulder.

'It doesn't look it. But I guess it *is* a rabbit.'

'Glad you're the one doing this,' she says, gagging as I remove the intestines.

'Can you dig a hole for the guts and stuff?' I ask. My fingers are stained red, it's under my fingernails. I can't remember the last time I ate food that doesn't come out of a can. I don't know if zombies would want to eat rabbit guts, but it's probably better to bury them.

When the hole's done, Poppy dusts off her hands and I dump the guts in there. I drag the dirt over them, then cover my hands in it. We don't have water to spare, so that'll have to do for now.

Dawn and Eve get a fire going, just a small, smothered one, and we rest a few stones in there. When they get hot enough we'll put the meat on – hopefully it'll cook.

We're all sitting next to the fire and it's way dark by the time one of us gets brave enough to eat some. It's Rhea. She bites down and screws up her face, but she keeps chewing. She's not dying so it's probably not poisoned or whatever.

Everyone grabs a piece, and we sit there silently chewing. The outside is tough and it takes me a sec, grinding my teeth, to get through the layer of charcoal. When I do, I bite down and it's the best thing I've ever tasted. The juicy warmth fills my mouth, and I moan.

Poppy laughs at me, nudging me with her elbow as she's biting down.

'So good,' Jojo says, and they're already finished theirs. They grin at me. 'You gonna eat that?'

I've still got half left. 'Heck yeah I am.'

Although it wasn't a lot, my stomach is sated. I sigh happily, letting myself fall back and lie on the cool ground, watch the stars. When we pile into the car that night to get some sleep, it's somehow more comfortable, like real rest.

***

Poppy and I volunteer to go in search of a river. There's not really a point moving the car just yet, we decide – camping on the highway is as safe as anywhere, really. No cars have come this way in two days, and we keep doing regular patrols for zombies. There are a few, but they're all pretty old and easy to get rid of.

There probably isn't a river but there's no harm in looking. Rhea mentioned she had a Melways but then realised she'd left it somewhere, so we've got no maps. The tricky thing will be figuring out how far we can walk before we have to turn around and get back before dark.

'We can't get lost,' Poppy says, dragging her feet to push aside the gumleaves and expose a trail of brown earth. 'Can you imagine if those cult people had found us? We'd be turned into baby-making machines.' She keeps dragging her feet every few steps.

'I don't even wanna think about it.'

We crash through the bush for a while, maybe only twenty minutes but it seems like the sun is rising too quick; we should have started out earlier. Soon we have to stop for a rest, so we sit on the ground and share the water bottle that's our only drink for today. I notice a trail of sugar ants beside me, crawling through the gumleaves and debris. As I let my eyes unfocus a little, I see that the whole floor of the bush is moving, alive.

Because everything's so quiet apart from the cicadas, we hear the screams.

'That's us,' Poppy says, turning in the direction we came. She screws the water bottle lid back on – we can't afford to waste any – and we pelt through the bush along her track. A branch cuts me on the face and I hold my palm to it, and then Poppy starts half-limping, she must have a stitch, but we keep going, feet pounding against the dirt.

Thirty-six

I'd rather have gone with Dee and Poppy, I think, than sit beside the car with Rhea worrying herself to death, while Dawn and Eve sit silently by themselves. Rhea's so jittery it's making me jittery. At every sound she turns around. She hasn't slept since we parked here, I think. One of her legs bounces up and down constantly whenever she's sitting. This is just like when we were stuck at home, waiting for Mum to come back.

I close my eyes because they're burning from the sun, the lack of proper sleep, the stress. I just want to give up, sit on this spot of the road for the rest of my life. Shitty shit fuck. I want to throw a tantrum, scream and bash my fists against the goddamn road. I sigh out angrily and Rhea looks at me, but I just shake my head at her. Don't want to talk right now because I'll sound like a whiny brat and she'll get even more annoyed. She raises her eyebrows but says nothing.

'Oh come on, I'm not being annoying, you are,' I say.

'I know I am,' she spits back. 'At least I don't bottle up everything.'

I roll my eyes at her like she doesn't secretly think everything is her fault.

'Come on,' I tell her and stand up. 'Let's play naughts and crosses.'

'Again?' She rolls her eyes, but she follows me. I gesture to the side of the road where there's a whole bunch of red dirt. Everything's red or grey out here. The gumleaves are green, sure, but dusty grey-green, and all the ones on the ground are brown and dead.

'Crosses,' she says as we sit down.

The dirt's cooler than the bitumen, doesn't burn my hands as I stabilise myself. 'Fine,' I say, and we play.

Naughts and crosses is the worst game to play over and over because there are only so many combos before you're just repeating yourself. Rhea says it's not really about skill but I can't see how. I don't know how I can keep losing, either.

We play maybe ten games before Rhea grunts and stands up. 'This is shit.' She runs a hand through her hair and tugs at the ends. It's getting longer – couple inches and I know she hates it. We should find some scissors.

'Do you want me to cut your hair?' I ask, standing up beside her.

'Eh?' She turns to me. 'How?'

'Your knife would work, right?'

'In theory. But like … scissors are two knives.' She pulls out her knife, grins. 'Let's try. Don't stab me in the ear.'

We sit back down in the dirt, and I grab a few strands and slice them off.

'Don't just do, like, a single hair at a time,' Rhea says, trying to turn around to see. 'Otherwise we'll be here all day.'

Dawn comes over and watches me get a grip on a bigger bit of Rhea's hair. I press down the knife and slice off a few more hairs, then I try sawing the blade back and forth. It's slow, but it works.

'Hold them tighter,' Dawn says, kneeling beside me. 'Here.'

I look at her warily, but she's just a girl. She's not going to kill me … I'm, like, ninety per cent sure. And Rhea would spin around and protect me in a second.

Rhea lets Dawn grip her hair, and I use the knife. 'Careful,' Rhea says, twisting her body out of the way of my sawing.

'Sorry.' I let her hair go once the chunk is cut off. 'This is going to take forever.'

'Not like I have anywhere to be,' Rhea says, shrugging. She hums something off-key and Dawn follows her, though they sometimes mismatch and make me think Dawn doesn't know the song. I've got no idea what my sister's humming so I don't join in, but Dawn's able to guess the next notes most of the time.

'How do you do that?' I ask her as she hums, holding out Rhea's hair. 'The song.'

She shrugs. 'Dunno. Just happens.'

'You're pretty good,' I tell her.

Eve walks to us from where she was sitting in the shade. She's so quiet I almost forgot she was there.

'Hey,' she says. Her voice is deep and soft. Even though she has that harsh ocker accent, she's soft. 'Listen for a sec.'

The sound of a car engine. I can't tell which way it's coming from and I spin around, trying to figure it out. Behind me, down the straight stretch. Fuck. My stomach goes cold.

Rhea shoves me towards the car. 'Move!'

They've seen us, they've fucking seen us. We were just sitting out in plain sight, in front of the car. They must've seen. Even though they were so far away, they would've seen us.

I start to ask, 'What weapons have we –?'

Rhea silences me with a *shh*.

'They saw us, Rhea, and if you're gonna deny it then …'

I don't wanna die cramped up in a fucking four-wheel drive with my sister and two strangers. Real shitty, can't even livetweet my own death. I don't know how serious I am. Maybe I'm already dead.

'Breathe properly,' Rhea says as she pats my back, and she hands me a knife.

Rhea has her machete, Dawn her knives, Eve her cricket bat. Up close now I see the wood is stained with old blood – guess no amount of washing would get that out without bleach. Maybe if it was one of those fancy ones with the wax and the price tag of six hundred dollars it'd be cleaner, but she's just got a shitty old bat from some kid's backyard.

My heartbeat is everywhere, in my throat, my fingertips. Everything is pulsing. The car gets closer, louder. Then it stops.

'Fuck,' Rhea breathes out.

Two doors open, but there are more than two pairs of feet out there. 'Come on out,' says a low gravelly voice. I've heard it before. I catch Rhea's eye and I know she recognises it too, but I can't place it.

'*Fuck*,' she says again, sharper this time. I start to ask her who it is, but she just opens the door to the car. 'I'm not going to die hiding.'

The sunlight blinds me for a sec, but I follow her out, shielding my eyes. Dawn and Eve follow us, not saying anything.

'What've we got here?' the person who spoke before says.

I blink a couple times, take my hand down and see who's talking. 'Fuck.'

The person is a man, Caitlin's dad, standing beside six big people I don't recognise. Their car's a big two-door ute, so five of them must have been riding in the tray. They've got knives, crowbars. Caitlin's dad's got his gun on his hip.

Caitlin's dad laughs. 'Rhea and Joe,' he says in his sandpaper voice. 'Well, shit.'

'You know these people?' Dawn asks.

I roll my eyes. 'Yeah, we're real close.'

'You killed me daughter,' the man says. I can't fucking remember his name. Wait – it's Matt.

'We did not,' Rhea says, stepping closer. 'A zombie did.'

'If you hadn't run away …' His face is getting redder. Now he steps forward. He's too close to Rhea. My hand grips the knife tighter, but I don't know how to kill a person.

'Then she would've died anyway,' Rhea says. 'Whatever you were doing with your weird rules and shit.'

He raises his hand, about to strike. 'You –'

Dawn runs up to him quicker than anything and stabs his arm; one of the others tries to grab her but she's too fast. She withdraws before Matt even screams. He hunches over.

'Fuck off,' Eve says. 'You keep driving.' That's brave of her, shit.

'You wanna say that again?' He stands up, clutching his arm, drawing himself to his full height and walking over to her.

Her jaw sets. 'Keep driving.'

'All right,' Matt says, and he laughs. 'Come on, then.' He reaches for his belt where a machete's strapped.

Eve steps back, then swings the cricket bat at him. *Crack*. She gets him in the mouth and he groans. His teeth are all bloodied, one's missing. There's a gun on his other hip but he doesn't draw it – maybe no bullets.

'You little dickhead,' he says.

Dawn knifes him again, this time in the leg. He swings at her with the machete and misses, but knocks Eve's bat from her hand.

'Well, go on then,' Matt says to his group, and they all start towards us.

One throws something at Rhea and she screams, piercing and quick. She falls and I rush over to her. Her cheek is bleeding, the one with the scar on it, but the fresh cut doesn't look very deep. 'Just surprised is all,' she mutters.

She flings herself up and cuts a person across their hands; they yelp in pain. Dawn and Eve are back to back, keeping people away with their raised weapons.

'We need to leave!' I shout over the fight as I fend off two people at once. One's got a crowbar, the other a belt, probably itching to put it round my throat – fuck that. I slowly move backwards, holding the knife out, as they get closer. Soon I'll be backed up against the car.

'Not yet,' Rhea says, and it's then I remember we should wait for Dee and Poppy.

But how can we?

'We gotta go,' I say. 'We're gonna die.' As shit as it is, I don't wanna die. And besides, we can always come back, right?

'No,' Rhea says.

She yells as she runs at Matt and buries her knife in his neck. But he doesn't go down, he's just screaming. The blade missed his oesophagus and is sticking through a lump of flesh, poking out the side.

I brandish my knife at the people approaching me but they don't care, barely even notice I'm armed. Once big boss gives the orders, I guess, they go.

Behind their ute I see Poppy and Dee run out of the bush. Dee makes to come for us but Poppy holds her back, points to the car. They get over there without being seen by anyone but me. Dee gets something out of the ute and then jams it into the front tyre. She wiggles it around for a bit before moving on to the next tyre.

I almost get hit in the head with a crowbar. 'Fuck off, mate,' I tell my attacker, but of course they don't listen. Asshole.

The crowbar hits me across my shins and I go down, just as Rhea screams. I look over and Matt's stabbed her in the leg, just below her knee. 'Rhea!' I yell. She pulls away from Matt and kicks him in the face. There's blood, but it doesn't look like too much.

The person with the belt gets closer, and I try to get up, my shins screaming in pain, but the crowbar whacks me across the back and I go down again. I smell the leather before it loops across my skin. Then it tightens.

I'm gonna fucking die like this, and it's shit. What'll happen to Rhea? She could look after herself, maybe, but I don't want her to.

Air is such a sweet thing, I think as I realise I can't get any. I claw at the belt, my skin ripping off under my nails, but my attacker doesn't let up, sitting on my back now. Whatever was left in my lungs whooshes out.

I'm seeing spots in my eyes, then it's getting harder to see, harder to move my arms and legs. And they stop moving. Vision's black, almost. I never knew my lungs could hurt this much.

And then everything comes back. I cough as the belt's released.

There's nothing to vomit but my stomach tries anyway, so many times that my eyes hurt, and Poppy pulls me up while I keep retching. Dee's got blood on her and I don't know whose it is.

I still can't see properly when my friends shove me into the car, and I feel Rhea land beside me; she grips my arm and I place my hand over hers. 'It's okay,' I rasp at her.

The car shakes as someone pulls a door closed and the engine starts. Poppy's yelling at Dee to keep driving, and we take off, the floor rumbling under my back.

I've finally stopped coughing and I sit up slowly, making sure I don't black out. 'What the fuck,' I say when I see Rhea's leg, more blood than anything.

'That guy you know got her,' Dawn says, her voice low and husky. She's wrapping Rhea's t-shirt around her wound. 'There's not too much blood, I think she'll be all right.'

'Fuck.' I run a hand through my hair. My eyes ache. They must be red as shit. My neck is covered in scratches, my own blood under my fingernails. 'Rhea?' I ask.

'It'll be okay.' Her eyes are closed. 'You asshole, almost got yourself killed, not even in a cool way. Don't fucking talk to me.' She laughs but I can tell she's in pain.

Eve sits in the corner, pressed in on herself as she watches us. When Dawn's done bandaging Rhea, she goes over to Eve and they lean on each other, hold each other's hands as they don't talk, only breathe.

'What happened?' Poppy asks from the front.

Rhea's grip is loosening on my shirt. His teeth are still gritted and she's breathing harder, trying to keep everything in.

I swallow and try to answer Poppy's question. 'We were just sitting around chatting, then we heard the engine but it was too late. That man, Matt – we met him a while back, before we ran into you. He was the leader of that cult camp, and he had a daughter.'

'Had?'

'We were trying to escape. Zombie got her.'

'Oh.'

'We should have stayed away from the highways.' I cough; my neck hurts and my voice is all raspy.

Rhea looks at me. 'Don't ever fucking do that again or I'll kill you myself.' Her eyes are still red. 'You shithead.'

'I love you too. How's your leg?'

'Not hurting as much. Maybe don't talk to me, I'll throw up.'

I glance out the window, see storm clouds coming up. 'Finally, some rain,' I mutter.

'Fuck,' Dee says. 'Petrol light is on.'

Thirty-seven

We take the turn-off an drive. First thing we see that ain' trees is a school footy oval, so Dee drives across the brown, crackly grass an pulls up in a car park. It's got a shit ton a cars in it, double-parked an all over the lawn.

'Come on,' Dee tells us, 'we can hide in that shed.'

There's another car jus like ours in the car park so I guess it don' matter if we leave it there, pretty camouflaged. An we woulda bin camouflaged before if we wasn' outta the car hangin round the highway like fucken arseholes.

Shed door's half-stuck but with a coupla wrenches with a crowbar it's okay. Inside is dark cause the windows are grimy as shit but we see rats crawlin round on the floor fore they scurry away from the noise.

'I don't know if we should stay here,' Poppy says, her voice higher. 'Cause, y'know, of Rhea's leg.'

I nod with her, cause I don' wanna stay with the rats. Especially don' wanna be found by those cult people, but then they don' have a car an don' know where we are. Though we didn' drive far before the petrol ran out, they're not gonna get here any time soon.

It's dead quiet as we go to the main school buildin. Usually there's birds or bugs, but nothin now.

'Why are there so many cars?' Jojo asks as we find a door. It's locked.

'It's a school,' Rhea says. She's so pale, looks like she's gonna faint. 'Lots of people at a school.' She closes her eyes, swallows a coupla times. She's not bin talkin, every time she does she looks like she's gonna chuck up her guts.

But there are more cars than parks, fucken everywhere. No one else says anythin but we're all edgy, cept Dawn who looks calm. Feelin for her knives.

With Jojo's machete Dee hacks the wood round the handle, an with a coupla kicks we get inside. The hallway's all messy with leaves an papers; half the lockers gainst the walls are open. The first classroom's windows are all smashed in. Half the chairs are gone from the desks an almost everythin's knocked over. There ain' a lot of bodies, some kids, some adults. School's a shit place to die. They're not in uniform, though, seems like everyone jus gathered here, maybe tryina find a safe place.

The next classroom has all its windows but less chairs. No bodies in it.

'We could camp here?' says Dee. 'Not like anything's gonna get in.'

'It's only got one entrance,' Dawn says. 'If something comes down that corridor we have nowhere to go.'

'I guess,' Dee says, shruggin.

We keep on past more classrooms. There's a big entrance bit at the end, with a reception desk. On the floor are lotsa pamphlets for all kinds of things – sport teams, bands an that. There are doors to the left, another corridor to the right, an two big closed wooden doors right in front of us.

Reckon this school's never bin this quiet durin the day ever. The wind's almost cold, an I stick as close to Dawn as I can. I don' take her hand, we gotta keep ready to fight, but I wanna.

'What about here?' Dee says. 'Got lots of exits, out of the wind.'

'I need to sit down,' Rhea says. She's real pale, an leanin a bit on Jojo. 'Please, can we stop?'

'Let's stop here for a bit,' Jojo says. 'It's getting dark, anyway.'

'Should check the rest of the school,' I say. 'Make sure it's safe.'

Rhea sits on a bench, an she winces stretchin out her leg.

A dead one walks in through the open door, the way we came. Rhea screams an backs up gainst the wall. I'm the closest so I try an get it with me bat. It was a younger person, maybe our age, an so it's tougher than normal. I whack it again, but it gets almost too close. I jump back, an it grips me arm with its cold fingers. Makes to go an bite me, an my heart kicks up. Not here, not in a school. Not after jus gettin away from those people.

'Eve!' Dawn cries out.

I can only see her. She knifes it, an it goes down, an her face is splotched with old blood.

'Did it …?' she asks, chokin out the words. My whole body's numb an I dunno where my hands are. She checks me arm quickly, hands dartin all over my skin, but no, there's nothin.

She sighs with relief an lies down on the ground. I crouch beside her, hold her hand, an she pulls me in to a kiss, fierce. I fall on top of her an she laughs, tears runnin down her cheeks, strokin my face. The others must be watchin but I don' care.

'Not dead yet,' Dawn says, closin her eyes as our foreheads press together. Her skin is warm; I miss sleepin tangled with her in our tent by the river. I reckon we gotta make that happen again, somehow. Find a quiet spot, near water, where no one's gonna find us.

There's a rumblin from the other side of them wooden double doors.

'Shit,' Dee says.

Poppy's eyes are wide. 'We should move.' The doors rattle again.

'Yes,' Rhea says, an gasps.

Down the corridor we didn' explore, zombies are comin at us, slow but gettin faster as they get closer. Some are school age, the rest is people who might've bin parents but some are too old. There's more behin the first group, an I haven' seen this many together since the start when we saw all the zombies from the factory.

How'd we miss em? Shoulda kept patrollin, let Rhea rest with Jojo in the car.

'Shit,' Poppy says. 'Shit, shit, shit. Rhea, can you stand?' She helps her up.

Rhea's wincin, but she can stand. Jojo worries beside her.

'It's okay,' Dawn says, an she goes over to em, jus at the entrance to the corridor we came from. 'We'll protect you, you just get her out of here. We'll meet you at the car, okay?'

'I'm a good fighter,' Rhea says. 'You all start going. You've got the car keys, Dee.'

'But Rhea, your leg,' Jojo says.

'Exactly, we don't have time, just go!' she says to the others.

The dead ones are gettin closer an I raise my bat, heart thumpin. It's fine, it's jus like sport. Jus focus on one thing at a time an it'll be fine. To see em all is too much, only focus on the front. *Focus, focus.*

Was always shit at sport.

A zombie lunges forward, an Dee goes at it with a machete, gets it in the face. The weapon's stuck, she yanks it out, but now more dead ones are closer. She has to back away down the corridor; Poppy's behin her.

One at a time, one at a time. Cricket bat ain' gonna do much good.

The doors next to me keep shakin, gettin louder, an I wonder how much they can stand without bein blown open.

One comes at me, only got one arm an it growls low. I get all me strength an ram the end of my bat into its face. Its head cricks backwards, but not enough. It comes at me again, pressin me away from everyone. Zombies get between me and the rest, between me and Dawn.

'Dawn!' I yell, but I can' hear her over the rattlin noise an the blood pumpin in my ears. Fuck.

Dee an Poppy're down the corridor now, an I can' see em. Fuck, fuck, fuck. Is Dawn with em?

Some zombies are getting past Jojo an Rhea, headin towards the others. An I can' take it if she dies. But the next one attackin me snaps its teeth, an I bash them out with my bat. More are comin towards me an I can' take em. There are too many between me an Dawn. I gotta get out or I'm gonna die.

I turn round an shove my bat through the bottom half of the glass doors, hit it a coupla times fore there's a big enough hole for me to crawl through.

I breathe in the fresh air an watch as the dead ones try an get me through the glass, but they haven' figured out how. Yet. Dunno if they have the brain power to learn how to crawl, but I ain' stickin around to find out. I gotta find her, gotta make sure she's okay.

Jojo an Rhea are still fightin like they know exactly where the other's gonna be. Rhea limps a coupla times, an Jojo ain' as good a fighter as her, but they're not down yet.

There ain' any dead ones out here in the dark. Storm's comin an I'm alone. I can' be alone. I can hear my heartbeat; I'm all shaky from almost dyin. Can still feel the grip of that zombie on my arm.

I could've not bin here. Dawn could not be here.

I swallow that fear an think for a fucken second. They were goin to the car. We'll meet there.

Thirty-eight

Poppy keeps muttering strings of swears beside me as we go down the corridor, and I can't see a way for Jojo and Rhea to get to us, but maybe they can find another way out.

'Where is she?' Dawn asks, her voice high with panic. 'There are too many.'

I don't know what happened to Eve, and soon we can't see Jojo or Rhea either. My breath catches at the thought of losing her. Rhea and Jojo seem to be doing okay, but I don't know how long they'll last like that, especially with Rhea's leg. They've gotta get out, but there are too many zombies.

It smells like death.

One of the younger zombies is a bit faster and starts to catch up to us. Dawn knifes it in the neck, then catches up to us. I don't know how she's so quick, so calm about it all.

I hope Rhea's okay with her leg wound, that she and Jojo don't get hurt. I hope Eve's still alive.

More zombies pour out and it seems like they're endless. Maybe it was Rhea's blood that drew them out?

'In here,' I say and grab Poppy's shoulder, steering her into a classroom. 'We can bottleneck them from here. Dawn, get that side.'

Dawn and I stand at either side of the door. She kills the first zombie in one swoop, while I tackle the second. First I get it in the top of the head with Jojo's machete, but it just bounces off the skull. The zombie stumbles towards Poppy, who's got the crowbar ready. I get it in the back of the neck.

'Careful,' Dawn says, as she kills another one.

When I get the next one its blood spurts everywhere, I close my eyes and feel it hit my face. 'Eurgh.' I wipe my eyes before I open them. 'Fuckin gross – shit!' I dodge out of the way of one coming at me. Number one rule: don't fucking close your eyes when being attacked by a zombie horde, for fuck's sake.

'Dee!' Dawn yells at me. 'There are too many!'

A zombie gets past her and me. I can't turn around to see if Poppy kills it; there are too many coming through the door. All I can hear is the groaning, and I can almost feel the wind rushing around the dead lungs, their ribcages, soaking into the air around us – how can they still walk?

'Shit,' Dawn says between gasps. She's sprayed with flecks of dark blood.

'Get to the window, Poppy!' I call out. 'We've gotta climb out.'

We're pushed back into the room, Poppy behind us trying to open a window. She gives up and starts smashing out the glass with the crowbar. We're just trying to protect each other. That's all we want. Just to go somewhere and not have to run. But we're being backed right up against the wall with the window, and a zombie gnashes its teeth at Poppy, I hear the snap right beside me.

She yanks her hand back, wide-eyed as she screams. 'Did it get you?' I yell.

I whack my machete into its neck and it turns to me; it's only got one eye and half a face, I can see into its mouth from the side. I keep hacking at it, because I am not fucking losing anyone else. We can't. I get halfway through its neck before it drops, arms useless.

'I'm good,' Poppy grunts out as she takes down another zombie. 'Window's almost done, keep them off me.'

I can barely see anything as I keep going, zombies dropping all around me as I try and remember how to breathe between the splashes of blood. It's all over my face, in my hair, on my arms, but I can't stop because I need to keep Poppy safe. I need to, I need to.

My blood's pumping so hard it feels like my arms are dripping with it along with all the zombie blood. The effort it's taking to clear the room is draining me, and it's tough to get myself to keep moving.

There's a break in the zombies and I pause, turn around and see Poppy with the window open. 'Come on,' she says, 'careful of the glass, though,' and then clambers out.

Dawn follows. I grip the edge of the window frame and step onto the sill, manage not to get any cuts.

'I've got to find Eve,' Dawn says after we land on the dewy grass beside Poppy.

Outside there's no one. It got dark fast. The zombies can't climb, so we're safe for a few moments. I press my hands into the lawn beside me, covering them in its wetness. I breathe in air that doesn't smell like corpses.

A few zombies come round the corner towards us, faster than the ones inside. They must've heard Dawn's voice, or the window. The three of us get up wearily and prepare to fight. The storm clouds are making the day darker but we can still see.

'Do you think they're still inside?' Poppy asks.

'We should check round the front,' Dawn says.

As she dispatches the first zombie, one of her knives gets stuck in its face. I get to the one that's about to attack her just as she wrenches her knife out. Poppy takes care of the third one. A few more are shambling towards us, but far enough away that if we go around the other side of the school we can avoid them.

We hear voices around the front of the school.

'That's Rhea and Jojo, and someone else,' I say.

I think 'heartache' is the wrong word; it's more that my whole chest has become a vacuum. I want to fall onto the ground and curl up so maybe it will stop, even though it won't. My hands are blistering from the effort of killing and my shoulders hurt, the muscles knotted.

This is too much and I don't know how I can keep going, it's not fair.

'Eve!' Dawn cries out, waving at a shape in the distance.

The shape pauses, and before it turns around I think it's a zombie, it's gotta be because we three must be the only people left in the world.

But then the shape turns around and it's her. Dawn runs to her and grips her hands; they're both covered in blood and they're laughing in relief, not even aware anymore that we're here.

Thirty-nine

Because we're clearly dangerously headstrong, Rhea and I try to keep the zombies from getting near the others. And it's worth noting that *because* we're clearly dangerously headstrong, this does not work. There's only two of us and there's a million of them and we're in such a small space.

'Super sibs out,' I tell Rhea, over the moaning and the groaning and the gnashing of the teeth. I'm surrounded by things that want to kill me and this is really not an ideal situation. 'I can't see the others anymore anyway.'

'Agreed,' she says. 'But we can't go down that corridor, zombies'll get us.'

'I think Eve went out those glass doors, but I don't think we can reach them.'

'We're gonna have to try the big doors,' Rhea says after stabbing a zombie in the eye.

'The big fucking doors with all the zombies behind them? Sure thing.' But I know there aren't any other options. And if we don't try something soon, we're just gonna be overrun. 'All right, but if we die I'm gonna fucking kill you.'

'Deal.' She holds the zombies back while I get the

door. It's not locked, just stiff. Which, depending on what's inside, could be really dangerous. I mean, like, you'd really want the room full of zombies to be locked.

'Ready?' I ask, and she nods while knifing another eye socket.

I let the doors open and maybe five zombies pour out. I look further into the room as I fight. 'It's mostly empty!' It's the indoor basketball courts and these zombies are the only things inside, plus a few corpses.

She turns around and we start running through the place, our shoes squeaking against the floor. It sounds exactly like it did at school. It's a slap in the face, the familiar sound in this situation.

We reach the doors on the other side and then we're outside, breathing in fresh air. We close the doors, lean against them, and it's fucking glorious to not be fighting for my life. I can't figure out how to lock the doors, but hopefully the zombies won't be able to get out. Depends on how many have followed us, I guess.

'Holy shit,' Rhea says.

'Yep.' I close my eyes and just feel the fresh air. Don't have to breathe in the rotting-meat stench.

'No,' she says, jabbing my arm. '*Holy shit.*'

I open my eyes and she's pointing at someone. A zombie … but no. He's a proper person, and it's Caitlin's fucking dad. Fuck.

'How did you find us?' I ask.

'Car,' he says. 'Ya car was leakin oil so I could find youse easy enough.'

'Fuck,' Rhea mutters.

'Like, could you just not? Did you just walk here?' I blurt out at him. 'What did we do to you?'

'Caitlin woulda been alive if it weren't for you,' Matt says.

'Where are your followers?' I ask, looking around. Maybe it wasn't oil, maybe it was petrol – would explain why we ran out so quick.

'Mind ya fucken business,' he says.

'What, did they say you shouldn't have followed us?' Rhea says. 'Bet they don't give a shit about Caitlin.'

'Don't you say her name,' he says, coming at us. He pulls out the gun from his hip holster and fuck, we really should have seen that before having a go at him. I've never seen him use it, maybe there are no bullets, but also it's hard to imagine no bullets when the gun's pointed right at you.

'All right,' I say, holding up my hands. 'It's cool, we're cool.'

'You killed her,' he says.

'Zombies killed her, dickhead,' Rhea says, and I jab her in the ribs.

'Don't really wanna get shot,' I mutter to her.

'What was that?' he says. 'Say it to me face.'

'Hey look, we don't want any trouble?' I say, like something from a movie. 'We can all just ... not be shot. And it'll be great.'

'Really, Jojo?' Rhea asks.

Matt raises his gun because we're not paying attention

to him, and I forget how to breathe. Seeing a gun in a movie is different to seeing a gun in real life, and that's very different from having one pointed at you and your sister. There's nothing I could do to stop a bullet. Like, if it's a knife maybe I could knock his hand away. Or if it was his hand punching me, like, one punch wouldn't kill me, hopefully. But bullets are a different story.

'We don't want to cause you any more harm,' Rhea says, slow and calm like she's talking to a dog. 'We'll leave you alone from now on.'

Not that we weren't, I'd say if I wanted to get shot. *We were fine forgetting that you and your weird heteronormative cult ever existed.* But I'm nodding vigorously along with what Rhea's saying. *Yes, yes, very sorry. So sorry.*

I think Matt doesn't know what to do; he should have shot us by now. Maybe he's got no bullets left. And he keeps staring at us, especially Rhea. She spent more time with Caitlin than I ever did with her, since I was being taught how to be a *man* or something, so she was the worse influence.

The doors behind us rattle and he takes a step back. 'What's in there?'

'Like a hundred zombies,' Rhea says. 'So careful or we'll unleash them.'

That is literally a thing she just said, oh my god. I would be embarrassed if this were any other situation. The doors rattle again. The zombies from the corridor must've followed us through the courts. And Matt's plenty loud so they can hear him.

'Why did you do it?' he asks, his voice cracking. He's got tears streaming down his face. But really, he barely seemed to notice Caitlin was there, too busy trying to get everyone to follow him, too busy trying to make that boy get with Caitlin. Took too much for granted, maybe.

'We didn't,' Rhea says, and it's back to the dog voice. 'We were running away, and in the dark it was hard to see anything. A zombie got Caitlin. It could have been any of us.'

My heart hurts. It could have been Rhea; it could've been me.

'She wouldn'ta gone if it wasn' for –'

We step back from the doors because the rattling's getting stronger. They must all be in there – those doors are gonna open soon. We need to get away but there's a gun between us and the car. Also, where the fuck are the others?

'She would have,' Rhea says, her anger getting the better of her at the worst possible fucking time, I swear to god. 'And she would have died on her own because anyone would, and it would be your fault because you were a shit dad.' She jabs her finger at him. 'You should have been there.'

'Rhea,' I say, touching her arm.

Matt raises the gun at Rhea. *No.* 'You dunno shit.' *No, no, no.* He steps closer; the heavy sound of his Blundstones is steady against the pavement.

Rhea steps back, raises her hands, and I don't know what to do. She's pale, he's red in the face. The seeds are still in my pocket, we're going to grow vegetables. She can't die. We have to find somewhere to grow things. To start again.

'Please don't,' I say, and there are tears on my cheeks, my nose is starting to run. 'Please don't.'

Bang.

I clap my hands to my ears as I scrunch up my eyes. There's no scream. I look over at her and her shoulders are tensed; she's ready to take the bullet but there's not one.

Matt's still pointing the barrel at us and he looks confused. 'Where'd it go?' he asks me, like I'm gonna fucking answer him.

Rhea and I look around – and there it is, in the door right between where we're standing. Guess it's harder to aim a gun than he thought.

He raises it again, does that thing with his thumb that reloads the cartridge or whatever.

And then the doors finally burst open.

'Fuckin run!' Rhea yells.

We bolt past Matt, who's still standing there confused by the gun. Not sure if he's mad because he wanted to shoot a teenage girl, or because he's a shit shot. And I ain' gonna stay around to find out, cause fuck that.

As we round a corner, I run face first into Poppy. I scream and she clutches my arms. 'You're alive,' she says, laughing, and pulls me into a hug. She's gripping me hard and her eyes are welling up. Over her shoulder I see Dee, Dawn and Eve standing together, alive.

'We gotta go,' Rhea says. 'The zombies are coming. Also … Matt is here.'

'Who's that?' Dee asks.

'The cult guy.'

'Right. Well –' Dee's cut off by a scream.

I poke my head around the corner and see Matt being ripped to pieces. As I watch, his screams get more desperate, then they stop. I turn away, all I feel is revulsion.

I notice yellow signs around this part of the school: evacuation point. I guess that's why there are so many zombies here.

'The car's out of petrol,' Dee says. 'And we need to get away from this place.'

'It's a petrol leak,' I say, 'so no point siphoning more.'

'We could just steal another car?' says Dee.

But on our way to the car park we find a big mesh cage with bikes in it, all the same navy blue, same brand but different sizes.

'School bikes,' Eve says. 'Let's get em. We don't need petrol, they're quieter, an we've got nothin to carry cept our weapons.'

I remind myself that I have the seeds in my pockets.

There's not time to argue, really. We find bikes that are the right sizes, their tyres pumped, ready to go. I take a bag that's hanging up – inside it's got a repair kit, extra tubes and a first-aid kit.

We take a moment to catch our breath, and I look

around at them all: Poppy and Dee, Dawn and Eve, Rhea beside me, without Jack or Zufan, without Caitlin.

Dawn kicks off first across the dewy footy ground.

We keep moving, because that's what we're good at.

Acknowledgements

This story was written on the lands of the Wurundjeri people of the Kulin Nation, and I pay my respects to their Elders past, present and emerging. This story was created on stolen land. Sovereignty was never ceded.

Everyone at Echo is wonderful to work with. Angela Meyer – what an absolute legend. You're my dream publisher and I can't believe it's real life that we get to work together. Thanks to Kate Goldsworthy for being a superstar editor and for making the story 100% better. Thanks again to Jo Hunt for another amazing cover and thanks to Shaun Jury for the wonderful layout.

Thanks to the #loveozya community: all the readers, writers, bloggers, YouTubers and Instagrammers! You are wonderful people to work alongside. Thanks to all my Patreon supporters for allowing me to have a space where I can write experimental short stories.

Highway Bodies is a book about many things, but for me it is mostly a book about love. Thanks especially to my fiancée Joni for more love and support than I thought could be possible, thanks to my friend Kat for reading a short story about Dawn and Eve and saying something that sparked me turning this into a novel, and thanks to my brother Ray for always being there for me.

IDA

*Winner of the People's Choice Award at the
Victorian Premier's Awards 2018*

How do people decide on a path, and find the drive to pursue what they want?

Ida struggles more than other young people to work this out, because of a secret ability that allows her to try alternative paths.

One day Ida sees a shadowy, see-through doppelganger of herself on the train. She starts to wonder if she's actually in control of her ability, and whether there are effects far beyond what she's considered.

How can she know, anyway, whether one decision is ultimately better than another? And what if the continual shifting causes her to lose what is most important to her, just as she's discovering what that is, and she can never find her way back?

Ida is an intelligent, diverse and entertaining novel that explores love, loss and longing, and speaks to the condition of an array of overwhelming, and often illusory, choices.

Learn more:
echopublishing.com.au

COMING IN 2020

Euphoria Kids

Alison Evans

Before the rose was there, the garden was full of moss. I started as a seed, under it, waiting for the right time to sprout. Clover waited, and waited, and tended the garden, and didn't listen to anyone who said she should give up. Moss, my other mother, she waited too. But Clover was the one who came out every morning and told me about her night, what she was planning on cooking that day, how Moss was going.

It was the first day of spring when I thought it was the right time. Clover knew this too, I think, and the day before she whispered through the ground to me that she knew I would be there soon.

When my first two leaves emerged, they knew I would be okay.

I didn't mean to be a strange baby made of plants and grown from a seed in the ground, but no one ever said anything. I don't know if anyone can tell. Only Clover and Moss talk about it.

After I emerged from the ground Clover fertilised the garden bed, and made a home for the rose bush with its moon flowers. Now it's as tall as me.

Saltkin flits over and touches a closed bud, waiting

for its time. 'Look at this, Iris.' He beckons me over. I have to squint to see him in the almost-dawn.

He's changed his skin, now he's a tiny fat boy and he's kept his wings. 'Your spring look?'

'Maybe. Not sure on the colour scheme.' He preens one of his bright green iridescent wings with his fingers.

'You look good.'

He smiles and moves to sit on my raised hand, crossing his legs. He's the weight of a bird. 'Are you going to change?'

'You know I can't change like you.' I wave my free hand around and he flutters so he's hovering in front of my face like a hummingbird. 'It's different for me.'

'I meant, you know. Like your hair. Or get some metal in your face. You love tattoos, you could get some of those.'

'I'm too young to get tattoos,' I say. I want to cover my body in art and stories, watch them move and flex as I go throughout the day. But not for a couple of years. I want to cover my body in flowers and vines.

'We can do something with your hair,' Saltkin says, touching a bit of it that's fallen out of the ponytail I put it in. 'You'd look nice pink.'

'Why don't you go pink? Keep the green wings, though.'

He closes his eyes and the snow blue of him changes to a peachy pink, with patches of orange.

'You look like a rose,' I tell him.

A couple of other faeries I've seen before but don't

know well come over and speak to Saltkin. I can't understand what they're saying; it sounds like music.

There's so much potential in winter, and the very beginning of spring is my favourite. It feels like anything can happen. The world is waking up again, and even now, in the dark backyard, the air is humming with new energy.

I walk around the garden. Clover tends it; sometimes I help but she is the reason it thrives. She grows us vegetables and herbs, and when there are flowers blooming there are always some in the kitchen in vases.

The rosemary has been here since long before Clover and Moss moved in, and when we're gone it will take over the whole backyard. I pinch off a stalk and, leaving Saltkin to his friends, return to the house.

The back door leads right into the kitchen. When I get inside, I switch on the kettle. As it starts to boil the kitchen starts to wake and I put the rosemary in a thin vase and place it on the windowsill. The scent lingers on my hands.

The light turns on and when I turn around, Clover is there. I hug her good morning and she sits, still blurry-eyed.

'You're up early,' she says. She always gets up at this time.

'It's spring.'

'Oh.' She looks out the window, though it's still too dark to see outside now that the yellow kitchen light is on. 'Of course.'

I always wake up early on the first day of spring.

I make us a pot of chai and I sit opposite her as it brews. She spoons honey into our cups.

'What are you doing today?' I ask as she pours the tea.

'Moss has the day off; we're just going to hang about I think. Do you want a lift to school?'

I think of Saltkin and his friends, and how my mothers have each other. I know lots of creatures, and I have my mothers, but I don't have my own people.

'I don't mind catching the bus. I like the walk.' It's not a long walk, maybe five minutes. Sometimes the stop is right outside the house. I'm not sure what that depends on exactly.

There are still a couple of hours before I have to go to school, and so I take the half-drunk tea to my room and get back into bed. The sun is rising and soft light is covering the garden. I can see the glitter that is Saltkin and the others, and I feel a tiny bit of annoyance

Just like that, Saltkin appears on my windowsill. 'Sorry Iris,' he says, pausing at the sill to see if I tell him to go away. Sometimes I do. It's hard to get privacy when you're friends with faeries. 'Are you mad?'

'A little.' I sip the tea and beckon him to sit on my bed. 'But I don't know if that's fair. I think I'm jealous of you.'

'The magic?'

'The friends. I don't have any friends.'

I'm envious of the magic, too, but we've been over that.

'We're not friends?' He looks up at me and I can see in his face I've hurt him.

'Sorry, I don't mean we're not friends. I mean I need human friends.'

He still looks a bit put out, and I feel like I would be too. 'Like how Clover has Moss. They understand each other. They're in love but they're friends too. And your other friends near the rosebush. You have a connection with them that we can't have.'

He nods. 'I'll be right back.'

He flits out the window and I stare after him for maybe five minutes before I wonder if he is not coming back. My tea has gone cold, so I lie back down. I reach for my phone and set an alarm, just in case I fall asleep and miss the bus.

***

When I wake for the second time that morning, there are herbs, flowers and rocks strewn all over the bed. I reach for the closest one, a rose quartz. It's polished smooth and it's not quite perfectly round, like it's been sitting on a river bed for a long time.

There is a tiny note on the bedside table. *A spell for friends* is written in loopy, thin, spindly letters. I assume it's from Saltkin. I've never seen his handwriting before.

My alarm goes off and I get out of bed, trying my best not to disturb the debris on the covers. I pull on my school uniform, in varying shades of blue, and pocket the rose quartz. The bus stop takes me twice as long to walk to today, and by the time I reach it I'm sweating.

There is a new person on the bus wearing our school uniform. I've memorised all the faces that get on, and what stops they belong to. But their face is new.

They've got straight black hair, cut so it's just shorter than their chin. They're wearing a choker, just a thin black one with a star on it. They're wearing a bit of eyeshadow, but it's just enough that no teacher is going to tell them not to.

Their school uniform is frayed a bit, so they might not be new. They have a denim jacket on the seat beside them.

They look at me, catch me looking at them, and I quickly look away. I can feel my cheeks burning as I stare at the scenery rushing past. We go through ten minutes of bush before we get to the town, and the school.

***

In science, that's when I notice that they're in my class. The new person. But no one is really paying them any attention. We're paired together because I have no friends and everyone else is paired up.

'Are you new?' I ask. They seem like they're not; they don't look lost. Up close, their dress is patched in a couple of places. It's definitely an old uniform.

'No.' They smile at me. 'But you probably just haven't noticed me. I'm Babs.'

'I'm Iris.'

'Like the song?'

375

I look at them blankly.

'You know. Goo Goo Dolls?'

'Oh.' I pause. 'My mums chose my name. But it's a good song.'

'I chose my name,' they say. 'I just liked the sound. I like how it makes me sound like an old lady.'

We smile at each other. We fill out the sheet our teacher gave us, and then the bell rings, and we have different classes to go to.

I think about asking them if they want to meet up later, but by the time I work up the courage, they're gone.

The next class I have is IT, but because we're on the computers no one is doing any work except me. I like to finish it early because then I won't have to do it all the night before assignments are due.

The school has most of the social media blocked, but not all the proxies, so it's easy enough to get around. I look up Babs on everything, but I don't know their last name, and I find nothing.

I can't wait to know them.